BATTLE FOR HELIOS

MICHAEL G. THOMAS

First published in the United Kingdom in 2014 by Swordworks Books.

ISBN 978-1-911092-40-7

Typeset by Swordworks Books
Printed and bound in the UK & US
A catalogue record of this book is available from the British Library

Cover design by Swordworks Books
www.swordworks.co.uk

BATTLE FOR HELIOS

MICHAEL G. THOMAS

CHAPTER ONE

Lieutenant Commander Sanlav Erdeniz was one of the unsung heroes of the Uprising. Starting as a lowly gunnery officer, he went on to develop the short-ranged railgun ammunition that would forever bear his name. His time aboard the Confederate warship CCS Crusader would pale compared to what happened at Yama City. Then a Captain, he led a group of survivors during the hostile takeover by the Echidna Union. In a matter of weeks, his forces waged a successful guerilla war against the enemy, and in the process saved hundreds of thousands of lives. Two decades later, the Lieutenant Commander was once again working with the Alliance Science Division, and this time his efforts had moved from weapons of war to the great secrets of the Rift generator equipment.

Heroes of the Great Uprising

Comet C34, now codenamed Leviathan was a massive

object, the largest ever faced by an Alliance attack force. Its bulk consisted not just of the Core but also the myriad of smaller chunks, many as large as ancient battleships. Millions of smaller pieces followed, each held onto its path by the gentle pull exerted by the Core. It moved at high speed on its elliptical pattern that had originally taken it well away from the Helion homeworld. Now, after all these centuries, the so-called Doomsday Comet was back and only a short distance away from the newly dedicated Helios Prime, the restored capital of the Helion League, and the Nexus for this part of the Orion Nebula. The naming ceremony had been a grand affair but it was nothing more than a branding exercise. The same problems remained, and Helios Prime, like its sibling planets in the same system were all still recovering from the violent insurrection started by the Zathee.

"This is Mauler A7. We are in position," said Captain Josevi Garcia.

It was a short, if direct announcement from the vessel. The Maulers were the only manned craft in the Alliance assault group. Just a few minutes away from the target, the massive group of tiny aircraft was no bigger than grains of sand compared to the comet. The Mauler was the largest and stayed well back to the rear of the group. Inside, it was filled with computers and communications equipment plus a dozen officers; each carefully trained and practiced in the command and control of semi-autonomous robotics.

There was a brief moment of static.

"Good work. The mission is a go. Send in the birds."

It was the sound of Admiral Lewis, the commander of the Helion Fleet. The man was a long distance away where he waited with the fleet. Captain Garcia looked out through the narrow slits on the front of the heavily armored Mauler and to the shape of the comet. It looked more like a moon at this close range. He'd volunteered for this mission, and he knew the risks. If Operation Needle failed, then it would be just Admiral Lewis and the fleet to protect Helios Prime. He looked back to the seated officers, each of them waiting for the word.

"Send in squadrons one through seven."

Forty-two craft of the initial attack comprised the bulk of the newly arrived X57 Avenger combat drones. Only six stayed back to guard the command Mauler and the two delivery Maulers, all carrying the primary weapons for the mission.

The drones had only just been delivered from the shipyards on Prometheus. Although new, they required no previous knowledge or training. All that came from a mixture of software and the skills and experience of the officers in the Mauler commanding them.

Captain Garcia watched from his view in the cockpit as the enormous swarm of drones rushed off ahead of him. They seemed large for only a few seconds and then shrank to pinpricks. Though a similar size to a medium-sized fighter, the X57 carried much heavier weapons and thicker armor. These robotic fighters were propelled not by one, but eight small engines, four on each of the bat shaped wings. The center of the craft would normally have been taken up by the crew and life support systems; instead it housed a massive quadruple barreled railgun. After years of research, an entire frigate gun system had been miniaturized enough to fit inside a single craft.

"What's your status, Captain?" asked the Admiral.

"Sir, the first wave is moving in. I'm holding the package in reserve."

"Good hunting. Do what you can. We're running out of options."

The swarm of robots split up in six-fighter squadrons and used their lateral thrusters to move further apart while maintaining their existing course. Nearer they moved, leaving nothing but a gentle, barely perceivable stream behind them. Captain Garcia almost believed the mission would succeed when they reached the first waypoint.

"Captain, I've got contacts!" said the tactical officer.

Before he could reply, the electronics warfare officer called out nervously.

"Heavy signal jamming and emissions coming from inside the Core. They're trying to block our control."

Captain Garcia had expected this, however.

"Switch to line-of-sight laser control only. Activate the autonomous package."

"Sir."

All of this would have seemed unnecessary, had Captain Garcia been able to jump ahead just three minutes. The planning, preparing, arming, and tactics would all have seemed simple folly. But none of this mattered, because the X57s were now halfway to the target. The deadly robotic fighters activated their weapon systems and spun up their primary guns. That was when the comet turned from an inanimate object and into a weapon of devastating power.

"Radiation bloom, something is powering up," said the tactical officer.

Six drones vanished in fireballs as precision attacks from hidden particle beam emitters vaporized the craft. They vanished from the Mauler's scanners as soon as they were hit. Captain Garcia felt the nausea hit him and for a brief moment was stunned into inaction. His training kicked in though, and he reverted to routine until his mind settled.

"Target assessment, what are we facing?"

"Uh…multiple particle emitters have deployed, and I'm detecting gun systems deploying along the flanks of the comet. Wait…no…it can't be…"

Captain Garcia looked back to the small cadre of officers, but it was clear from the looks on their faces that the mission was going far from well.

"Captain, launch bays are opening. We have incoming targets. I read three cruiser class ships and ten, no twenty-six fighters."

The man turned about in his seat to look toward the cockpit.

"They must have been waiting for us, Sir."

Captain Garcia sighed and wiped his brow.

"We're here, and we have a job to do. Squadrons one through four engage their fighters; the rest clear a corridor to the target. It's time to release the packages."

The warfare officers directed their robots into battle with great speed and skill. Even as the fighters from both sides engaged in a massed dogfight, the X57s proved more than equal to the task. The following Maulers opened up their bomb bays to expose the bank of four long-range standoff missiles. The original plan had been to launch then from long distance, but that was now clearly the wrong decision. The missile racks lowered underneath the Maulers and opened the release ports.

"Sir, all missiles are locked, armed, and ready."

Captain Garcia's memory flashed back to the briefing six hours earlier. It had been the last time they were able to discuss the plan in detail. He recalled the scientists explaining about where the nuclear weapons would need to impact to cause the fissures. It was complex, but he'd left the targeting to them. His job was simple, to get the package to the target and to release it.

"And the depth penetrators?"

"Also ready, Sir."

"Then launch them, now!"

Not one officer questioned his orders, and the signal was spread throughout the strike force. First to launch were the inert penetrators. At first glance, they looked like any other missile, but in reality were slightly bulkier and built for impact only. Made from a combination of hardened alloy, they would strike the target first to create an impact crater deep enough to insert the nuclear weapons. The sixteen projectiles screeched off from the Maulers and toward the comet.

"All Maulers return to the fallback position. It's time for the machines to do their work."

The three manned craft banked away from the battle and accelerated from the unfolding dogfight. Half of the Avengers had been crippled or lost, but they were doing their job. Over twenty Biomech fighters had been destroyed, and the missiles were on their way. Captain Garcia watched their progress and almost believed it would work. First one missile vanished from his scanner. Then one by one they vanished into dust as the particle emitters based around the comet vaporized them in seconds. The attack was over before it had even begun.

"Sir, the remaining drones?" asked the tactical officer.

Captain Garcia lowered his face into his hands. The only good thing he could think of was that at least they'd only lost machines, not fighter pilots.

"They can't escape now. How many are left?"

"Just seventeen, Sir."

"Very well. Send them in close to the comet. Collate as much data as you can on their weapons, firing patterns, and capabilities. Anything we can learn may help us later."

"Yes, Sir."

The man turned away and sent the commands to the other officers. Once the last had gone he looked back.

"Sir, what do you mean, later? We're going to hit them again, right?"

Captain Garcia swiveled about in his chair and shook his head.

"Based on this course and velocity? I don't think so. Admiral Lewis is assembling everything we have. If you ask me, this whole thing is now going to be decided in orbit over Helios Prime. The Admiral is going to have to draw his line in the sand, and Helios Prime is that line."

* * *

The Biomech lander screamed overhead at a height of no more than a hundred meters. Even as it vanished into the distance, Wictred tracked the movement of its flank gun turrets. They moved about in quick jerks of movements, much like the way a bird would twist its head about. The right-side turret tracked back almost enough to point at him and then it was gone.

Close.

12

The heat from its engines registered inside Wictred's helmet, but he knew it would be foolish to even consider moving. Once he was sure it had moved away, he looked back at his small unit. They were spread out and using any cover they could find as they entered the outskirts of the small town.

Ten seconds earlier, and they would have had us.

He could feel a sickness in his stomach, one of fear. It wasn't of injury or even death. It was the fear of risking and losing those that were left. Wictred wasn't an officer, but right now he was effectively their commander, and it was a very heavy burden for such a young marine. The unit moved off the street and past the derelict guard post marking the entrance to the place. There were a number of abandoned vehicles dotted about, but it was the large military truck that he had in his sights.

"I'm going in," he said over the intercom.

Increasing his speed, the towering figure of Wictred lurched ahead until he reached the rear of the truck. Feeling exposed, he took cover behind the remains of the wreckage as best as he could. The markings down its flanks showed it had been a New Helion Army truck, at least during some part of its life. Hiding behind the vehicle was no easy feat, due to his size and armor, but at least the truck was one of the larger vehicles used by the NHA. He moved carefully, avoiding stepping on the broken pieces of metal lying about that might make a noise and give away his position. He paused and glanced briefly at the vehicle, taking in as much information as he could. He estimated the size was somewhere in the region of twice as large as a Bulldog and much more heavily built. The design of the armor plating suggested it had been retrofitted and was actually a lightly modified civilian vehicle rather than something purpose built.

"Stay low, move up."

Two of his marines sprinted across the open ground to join him, and then moved past him to take up their positions at the end of the long vehicle. Neither carried much in the way of heavy weapons, but the taller of them did have one of the older L48 rifles. Back in the Uprising, they had been the standard issue weapons but were now relegated to use as a support gun. Wictred moved a short distance behind them and checked the lower sections of the truck as they continued onward.

Yeah, that's where the mine got them.

The lower part of the bodywork and part of the underside had been blown out by something in the ground. Wictred bent down and spotted the crater underneath the truck. An Alliance vehicle would have been much better protected with its combination of layered plating and a v-shaped hull. Years of fighting in the Uprising had shown a need for simple vehicles that could withstand a variety of attacks using improvised weapons. He moved on a little further and looked at a line of holes the size of his arm that ran alongside the left side. Not far from the mine damage were several areas of congealed blood, marking the spot where its crew had once been. The entire side had been torn out by an explosive shell, and tracks marked where either the bodies or prisoners had been taken.

Idiots, all of them! They tried to get out and instead lost most of their soldiers. They should have waited for help.

He did feel some sympathy for them, but he felt more for the rest of his unit who'd spent the last four days trekking across open country to the town. According to the last contact from Colonel Gun, this was one of the many remaining civilian outposts with an intact NHA garrison. The one thought that kept coming back to him though, was that these could have been the reinforcements. In which case, the town would be under enemy control. He looked back to the town and checked for heat or movement readings via his visor. It took only a few seconds to do a full scan, and as before, it came back negative.

So what will we find in there, machines, Helions, Khreenk, or just bodies?

The town had been the nearest Helion location, and even though they'd been unable to reach the place via line-of-sight communication, they had made the arduous journey. He hadn't told the others, but this was the only plan he could come up with. It was either that, or stay out in the open, and just hope somebody would find them who didn't want to kill them. That wasn't Wictred's style.

He would rather risk it all in some dramatic firefight than lose his people one by one to heat, starvation, and even radiation sickness. A blip caught his attention but vanished just as quickly as he'd spotted it.

"Any contact yet?"

Lance Corporal James shook his head. The young man had proven a natural ally to Wictred, and there was little they disagreed on in terms of their short-term plan on Eos.

"Nothing, Corporal. It's like there's nobody out there."

Wictred turned back and looked at the shape of the town. It was small, home to perhaps no more than five hundred people, and based around the wide road that ran down one side. None of the buildings were more than two stories, and the entire place was covered in a thin layer of dust. If it hadn't been for the wrecked truck outside, he'd have considered it abandoned.

"There's something in there. The first signs we had three hours ago showed heat signatures on the perimeter. That Hunter-Killer was in this area for a reason."

The Alliance forces generally knew the lander as a Bioray, but since their abandonment on Eos, the powerful craft had taken on a completely new role. They were large, tough, and carried a varied contingent of warriors. Wictred had watched two squads of marines and an NHA patrol as they were totally destroyed by the firepower of the craft over the last days. Only the marines had managed to hold off the lander, but it had then simply deposited a number of warriors to finish the job. The name Hunter-Killer was well deserved.

"Wait, movement!" said one of the other marines.

All eyes turned to the town and the glimmer of metal in the distance. A small number of yellow flashes marked out hidden gun positions, followed by shouting.

"Stay down!" Wictred said.

It was an unnecessary order, but after the last few days, Wictred was taking no chances. He was no officer, having only recently been made a corporal. Yet since the disaster at the fort, he'd become the leader of the tiny band of marines, and so far he'd kept them alive.

"There!" Private O'Hara whispered.

The young female marine wore a heavily dented set of armor, with the unusual distinction of having a section of a Biomech blade still partially embedded in the right arm. Luckily, it hadn't made it all the way through. She dropped down to her left knee and lifted her L52 Mark II carbine. She carried a pair of helmets, taken from fallen Biomech foot soldiers, on a number of hoops attached to her belt. It was a grisly set of mementos from a savage few days' fighting and hiding, and did little to dilute the look of feral savagery that had befallen her.

"There's something near the low building, to the right. Three o'clock," said Private Harvey.

Even in this stressful environment, Wictred could hear

the faint pangs of pain and exhaustion in the man's voice. The man was one of the many stragglers Wictred had added to his unit, but he was different. The neutron missile bombardment had destroyed most of the Biomechs, but a small number of marines had also succumbed. The Private had been caught near the blast zone, and his armor hadn't been able to stop him from absorbing a significant level of radiation. According to all the information to hand, the man should already be dead, but he refused to go, and Wictred had decided he'd give the man the best possible chance of a good death. Wictred grimaced as he moved his attention from the marine and back in the direction of the possible enemy sighting.

"I see it."

The shape was nothing out of the ordinary, just a man-sized figure moving around the outside of one of the many buildings. From this distance, it wasn't easy to identify much in the way of details, especially as dust and dirt seemed to make them all look roughly the same. It staggered back and then landed on the ground, just as the sound of two gunshots rang out.

Where are you?

Wictred's suit tracked the bullets as well as the sound, quickly locating the source of the gunfire. He'd expected it to be from one of the buildings, but it was actually coming from another of the wrecked Helion trucks.

"Harvey, with me. The rest of you on overwatch."

Wictred moved out from cover, lurching off to the right and the cover offered by more wrecked vehicles. He made it halfway when the gunfire started. A few rounds hit nearby, but the return fire from the marines quickly subdued whoever had opened fire to begin with. He kept moving, and Private Harvey followed him until they were behind the vehicles and moving down the road parallel with the main one. A few more sporadic shots rang out, and then there was a large two-story building blocking the line of sight.

"Corporal!" Harvey called out.

Wictred moved his eyes to the right in time to spot the four Biomech warriors. They appeared just as surprised as him as they continued to pull apart the innards of machinery attached to the side of the building. One cried out something in its alien tongue and then lifted a rifle. Wictred ran at them and didn't even bother shooting. Two rounds glanced off his thick JAS armor before he crashed into the group. Wictred's size and overall bulk forced the group to the ground where he had an easy time dispatching the first two with his bare hands. The other two rolled out of his reach and opened fire at point blank range. The shoulder of his armor was quickly penetrated, and he resorted to the arm's built-in blades to decapitate the next.

"Get down!" Harvey shouted.

Wictred obeyed without thinking, and a burst of L52

gunfire blasted over his head and tore holes out of the creature's chest. It staggered back and fired a single round before collapsing backwards. Wictred sighed and looked back to see Harvey dropping down to his knees.

"Harvey!" he muttered.

The large Jötnar towered over his comrade as he looked down to check his wounds. A small hole the size of a finger marked the point where the round had managed to find a crack in the visor and had allowed the single round to smash through and embed directly into the poor man's forehead.

"Bastards!"

Wictred lowered the man to the ground and turned back to the direction of the original gunfire.

"Marines, how are we doing?" he asked over the secure communications network.

"All good here, Corporal," Lance Corporal James answered.

"Good work. Harvey is down. We still have work to do, though. Watch my back. I'm moving in."

There was no time to mourn the dead on Eos. Every hour brought more death and tragedy to the marines. Wictred moved on past the bodies of the Biomech warriors and to the corner of the building. He leaned around just long enough to look at the damaged truck parked at the end before slipping back into cover. His built-in camera gave him a detailed series of images to examine from the safety of the cover.

What do we have, then?

The two roads joined at the intersection and were surrounded on three sides by buildings. The windows were boarded up, and three Biomech bodies lay out in the street. Then Wictred spotted the movement at the rear of the truck. One of the wheels was shattered and right behind it the shape of two people, each huddled around a large weapon mounted on a bracket.

Clever.

Wictred recalled from his training in the Corps the best places to site snipers. Most people, of course, assumed it was to choose the prime shooting location, perhaps the high ground or the area with the optimum line-of-sight. They had been quizzed on this so many times, with the classic example of the house on a hill or a tower structure. As a rule, they had all been trained to avoid the obvious hiding place, and to instead set themselves up somewhere near this place but not directly on it. It was a minor detail, but a way of achieving a good shot while not getting yourself killed. He watched them carefully, noting how a pair of the Biomech soldiers was trying to work their way around the side of the truck.

They can't hold forever.

"Marines, watch your fire. I'm going in."

He moved out from the relative safety of the corner of the building and to the other side of the street before one of the warriors spotted him. It pointed and barked something. Another dozen of the things came from the shadows, and most aimed their weapons at him. The marines opened fire and dropped two of them where they waited, but the others put out so much gunfire, Wictred was forced to take cover behind a partially destroyed wall.

"Move in and watch for friendlies."

The other marines had already taken their own initiative and moved up the street and toward the smashed truck being used as a sniping position. There were now only seven of them left including Wictred, and all of them bore the marks of battle and damage. Private O'Hara was the first to move to the right of the street and slid down behind a heap of rubble. A shot glanced off just a few centimeters from her leg.

"Keep down!" Wictred shouted out.

More of the marines went ahead, and soon they had the vehicle boxed in on three sides. A quick rush might have ended the fight, but Wictred had no intention of losing any more marines.

"Canners!"

From his position further back on the street, Wictred spotted the pair of arachnid walkers jump out from the building behind the truck and land heavily on its roof. With terrifying efficiency, they hacked and smashed at the vehicle to gain access to those inside.

"Marines, forward! Bring them down!"

As one, the entire group of seven pushed ahead, each with their rifles and carbines raised and pointing directly at the fearsome machines. The carbines blew small holes in the metal, but it was the high-explosive charges of the L48 rifles that dislodged them. The machines tumbled down to the floor, but suddenly one of them jumped up and threw itself at the advancing line of marines. Wictred tracked it with his shoulder mounted gun system, and when he was satisfied there was nothing else nearby, he opened fire. The muzzle flash extended out almost a meter, and the blast instantly stopped the machine. As the dust cleared, the marines watched two Helions emerge from the wreckage.

"Who are you?" Wictred asked.

The first to emerge was a young woman wearing long, dirty clothing wrapped about her body like a snake. She wore a mask, yet her long hair ran down over her shoulders where it was partially concealed by a light quilted cloak. In her hands, she carried an alien looking rifle, and its barrel pointed directly at Wictred. She said nothing and simply waited for the second, a young boy, to join her. He was unarmed and carried a box, presumably ammunition.

"Corporal?" asked a voice from above.

Most of the marines looked up, and to their surprise found the upper body of a marine looking back down at them.

"Corporal Wictred, who is that?"

The man leapt down from the level above them, hit the

ground, and then bounded up alongside the two Helions. He wore the same PDS Alpha armor as the rest of them, but his was remarkably smarter and better looked after. His visor snapped open, revealing a young man with a thin black mustache.

"Captain Carter, at your service."

Wictred quickly saluted at the officer.

"Wictred you said? You were part of the unit that fought with us on Helios Prime, at the transport hub, if I'm not mistaken?"

Wictred nodded.

"Yes, Sir."

The young man smiled almost apologetically and extended his hand to shake Wictred's.

"Well, Sir, in that case I am amongst friends."

"What happened here?" Private O'Hara asked.

The Captain grimaced at the question.

"My Mauler was hit on the way out. Only three of us made it out of the wreckage before one of those Biorays found us. Luckily a NHA column was moving through the area. I was the only one to make it away alive."

"What about these civilians?" Wictred asked.

Captain Carter looked at them, tapped the boy on the head, and then turned back to Wictred. He pointed out to the wrecked truck.

"We made it this far before the damned Animosh hit us. The NHA put up a good fight and routed the whole lot of them. Still, they lost half their fighters, and they are needed back at the air base."

The mention of that one word seemed to get all their attention, and the Captain could see that.

"There are a dozen small towns and hamlets within a hundred kilometer circle of the air base. I volunteered to help protect this one while the NHA left to move back to their main base."

Wictred looked confused.

"Why not go with them?"

"They took as many as they could carry. That was three days ago, and still there's been no help. They will be back, but until then we hold."

"How many of you are there?" O'Hara asked.

Captain Carter turned about, put his fingers in his mouth, and let out a loud, piercing whistled. A dozen windows slid open on three different buildings, and gun barrels pushed out to face the marines.

"Fifty plus civilian workers, four NHA soldiers, and a rather unusual fellow called…"

"Vadi!" Wictred exclaimed, upon seeing the figure of the synthetic warrior.

He was a head shorter than Wictred, but still much larger and stronger than any Helion, and came out from cover to move toward the marines. By now all of them had lowered their weapons, though Anton dropped into a defensive fighting stance as Vadi increased his speed and then crashed into Wictred. Private O'Hara reached out and held back the marine.

"They're old friends."

The marine was much bulkier than O'Hara; yet somehow she held him back long enough for the two to exchange laughter and a few blows. He looked back briefly at O'Hara who then let go of his arm.

"I know who he is."

"Jack, where is Morato?" Vadi asked.

Wictred laughed at his barely understandable language.

"I see you've been working on your language. Jack is not here. He is heading to Helios Prime for the big fight."

Vadi didn't look as though he fully understood, so Wictred point to the sky.

"Jack is in space."

A door opened, and out came three more Helions, each covered in layers of cloth to disrupt their outlines. As they approached, more could be seen, with the majority completely unarmed.

"What's the plan, Captain?"

The young man wiped dust away from his visor and then looked back into the grimy looking town. It was nothing special, just another inhabited area on an alien world. He nodded as if somebody was speaking to him and then looked back to the marines.

"We cannot make it to the air base without help. The last message said the NHA were securing the outlying areas one at a time. They will come. For now we have a simple job. We reinforce the town and hold it until relieved."

He was met by silence. Wictred finally spoke to break the uncomfortable silence.

"Against whom? The Animosh or the Biomechs?"

Captain Carter nodded slowly as Wictred asked his question.

"The Animosh are being hunted, just as we were."

Anton stepped closer and pointed at the wrecked armored vehicle.

"They are still fighting though, aren't they?"

Captain Carter shook his head.

"No, not all of them. We have four of them guarding the northern perimeter road."

He knew what he was saying would be contentious and decided to continue.

"Their insurgency is splitting apart right now. Some have turned against their commanders to fight the common enemy. That's what this group did."

Wictred looked unimpressed at this change of events.

"Wait, you're saying you have Animosh guarding the northern approach?"

He made to move, but the Captain lifted his hand.

"Yes, that's exactly what I'm saying. When we arrived here, a group of fighters ambushed our column. In the middle of the firefight, another party of Animosh turned on them and fought them off. They are no friends of the

Zathee government, but they have all vowed to turn their attention to the real enemy."

"The Biomechs," said a thickly accented voice.

Attention moved to the cloaked man as he stopped and removed his hood. The tattooed face of an Animosh warrior looked at them. He turned his head to show his neck where the mark of his clan had been tarnished.

"We will fight the machines."

Wictred stepped closer to the Helion and looked at him carefully. He was the same size and build as the Zathee, but his disdain for the civilians around them was obvious. The female sniper spat on the floor as he spoke but made no move to take her complaint any further.

"When this war is over, we will resolve this..."

He looked to the female as he spoke and then turned back to Wictred.

"We pledge ourselves to the destruction of the enemy."

Private O'Hara moved to Wictred's flank and gazed into the face of the mysterious Helion. His clothing was stained from the dust of Eos, but he stood tall, almost aloof. She shook her head in irritation.

"Typical damned religious Zealot."

Captain Carter smiled. "I can see you're not from Carthago."

She seemed to grimace at this suggestion. The mention of Carthago was a bitter one for her, but she saw no need to say anything else on the matter. The Captain appeared to think differently though. He moved closer to her and continued to speak.

"We have our own history of dealing with religious persecution and discrimination, do we not? These Animosh may not match your ideals, but they are not our people."

The young marine could feel her blood pressure increasing as he questioned her.

"Captain, I've seen what special treatment for religions does; it empowers them against those that have…"

"No faith," finished the Animosh warrior.

Both of the marines moved their eyes to watch him. It was rare to find a single Helion who could understand, let alone speak any of the human languages. Yet this one seemed more than fluent. He turned his attention specifically to O'Hara.

"There is no such thing as no faith. There are many Animosh who trust in science, more than those who believe in any of the old or new religions. It is harder to not believe in something bigger, like a god, wouldn't you say?"

She looked at him, and there in the dust of Eos, they came to an unspoken understanding; because deep down, she knew that not believing there was a god out there with a plan for them all, was more terrifying than facing the wrath of any actual god.

"Good," said Captain Carter, "Let's get you into the

town and acquainted with our facilities and defenses. Can I assume you could do with some food and drink?"

Wictred shook his head.

"Not yet. First we deal with our dead."

CHAPTER TWO

The Steersmen were the great mystery of their time to all races, including humanity. Having allied themselves to a similar race known as The Twelve, the Steersmen were granted a home on Taxxu, one of their planets. For generations, this gifted race of scientists and engineers managed to explore the galaxy and made contact with a myriad of peoples. For all their advances, they succumbed to a great plague that devastated their species only a short time after having met the Helions. After failing to cure their failing bodies, they used their technology to encase themselves into machine bodies, and for those too weak for the process, their minds were meddled with technology known only as Cores. These Biomechs, as they were now known, turned on their brothers among The Twelve.

Taken from the accounts of Z'Kanthu,
Warlord of The Twelve

The battle-scarred shape of ANS Conqueror limped

toward Helios, along with her collection of damaged ships following behind. The two Battlecruisers had taken the lead position. Though similar in design to the much more common Crusader class, they were substantially wider, and this additional girth provided space for more fighters, landers, and marines. All of this had proven useful during their journey from Eos as they took on casualties from the other ships, as well as swathes of marines. The three Crusader class ships, ANS Crusader, ANS Victory and ANS Devastation flanked them. The bulk of the remaining ships were Crusader class, with a smattering of Hunter class frigates providing a skirmish screen. It was no more than a shell of the original fleet that had fought at Eos, but it was no less effective.

"They fought one hell of a fight," said Admiral Lewis.

General Daniels and Colonel Gun both nodded in grim agreement.

"Eos was a victory, of sorts," answered General Daniels.

Colonel Gun looked unimpressed.

"A victory? We can't afford many more victories like that. Eos might still be ours, but what price did we pay?"

General Daniels sighed, and Gun could see the struggle he was putting himself through. Gun placed his hand on his shoulder.

"Spartan gave me a book many years ago about commanders on Earth. I remember something an American general once said about war, and I think you'll appreciate it."

General Daniels raised a single eyebrow and closed his eyes briefly.

"Go on."

"It was something like this. To be a good soldier, you must love the army. To be a good commander, you must be able to order the death of the thing you love."

They watched the ships in silence for a short, uncomfortable silence that was eventually broken by Admiral Lewis.

"I believe that was General Robert E. Lee, commander of the Army of Northern Virginia in the American Civil War. He was right, of course. If you're not prepared to risk what you have, then you will never be able to fully commit to an operation. On reflection, it would have been better to draw in the Biomechs to a trap and then use the nukes."

"True. Hindsight is one hundred percent effective," replied General Daniels.

His voice was bitter, and though he understood the message all too perfectly, it still didn't help him with the heavy losses sustained by his marines.

"General, the 17th took just as much damage as the 8th down on Eos. Both of our combat strengths are down to just over half combat effective. Lieutenant Colonel Diego Koerner lost his leg in the evacuation. He's still in the medical bay."

The General looked out at the planet of Helios. It was an annoying name for him and his other officers, as the Helions themselves had named both their world and their star the same. He was just glad that as part of their reunification plan, they'd decided to rename the capital as a reminder that this one world was key to the Helion system.

"This place, it's going to take many more lives."

Gun nodded.

"Agreed. At least General Rivers has managed to get more troops into the area. What have we got so far?"

General Daniels moved over to the tactical display and activated a chart that showed current dispositions.

"Marine and Colonial Guard units are now fully activated. Every Alliance colony is at maximum security alert, with Colonials protecting key installations. Marine Corps reserve regiments are being shipped out to reinforce our existing commitments."

Gun tapped the screen and concentrated the area to those Alliance and Helion holdings in the Orion Nebula.

"So we have our own territory in T'Karan, plus five Helion star systems all on the frontline. I thought the plan was to get everything on or around the Helios system. Something has changed? What exactly is the plan?"

General Daniels pointed at the other four stars in a circle around their primary star.

"Out of those four stars, there are only three inhabited

worlds. Two are heavy industrial sites and one is a partially abandoned military research site."

"And the fifth?"

"Dead."

Gun looked surprised.

"So they have more valuable colonies around Helios than the rest of their Empire combined?"

"Indeed. Since the last war, they have spent most of their time looking inwards."

"Stagnating," said Gun.

General Daniels allowed himself a tiny grin at the word. Gun was a very different person to the one he'd met back in the War. It reminded him of Spartan and their various arguments and battles in the past. A brief wave of nostalgia waved over him that was quickly erased by the face of Gun.

"So we are concentrating on Helios Prime only? What about the other races?"

Admiral Lewis answered.

"No, not just Helios Prime. We have more ships arriving every hour from T'Karan as well as from the other races. Even the Helions have got off their butts and brought in most of what was left of the Narau Fleet that had been commanded by Admiral Lanthua. It's mainly Helion, but there is also a smattering of Klithi, Byotai, and some Khreenk mercenary ships that were persuaded to stay. So far, there are more than two hundred ships."

"What happened to Lanthua?" Gun asked.

Admiral Lewis shrugged.

"Unsurprisingly, after the evacuation of Helios Prime, his Khreenk mercenaries and forces vanished, along with Dictator Justitium Lyssk. The last sighting of them had their forces making for the Anicinàbe Rift. I'm sure we'll be seeing them again soon."

Gun looked impatiently at the two men before finally asking again.

"And the plan?"

General Daniels looked to the Admiral and then tapped a button on the display next to the table-like tactical display; an image of General Rivers, the Chairman of the Joint Chiefs.

"Gentlemen, I have attached detailed plans for the Orion strategy as developed between myself and Admiral Anderson, with input from the Joint Chiefs. The crux of it is pretty simple though."

Gun, Admiral Lewis, and General Daniels shared a quick glance before he said the next part. The imagery changed to show a wider view of the entire Helios systems, with the paths of the inhabited planets shown by light gray circles.

"The comet is slowing and moving into the projected high orbit around Helios Prime. Data from the Helions' reconnaissance drones confirms that three sections have detached from the main body. These sections have adjusted their course, and we have plotted their targets."

Admiral Lewis shook his head as he looked at the imagery.

"The other planets."

"We suspect this is part of a diversionary tactic to pull our forces from the defense of Helios Prime. That, or they are just being thorough in the deconstruction of the Helion defenses. Either way, based on detailed projections, all these objects are heading for planetary orbits. That is all the more reason why the bulk of our forces will remain where you are. Two full Marine Corps regiments will be on Helios within the next ten hours, that's eight complete battalions of veteran troops. I want you to take what you have left to prop up the NHA garrisons of Micaya and Libuscha. You will be supported by territorial Marine Corps units comprising of two more regiments."

The group was stunned at this news and not one of them spoke. The message was prerecorded from Terra Nova and continued even as they struggled with what they were hearing.

"General Daniels will assume command of the defense of Helios Prime. Colonel Horst Brünner will take the 4th Heavy Battalion and take command of the defense of Libuscha. Colonel Gun, you will take the combined 17th and 8th to Spascia. We cannot afford to send more ships other than a token force to each world. The rest of the fleet will assemble alongside the Narau over Helios Prime, plus a small contingent will meet at Micaya, safely behind the frontline to assemble a strong reserve, when and if the extra ships promised by the others actually materialize."

The display showed the worlds as well as the disposition of the fleets. Though there were sizable forces at each point, there were still as many ships around Helios Prime as there were with all the others combined.

"The Biomechs can only have one of two primary strategies in this campaign. Either they will attempt to bombard the planet into submission, or they will assault it, just as they did with Helios Prime in the past. The fleet will do its best to thin the herd, to cut the numbers for the defenders on the ground. If we're lucky, they will choose the first option, and I will be able to engage them while they are vulnerable, trying to bombard the planet."

He lifted the nearby glass and took a quickly gulp of water. It had gone slightly tepid, but it still managed to cool his throat.

"Now, we also have diplomats on the capitals of all the other races, each pushing for help before Helios Prime is hit, but I'm not expecting much help anytime soon. I suspect they are waiting to see what, if anything, we can achieve. They will help, but only if they think we can win this thing."

The General continued speaking, but all Gun could find himself doing was checking on his modified secpad. It took a few seconds to find the data on his new objective.

It didn't take him long to read the details, and he wasn't amused.

"Spascia? It is a ruin. Why the hell is Rivers sending me there? I'm needed on Helios Prime!"

General Daniels looked at him and then to the screen.

"Colonel, I think he chose you because that place is already a ruin."

Only somebody familiar with Gun would have dared to suggest such a thing, and the response it obtained was a great roar of pleasure from the old warrior.

"Yes, that sounds more like it!" he growled back.

He tried to hide it, but the General knew his face too well. He smile was an impossibility to disguise. General Rivers continued his briefing with the shape of four images, each showing a large structure that looked like a combined weapons and communication array.

"As you know, the Helions and T'Kari maintain a station and a small garrison at the Black Rift. The equipment fitted there can destabilize and collapse any Spacebridge for hours though usually days. If you recall, our T'Kari friends did this during our first encounter with the Biomechs here. If enough energy is used to disrupt the Spacebridge, the effect can last a number of months."

"So why don't they come right through?" Gun asked.

The communication was all prerecorded, so there was no way General Rivers could reply. Instead, the rest had to wait patiently as the senior commander explained.

"The security force at the Black Rift can shut the thing down the second it opens, and this makes an assault useless. Each time they shut it down, it blocks access for quite some time. If you recall, the last time a Biomech ship made the run for the Rift it was intercepted by our own forces. Even if they make it, they would have to eliminate any ships fitted with the defensive Rift collapsing technology, and then find a way to activate the Rift so that it can mate with whatever system is in Biomech space. Until the defensive systems of the T'Kari and Helions are disabled, the Biomechs will be unable to send through any kind of significant force."

He paused, letting that new information sink in before getting to the crux of the problem.

"So why is the comet heading for Helios Prime? You'd think an assault on the Black Rift defenses would be first?"

The General smiled at this part.

"That, Gentlemen, is the million dollar question, and that is why you are being sent to each of the Helion worlds. It would seem our Helion allies have been keeping their backup plan to themselves. Only the larger and more advanced Helion and T'Kari ships have the technology for collapsing Rifts. Even if every ship is destroyed, or some great misfortune falls upon the Helions, they still have a way to close the Rift directly from their own worlds."

Again he pointed to the images on the screen.

"Helios Prime, Spascia, Micaya, and Libuscha all have

a city-sized weapon system built directly into the northern poles of each planet. Any one of these can provide the energy and power to shut down the Rift for months with just a single burst of energy. The problem, Gentlemen, is the time it will take the energy beam to reach the Rift, assuming they have line-of-sight at that time of year."

The image zoomed out to show the Helios star along with its planets and the Black Rift out on its own.

"The Black Rift is two hundred and twenty-four light minutes from the Helios-T'Karan Rift and Helios Prime itself. That means if they can open the Rift, they will have a three and three-quarter hour window before the energy beam from Helios Prime could shutdown the Rift."

Admiral Lewis nodded as he listened.

"That's enough time to bring in a massive fleet, maybe even to establish some kind of deflector system near the Rift to block the signal. It's too big a risk."

"Obviously, the planets are always moving, and depending on the time of year, the planets will be at different positions and distances from the Black Rift itself. That is why, from today each of the Helios planetary weapon batteries will fire each minute according to a specific preset sequence. The dormant Rift is being hit every fifteen seconds with a blast sent from these worlds. Even if the enemy opens the Rift, it will be shut again in seconds, for long enough to stop them sending in more forces for weeks or months to come."

Gun and the others knew in an instant what the plan was, but the final words of General Rivers explained it more succinctly than they ever could.

"The planets are the guardians of Orion. As long as they remain, the Biomechs will never be able to bring in substantial forces. The plan is simple. For there to be a victory in Helios, we must ensure that at least one of the planetary weapon systems remains operational. Then, and only then, can the system be kept secure."

He paused before finishing with just one more point.

"Be under no illusion, Gentlemen, the Biomechs have a bitterness and hatred for the Helions that is unmatched. They will not want their surrender. They will want nothing less than the destruction of every city, and the death or enslavement of every person they find. After that, they will move through the Rift to each connect world doing the same. They tried it once before and nearly succeeded. This time we're here, and we will not let this happen, not on our watch."

* * *

Jack eyed the small group of Khreenk warriors carefully. There was little different about the Khreenk in terms of build or strength, but their individual augmentations gave them a number of unique advantages. One of the most common was eyesight improvement, but there were also muscle and limb replacement, plus the addition of computer overlays and communications gear.

One of them tapped his left arm, and it emitted a buzzing sound for a brief moment. He struck the arm, and it quickly stopped, much to his comrades' amusement. Jack looked to Riku who waited patiently at his side.

"What the hell is that?"

Jack shrugged. "I have no idea."

They looked back to the Khreenk and readied themselves for the fight. Each of their opponents was dressed differently, yet that disparity gave them a look unlike anything in the Alliance. All four of them wore close-fitted gold colored breastplates, with carefully detailed imagery across the section directly in the center. Every one of them was battered and scratched, and one had a continued series of long marks that ran diagonally along the middle. The rest of their protection was what separated them from each other. Small pieces of armor varying from matt black to a smooth iron covered them from head to toe. One warrior's armor comprised mainly of rings and hoops, each connected via articulated sections. Another had a mixture of plates and scales while yet another used a bizarre mix of the two.

"You ready?" he asked Riku.

The marine looked at him through her helmet, smiled, and then clamped down her visor to protect her face. It sealed with a clump sound, and the partially smoked visor hid most of her face. He could just about spot the curve of her smile as she spoke.

"Oh, yeah, I'm ready all right."

"Fight!" came a voice from a short distance away.

Jack felt his pulse quicken as if he'd just been injected with some fiery substance. It was of course nothing more than adrenalin, but it gave him exactly what he needed in the coming fight. Jack and the other three marines ran into the center of the training hall with their long synthetic sticks held like medieval swords. The weapons were long at nearly two meters and could have represented anything from a club or spear through to an ancient German zweihander. The Khreenk mercenaries advanced in a loose line, each carrying the same weapons as the marines. Two held them low while the others lifted them up high like the marines. The tall and commanding figure of Private Callahan moved out ahead of the group, with Jack and Riku moving off to his right. Private Jenkell stayed close to Callahan's flank and looked half his size in this particular match.

"Watch your flanks!" Jack called out.

He glanced to his right and then his left as they moved forward. Experience had taught him the value of watching your flanks, especially when fighting in such a confined battle. One of the Khreenk warriors launched a series of cuts at Jenkell's head, and she parried them quickly before rushing in after them. Callahan tried to move forward to help, but she'd moved too far and pulled away from him.

"Get back on the line!" Jack shouted, but it was much too late.

The largest of the Khreenk, their leader and the man they'd captured on Eos, blocked his path and swung for his head. The blow was quick and started low, as the enemy warrior brought the weapon up fast and then whipped it around to try and hit Callahan in the face.

"Nice!" he muttered, as he clumsily parried the blow.

He then sidestepped and swung his weapon down from the upper-left to hit the Khreenk in the shoulder. He actually managed to strike his foe; much to both of their surprise, but instead of knocking him down, there was a clunk sound. The Khreenk laughed and beat the weapon aside. Only then did the marine notice the robotic arm that had deflected the blow.

"Typical," he grumbled.

Both sides exchanged more cuts and stabs as they tried to find an opening they could exploit. At the same time, they were forced to watch their opponents who were desperately trying to do the same to them. A few months ago, this could have been fought on the surface of Eos with live firearms and blades. All the bitterness and anger the marines held toward the Khreenk had long vanished. The journey from Eos to their final destination at Helios Prime had seen much change in both the marines and the Khreenk. Even so, this sparring session was more than a way to break out a sweat or to practice moves. This was a test of human versus Khreenk. Jenkell was out on her own now, and the two Khreenk surrounded her, beating her down with a fusillade of cuts to her head and torso. The training armor took the impact, but that still didn't stop her falling to the ground, and finally dropping her weapon and submitting.

"One down!" called out a voice in the background.

Jack and Riku had been working their way slowly around the other flank of the Khreenk when he saw the fall of Jenkell.

"Help her!" Riku called out.

The two women were far from being friends, but that didn't stop Riku wanting to beat the Khreenk. She took a step forward, but Jack grabbed her, yanking her back just as the Khreenk leader swung his blade. It missed by just a few centimeters.

"No, she's gone. Now watch my flank."

Jack pressed in on the Khreenk warrior and swung hard while Riku moved up right next to him. Each time Jack attacked, she readied herself for the opening. After the third attack, the Khreenk warrior had no chance but to lift his weapon. Riku leapt forward and stabbed the blade into his chest. The impact made him grunt, and then Jack was on top of him and sending him to the floor.

"Two down!" said the voice.

Jack pointed to Callahan where he had three of the

Khreenk hacking at him.

"Help Callahan."

Riku turned back and ran to the large warrior's flank in time to parry two quick cuts.

"Good timing, little lady," he laughed.

Jack, meanwhile, ran behind the Khreenk and managed to land a blow on the one directly in front of Callahan. The blow came down hard on his foe's collar, but instead of waiting, he lifted the weapon again and hurled himself at the others. The attack was wild but did the job of confusing them. One continued to fight Riku, but the other two turned about, only for Callahan to knock one down to his knees.

"Three down!"

The Khreenk still held their ground, and the remaining fighter moved in tightly around its leader, both of them waiting for the right moment before hacking and stabbing. Their attacks were shorter than before; each one intended to bait rather than to over extend. Even Jack was impressed, as he moved around them, looking for an opening. The Khreenk leader saw a chance, took one step forward, and stabbed at Riku; an attack she barely avoided.

"This is the Colonel," said a gruff voice over the loudspeakers.

"It's Gun," said Riku.

Jack lifted his hand to silence her and lowered his weapon. The others threw a few more cuts and then also stopped. One of the Khreenk moved off to help his vanquished comrades from the dusty floor. As Gun spoke, the translator circuits worn over the ears of the Khreenk made low volume sounds.

"We have arrived in orbit over Helios Prime, and things are about to get interesting. Your unit commanders will give you the specifics. The short of it is that we're being replaced."

The sound of footsteps brought their attention to the entrance where the shape of Corporal Frewyn arrived. He nodded as he moved inside while listening to the voice of Colonel Gun. He didn't seem particularly surprised by what he was hearing, unlike the other marines. He was stoutly built, and his right arm was still locked in a synthetic arm sling that allowed only movement at the wrist and shoulder.

"We took a pounding on Eos, and our number is down to less than half. We are supposed to be joining ground forces on Helios Prime, but instead we've been reassigned to help organize the defenses on Micaya."

"Micaya?" Riku asked.

Jack nodded as though he had a firm understanding of both the strategy of the Alliance, as well as a deep understanding of the Helion political system.

"Micaya is a strategically significant world of the Helions. It must be a major potential target for the enemy. Doesn't it have a massive population?"

Corporal Frewyn shook his head with annoyance.

"Thank you for that pointless interruption, Private."

He turned back to Riku and the others.

"As we already know, the call has been sent out to every planet we know of. That includes all of ours plus probably the Helions, T'Kari, Byotai, and the rest."

Jack shook his head as he spoke and pulled out his secpad to show them a map of the system.

"We've already seen the report, Corporal. Look, the transfer reports show we have additional forces converging on this area from the T'Karan Rift. If you ask me, we're mobilizing everything for a massive last stand, right here."

He thumbed at the center of the image where Helios Prime was displayed.

Corporal Frewyn wiped his brow and sighed.

"Jack, can you bring it down a notch? I'm trying to explain something to you, information that has only just come to light and is being sent down through the chain of command."

He leaned in as though he was about to expose some great secret.

"Rumor has it that General Daniels is taking over command of the 3rd Marine Corps Regiment on Helios Prime. They are already there along with a lot, and I mean a lot, of other units."

The loud speakers blared their song once more.

"Marines report to your stations and await orders. We

49

will be accessing the local network shortly. "

"See, I said we wouldn't be staying in this system," said the Corporal.

They each removed their helmets, and even after such a short time, the group of eight dripped with sweat. The leader of the Khreenk approached Jack and nodded.

"That was interesting," he said through his low-pitched translator.

Jack did his best to smile.

"What do you know about this place?"

The Khreenk looked confused.

"The gas mines of Micaya?"

Riku approached. "Yeah, why are we going there?"

The Khreenk shrugged.

"It is an industrial world, many mines, advanced transportation, and heavily populated. It is just one of the inhabited worlds around Helios."

"Yeah, but why are we going there?" repeated Riku, "If the Biomechs take Helios Prime, they won't need to bother with the rest, will they?"

She didn't sound particularly confident in her own thesis.

"You don't know because you don't listen," said the gruff voice that had been counting those knocked down in the sparring match. Corporal Frewyn hadn't moved from where he'd been standing. He walked up to the small group and stopped at reaching Jack and the Khreenk warrior.

"Jae Jaan, I've been meaning to speak with you."

The Khreenk bowed politely.

"Of course, Corporal Frewyn. We've run into each other on several occasions since Eos."

"Indeed, and at least once before."

The marine's tone was far from conciliatory. It was true. They had met before the fighting on Eos and even before the Biomechs had landed. Things had changed since then though, and Frewyn had spent most of his time in the medical facility aboard one of the troop transports ever since that battle.

"I thought you had a different name on Eos?"

The Khreenk raised one of his eyebrows in amusement.

"Jae Jaan is my...uh...professional name, the one I use for my new employment."

The Corporal looked back to Riku and shook his head. He was clearly not completely comfortable with the new role being played by the small contingent aboard the ship. Their assistance in the final stages of the fighting on Eos couldn't be ignored though, no matter how much he wanted it.

"On the trip back, Jae Jaan and his people have proven very useful. They've given us detailed tactical information on the Helion worlds."

"And Jae Jaan helped us sort out several security issues," Jack said.

Even Private Riku stepped forward and added her support.

"True, don't forget the little issue with the Biomech infiltration team."

Corporal Frewyn had little love for these mercenaries, but he couldn't argue with their assistance a week earlier. He recalled the reports he'd read concerning a six-man infiltration unit of human spies. They managed to knock out the ship's engines and almost jettisoned the crew into space before being tracked and found by Jae Jaan and his people. They had done this while under strict marine supervision and had proved to be trackers of incredible skill and quality. He looked back to Jae Jaan.

"We have you and Private Morato to thank for that, I believe?" he said.

Both Jack and the Khreenk commander nodded ever so slightly.

"Private Morato took a chance on us after Eos. We fought as your enemies, but when it came to the Biomech attack, your own pilot's craft risked their lives to rescue us. One of your captains lost his life during the rescue, for that both I and my entire clan owe you a blood debt."

Corporal Frewyn considered his words carefully.

"Thank you. We could not let you stay behind to fight those things on your own. Politics are not our business. We are soldiers, not politicians."

Jae Jaan bowed slightly before the marine.

"Agreed. Khreenk are a shadow of what remained from the last war. Now we offer up our skills and services to whoever pays us. We will only take on honorable military work, and we honor our contracts until complete. As you know, we take no sides in the politics of race and nation."

He expanded out his arms as though to encompass the entire group.

"But since what happened on Eos, we can see what is coming, and it is a return to the dark times, one that none of my people can remember. We can see the damage done in the past though, and we also know the prophecy of fire. This enemy was banished, but it was foretold that they would return, and this time they will smash their foes and turn our worlds to ash. These machines have long memories and long lives. If Helios falls, our own will follow soon after."

He smiled, a look that never seemed to fit on a Khreenk's face.

"Your people, humans, are an interesting one. You are many generations behind us in technology, yet your numbers and your resilience are impressive. You have provided the rock on which the defense of Helios Prime will rally around. My commando unit has pledged itself to stopping the machines from ever returning to our worlds."

Jack hadn't heard this particular part. All of them had read the stories circulated by the T'Kari, and to a lesser extent by the Helions. The Khreenk had been something of a mystery, going right back to the Alliance's first contact with them. He listened with interest as Jae Jaan continued explaining.

"In the last War, the enemy came to my worlds as well. Back then our territory was wide and our people strong. They came and we fought them. Our people even took on some of their attributes, the enhancements, and the weapons to try and even the balance. It didn't work though, and our civilians paid the price. Our central government collapsed, and after the surprise victory, we were left with only two stars and ruined worlds. Now we live in ships, stations, and domes, fighting for whoever pay the highest. All Khreenk are now warriors."

He looked to Jack.

"Your people are the only race we know of that has fought against a Biomech rebellion within your own borders and won. For a chance of victory against the machines, my team will side with your forces."

The Corporal didn't seem particularly impressed.

"And the rest of your people. Will they join with us so easily?"

Jae Jaan laughed.

"Of course not. But if you pay them enough, they might consider it."

Frewyn sighed and looked back to Jack.

"That's the trouble with mercenaries. They are good fighters but only when you have the money to pay them."

Jack couldn't disagree, and he looked to Riku who also had nothing to add. Both of them shook their heads.

"I see. Well, you wanted to know what we're doing heading for Micaya?"

Riku and Jenkell turned their attention fully to their Corporal, but Jack answered him.

"All we've heard so far is that the local Rifts to the other Helion planets in this system are partially operational. The rumor is that we're going to Micaya. Nobody knows why though."

Corporal Frewyn seemed amused at this.

"I only know what the others in the unit have been saying. With these local Helion Rifts open, we have access to four of their five worlds, and they are all preparing for war."

This seemed to interest them, especially Jae Jaan who waited patiently at the rear of the group.

"The Eos Rift is still out of commission because of the attacks in the Helion Uprising. We can thank the Animosh for that bit of terrorism. Micaya is the furthest world from the approach of Comet C34 and it is connected to the local network."

"So?" said Private Jenkell.

Riku threw her a look of scorn and then moved her attention to the Corporal.

"That still doesn't explain why we're going to Micaya. What are we doing going there, then? I thought we were part of the fleet around Helios Prime? Isn't defending this place the whole reason we're here?"

Jack seemed to be in agreement with that statement.

"True. I think it is a bit more..."

A shape entered the room, and all of them straightened up as the form of a grim looking Sergeant entered. His uniform was smartly pressed, and his faced looked as hard as rock. He moved right up to the group, stopped, and then looked directly at Corporal Frewyn.

"Okay, Ladies, you've had your fun for today. Twelve minutes and we hit the Rift."

They waited for what was coming, as there was little chance the Sergeant had just appeared to tell them what they already knew.

"I've just finished with the transfer papers. The platoon, and this squad in particular, is being reinforced. Units from our battalions are being merged together to get squads back to full-strength. You'll meet your new friends when we meet the rest of the fleet and get our assignment."

"Fleet?" asked Riku.

Sergeant Stone smiled with the kind of grin that all of them knew was completely artificial. Jack looked the most interested at this news.

"So it's true, the others are sending help?"

Sergeant Stone looked at Jack carefully. He could remember their first meeting, and it had been less than inspiring. There was still a lot to like about the young marine, but he'd also made plenty of mistakes.

"They don't give us all the information, and I give you even less than that. I do know only part of the fleet is here. Admiral Anderson, in his wisdom, is keeping back a large force in T'Karan to protect our bases."

"Makes sense," said Corporal Frewyn.

He looked to Jack.

"Helios Prime is important, but T'Karan is our way home. Without it, we'd be trapped out here."

"That brings me to the real news," said the Sergeant.

His tone was impatient, and he cleared his throat to remind them he was there. For a moment, the other marines had almost forgotten him. His expression suggested otherwise, and all of them straightened at hearing the tone in his voice.

"The comet's course has adjusted again, and the official word is that it's preparing to release forces in order to assault the rest of this system simultaneously. Three sections have already detached from the main comet, and each one has been built directly from the comet. One each we suspect for the planets Libuscha and Spascia, and another one that will make it to Micaya, eventually."

"And the comet?" Corporal Frewyn asked.

Sergeant Stone smiled that grim expression once more.

"The comet is the largest of the four elements, and it is heading right for Helios Prime. High Command is classing all these objects as super-carriers, but who knows what kind of assets they will have access to?"

The Sergeant then turned to Jae Jaan.

"What do you know about these worlds?"

Jae Jaan seemed surprised at the question, and his answer started off slowly as he build up speed.

"Libuscha...it is a small world, fully terraformed after the War. It is where the Helion elite live out their lives. You will not find a richer or more decadent place in the Helion League."

"And Spascia?"

Jae Jaan grimaced.

"We lost many brothers fighting with the Helions on Spascia in the War. This is the traditional homeworld of the Zathee. This place is as urbanized as Helios Prime, but is poor and rundown. Billions live in squalor. It is the opposite of Libuscha; a place visitors never get to see. Nearly half of the world is now abandoned; that is why they call the massive city the Ruins of Spascia. As if nobody lives there anymore."

"But they do?" Jack asked.

Jae Jaan nodded. "More than a few."

Sergeant Stone listened to the Khreenk warrior with interest. As a relatively low rank, he was privy to only a limited level of information. This direct line to the intelligence on the Helions was just the thing he'd been sent to collect from his contact with the Khreenk.

"Good. Well, there's a major summit on Micaya right

now, and that's exactly where we are going. Representatives and commanders from the different races will be there, as well as a small contingent of your own people."

He looked to Jae Jaan, but the Khreenk seemed disinterested.

"I have orders from Lieutenant Elvidge. He says your team is to come with us on our own mission. Apparently, your presence has been requested by the Khreenk contingent already on Spascia."

All the marines turned their attention to Jae Jaan. Jack had spent the most time with him, but they'd not discussed his role or position within the Khreenk.

"They want you, why?"

Sergeant Stone grinned that dishonest smile that all of them recognized.

"Yeah, I have the file on you Jae Jaan."

He pulled out his secpad and turned it to face the marines. It was all a mere gesture, however, as he quickly replaced it before they could see anything.

"It seems our friend here is a member of the Khreenk Brotherhood."

None, not even Jae Jaan himself seemed to understand what he was saying. Sergeant Stone continued to explain.

"They are part of the political elite of Khreenk society. Can we assume that your assistance to the Animosh on Helios Prime was more than just another job?"

Jae Jaan now smiled.

"Everything is a job to us. Yes, I am of the Brotherhood, but I remain apart from the Khreenk in general. We had…"

"A what?" asked the Sergeant.

"A disagreement."

The Sergeant scratched his head, considering his words before looking to Corporal Frewyn.

"Well, in any case, we've been reassigned to Spascia. Due to this squad's experience and exposure to the Khreenk, we've all been assigned to work alongside them."

Corporal Frewyn was not impressed.

"Work, Sergeant? We're to be their bodyguards, on Spascia?"

Jae Jaan began to laugh and looked to his three comrades. They shared a few words in their own language before a great roar of laughter spread about them.

"No. I've got my orders, and the LT says that Jae Jaan's fighters are just a part of a larger force that have already arrived. They have experience of Spascia, experience that could prove very helpful in a stand up fight."

Jae Jaan looked at a computer interface unit on his arm and tapped several buttons before looking back at the humans.

"That is correct. My brothers are on Spascia, on my orders."

Sergeant Stone didn't seem impressed that Jae Jaan had been able to communicate off the ship, and he threw a quick glance at Jack as though he must have had something to do with it. The young marine lifted his hands defensively.

"Hey, Sarge, don't look at me."

Jae Jaan nodded to the Sergeant.

"I was asked not to speak of this until we reached Helios Prime."

He could see Jack looked almost offended at having been left out of the loop.

"Since the incident with the infiltration team, I have been in talks with your commanders. My blood debt is with your marines, Sergeant, but our commitment to keeping the Biomechs out of our territory is even greater. The Brotherhood has been tasked with assisting your forces in any way we can, and every one of them reports directly to me."

"How many are we talking about?" Jack asked.

Jae Jaan wiped his lip with the back of his hand.

"About thirty."

Jack raised his eyebrow and sighed.

"Thirty Khreenk? All this fuss for thirty warriors."

He turned and walked about muttering, but Jae Jaan merely chuckled.

"No, not thirty warriors, thirty Khreenk Corsairs. They are not of the size or power of something like this ship, but they are useful vessels."

"Tell me more," demanded Sergeant Stone, "How many warriors can you supply us with?"

"Thirty ships, each with about a hundred warriors on

board, plus crew. As I said, they are Corsairs, designed for…well…privateer work. The ships will be useful raiders and scouts. My brothers will meet us on Spascia. They are surveying the defenses as we speak."

Jack moved back and looked at Jae Jaan carefully.

"What kind of warriors are they?"

Jae Jaan pointed to his three comrades.

"Just like these."

He then looked back to Sergeant Stone.

"I have already spoken with your commander, Colonel Gun. It is with him that I made the deal. My brothers will honor their oath. They are all strong, able fighters, and they will serve you well."

Sergeant Stone nodded and turned to look at the odd assortment of marines and Khreenk. All were physically tough, and he had little doubt they would put up a good fight, if it came to it.

"Spascia is not a second-rate posting. Alliance Naval intel says that these objects are definitely adjusting their courses onto intercept vectors to move into orbit around all four worlds."

He lifted his secpad to check the figures.

"According to the number crunchers, we have thirty-three hours before the first of these objects arrives. Helios Prime is in five days, Libuscha in nine weeks, and the last will reach Micaya in thirteen weeks."

Jack had been quiet for the last minute, but the timetable

seemed to wake him up.

"So these things will be in orbit around every Helion world in less than four months? Is that why we're being sent to Spascia?"

Sergeant Stone smiled, and this time it was a cruel expression, one that almost made Jack shudder.

"Spascia will be the first to face the full wrath of the Biomechs. That's why High Command has flagged the planet as the site for first contact in this war."

"Uh, what about Eos?" Jack complained, "I think we kind of fought a hard fight there, didn't we? And that was against the Biomechs."

Sergeant Stone shook his head.

"No, Son, it wasn't. These four objects are as large as a small moon, and scans show massive emissions from there, so they are probably occupied. The word is the force that hit Eos was a minor scouting party."

"Bullshit!" Corporal Frewyn snapped back, without thinking.

"Secure that crap, Corporal."

"Sorry, Sergeant."

"In any case, we just don't know. That's why Command is throwing our most experienced warriors to Spascia, and they are expecting hard intel from us when the Biomechs arrive. It won't just be us there. We'll have substantial Khreenk and NHA support."

The look on the faces of the marines was far from the

keen expressions he'd expected. Instead, he saw a mixture of bitterness and resentment, especially on Private Morato's face.

"Son. This is important. Anything can learn on Spascia will help with the main event on Helios Prime. This war is about to get biblical, and we need every marine primed and ready. You got me?"

"Yes, Sergeant!" he replied, in exactly the manner that had been drilled into him since his days in training. The rest of the marines joined in the chorus while the Khreenk watched on patiently.

"Good. We'll be through the Rift very soon. I want you all in full tactical gear and with everything stowed within the hour. We're going to war, people, and this time we're gonna make those bastards pay!"

He turned away and marched out of the room to leave the mixture of humans and Khreenk watching on.

"Well, there you have it, then," said Corporal Frewyn.

Jae Jaan bent down and picked up one of the discarded training weapons.

"We have time for perhaps one more bout before we prepare for this deployment?"

Jack opened his mouth, but Riku stepped out to his right and shook her head.

"Another time, Jae Jaan. We have some things to attend to."

Jack looked at her in confusion.

"We have what?" he asked.

She moved closer, ran her fingers over his mouth, and then leaned in to whisper in his ear.

"Come with me. We don't have long."

CHAPTER THREE

ANS Dreadnought marked a turning point in ship design as the venerable Crusader class was modified once more. The Conqueror class Battlecruisers had proven capable heavy warships, and initial combat had shown a need for an up-gunned version. Dreadnought, named for the British pinnacle of ironclad battleship technology, combined everything learned since the Great War. The flexibility of the modular Crusader layout remained, but with the additional slats designed to fit onto the existing model. The end result was a Conqueror class with twenty percent additional bulk and even more turret guns systems.

Ships of the Interstellar Navy

There was only a short time left to go before they had to assemble in the landing bay of ANS Conqueror. Riku was in the shower, and as had become something of a tradition for Jack, he used the time before a major operation to check his account for messages from his friends or family. He'd sent a message back home just the day before, and to his surprise there was a message waiting for him, already pre-screened and decrypted. He entered his access codes and waited for the final conversion.

"Jack, I just received your message. Your father and I are safe, and we'll be back together again soon…"

Those were words Jack hadn't expected to hear in a long time. She went on to explain about her new posting, and that she'd been given command of a new unit on the planet of Prometheus. All of it seemed to pale to insignificance when she got to the part about his father.

"I've seen footage of Spartan. He's in a bad way; the machines had him prisoner for a long time. As soon as my job here is done, I'll be getting to Sol as quickly as I can. Good luck, Son. We'll both be in touch soon."

He would have liked to have spoken with Spartan, but as was almost always the case, his father was nowhere to be seen, and now that the Sol Rift was down there was no chance of getting a message to him. There were his two half-brothers, children of his mother's previous life, but they were anything but friends to him; just thinking about them made him angry. As he sat there in his pants and training shirt, he felt a hand run along his shoulders, and his worries began to tumble away.

"Jack, wouldn't you rather do something else?"

He looked to his left where the voluptuous form of Riku waited. She wore nothing but her Marine Corps cap and moved around him to sit on his lap. He looked at her, and though his mind had drifted about, he found he couldn't take his eyes off her face. He usually avoided looking at the long scar that ran along its side, but even her nakedness couldn't stop him gazing at it. He ran his hand over the scar; feeling the soft, cool skin and the tiny ridge that marked where she'd been badly injured so long ago. She leaned in and kissed him, to feel him trembling beneath her. She stepped back from his lap and then pulled him to his feet.

"We should get ready. We're supposed to be ready in..." Riku shook her head.

"No, Jack, you should be exactly where I want you."

She grabbed his arm and threw him onto his small bed, narrowly avoiding hitting his head on the raised bulkhead that ran directly through the room, instead striking his face on the wall. He grunted more in surprise than pain, but before he could orientate himself she threw herself at him, and the two collapsed onto the bed in a tangled mess of flesh.

* * *

The journey through the Helios-Spascia Rift was short and uninteresting to Jack. Some of the marines had only done this kind of trip a few times, but he'd lost count years earlier. It was as interesting to him as putting on his PDS Alpha armor. Jack had been waiting alongside the rest of his comrades in the landing bay, doing his best to hide the bump on the side of his face where he'd struck the wall. It was cramped, especially with so many other marines being stationed there. The shuttles, landing craft, and other vehicles had been moved to their flank stowage areas. The long lines of marines were silent, each waiting for their commander to arrive. Unusually, they were all wearing their full combat gear as if they expected an attack at any moment. The only concession was that their weapons were onboard their craft and their visors open.

The first indication that something was changing was the metallic clunk of somebody approaching. From the far end came the great shape of Colonel Gun, the Jötnar hero of the Uprising and now commander of the entire battalion. He marched between the two large groups of marines, along with his small entourage of Jötnar guards and senior officers before stopping and looking at the marines.

"Marines, we have a new mission."

None of this was news to Jack, but he found it reassuring to hear the sound of his old friend's voice. It reminded him of time spent years earlier in the company of the Jötnar, hunting on Hyperion or off on private security operations with Wictred and the others. It was a time between wars, when few thought another struggle like the Uprising would happen in their lifetimes.

How wrong we all were.

"The 17th and 8th put up one hell of a fight on Eos. I've received official commendations from General Rivers, but I know that's not what you want to hear."

Jack looked about the group and could see Gun had identified the mood perfectly.

"By now you will have heard the news, and yes, it is all true. The 17th and 8th are being merged in time for our new mission. This mission is not some backwater posting. It will be right on the frontline."

One of his junior officers tapped the wall-mounted display, and a massive image of the planet of Spascia appeared. Gun walked closer and examined the image carefully, as though he was trying to find something important. Finally, he stopped and pointed at the center.

"This is Spascia, one of Helios' five worlds. This particular hunk of rock is the home to billions of civilians and is littered with cities on every continent. This place is one of the hottest worlds we've ever found that is inhabited. That's why Spascia City was built around the northern pole. This was the ancient capital of Spascia, but now it is a ruin."

He pointed again at one section of the planet as he mentioned the ruins.

"People still live there, right in these ruins to take

advantage of the milder climate. The terrain is rocky, and there are mountains and valleys throughout the northern continent. There's also something else that is critical to the war effort, and that's why we're going to Spascia. At the heart of the Helion world is a weapon system. They have some alien name for it; we call it the Doomsday Gun."

The image moved in closer and every single one of the marines looked on with interest. Even the small party of Khreenk mercenaries appeared captivated at the information.

How the hell didn't they know? Jack wondered.

"These weapons are powerful enough to shut down a Rift for months. They are a guarantee that Biomechs will be unable to enter the Helios system from their own worlds. They are also able to target all year round, due to the sites being placed at the top of each planet, with their power plants and facilities buried deep underground."

Colonel Gun looked out to his marines and grinned. His wide smile showed a hidden line of gleaming teeth.

"Our mixed unit will provide the backbone of the Spascia's defense force. General Daniels is taking command of Helios Prime to do the same. That's right. So as of today, I am the commander of all Alliance forces on Spascia, and we will not let the world fall."

The marines cheered, but it wasn't as loud or passionate as he had expected. He looked about the group, noting the fatigue showing on their faces. He forgot sometimes how the average marine saw combat, unlike him and his kin. He took a long, deep breath before continuing.

"We have Jötnar reinforcements from T'Karan, as well as help coming from the 22nd Regiment. The Khreenk Brotherhood is supplying almost three thousand ground troops, as well as robotic hardware that will prove useful. This is a major force of thousands of warriors."

Again there was little excitement in the group. He looked about and spotted Jack in the crowd. He couldn't say anything right now and didn't give the young man a nod of acknowledgement. It reminded him of what he'd heard prior to leaving Admiral Lewis and the General.

"I have news that Spartan himself has been found and has valuable information on the enemy and their plans. If Spartan is back, then you all know what that means. He was last heard of on Earth where he was joining Earth forces in an assault on Mars. That's right, Spartan is back, and he's waging a personal war against these things."

It wasn't much, and he'd already modified the story to fit his needs, but it seemed to be having the desired effect. Several of the marines were already chatting excitedly at this change of events.

"When Spartan raises his head, our enemies begin to panic, and for good reason. Spartan and I have a long history together. More than that, between us we have killed more Biomechs than you've eaten hot meals!"

It was a bold boast, but the marines enjoyed it. Gun

looked like a monster alongside them all, and the more excited he became, the more they responded.

"The Biomechs are sending a large force toward Spascia, and we can expect one hell of a fight. Eos was a walk in the park compared to what we're expecting on this new planet. I can promise you that this time we will not be forced to leave. No matter what they throw at us, the Marine Corps will stand, and we'll make these soulless machines burn. Won't you?"

This time the noise from the assembled marines increased in volume. It wasn't much, but he could definitely sense the improvement.

"Now, to your landing craft and Spascia. Report to your junior commanders and get to work. We have a lot to do and little time to do it."

* * *

The Alliance deployment over Spascia was as impressive as anything Admiral Lewis had ever seen. General Daniels was now long gone, along with the entirety of his senior command staff. They had left with dozens of other landing craft and Maulers as they made their way down to the surface of Helios Prime, just minutes before the ship had entered the Rift to Spascia. Colonel Gun had remained at his side to watch as the fleet assembled, and he seemed genuinely excited at the prospect of another confrontation with the enemy.

"They did as they promised," Gun said calmly.

Admiral Lewis nodded.

"True. Every ship that said would be here, is here."

"Did General Daniels tell you the news from Eos?" Gun asked.

Admiral Lewis turned his head and looked a little confused.

"What news?"

Gun could sense the raw nerves as he asked and realized he'd been a little too vague in his comments. He'd been getting much better, but even experienced commanders like Admiral Lewis were vulnerable to the impact of difficult news.

"A message got through to me less than twenty minutes ago from Eos. It was rerouted back from General Daniels. There's news from Eos and Captain Carter."

The name took a moment to register.

"Ah, the man we sent down to Helios Prime. Yes, he is one of our Black Ops specialists. What is the news?"

Now Gun found it hard to conceal his pleasure.

"Wictred and a handful of marines have found him, and they are assisting in the defense of settlements against the last Biomechs. By all accounts, the NHA is finally doing something useful."

Admiral Lewis looked less impressed.

"Well, we did hit the bastards hard with a barrage of

nukes. Still, if they can clear Eos, it would give us a place to operate from away from these new arrivals."

He looked back at the fleet ahead of them. Gun nodded slowly.

"I agree. Eos could prove a real pain for them to deal with later on."

The Admiral watched a pair of Crusader class warships move across their beam and toward a small group of Alliance transports that had just moved in through the Rift.

"Gun, that isn't what worries me though. Just look at all of this."

Gun did as he said and couldn't quite see the problem. The 4th Heavy Strike Group was now just a component in what was being called the Spascia Fleet. Additional ships had arrived, including a fourteen first generation Crusader class ships. He could tell the difference by the hull configuration. There was even a small number of the new Liberty class vessels, ships capable of performing the role of frigate and light-cruiser equally well.

"What's the problem? I see lots of ships."

Admiral Lewis looked as glum as he'd been ever since they'd withdrawn from Eos.

"True, we have over thirty Alliance ships, quite a fleet in anybody's eyes. It would be even bigger if we'd been able to bring the damaged ships with us too. On top of ours, we have a similar number of Khreenk ships and seven

Helion cruisers. Even so, sixty-seven ships will not stop the kind of forces I'm expecting from the Biomechs."

Gun looked out at the formation.

"This number would have stopped them at Eos."

The Admiral looked at them for a little longer.

"You're right. We could have stopped the assault before most of them even made it into orbit."

He then looked at the screen to his right and the details obtained so far on the objects breaking away from the comet.

"These things are unlike anything any of us have ever seen before. Even the T'Kari say there is no precedent. The object heading for Spascia has expanded and lengthened in the last few days. It is now over five kilometers in length. Initial readings show it is constructed in the same way as the rest of the comet, but most of its mass is artificial and extending out behind the remnants of the comet."

"So they're breaking off chunks of the comet and directing them to the orbit of the Helion planets. I thought you said they were manned?"

Admiral Lewis tapped the image to show just one quarter of the nearest.

"They are powered by something massive, a reactor of a level we've never come across. They are capable of course change, and we're detecting massive levels of digital communication. They are not just mobile rocks, Gun. Each of them is a self-contained starbase or massive battleship, and if our estimates are correct, they could be carrying substantial space and ground forces. It's why we're calling them Arks. At least until somebody comes up with a better name."

Gun rubbed his right hand along his chin.

"So, they've spent the last hundreds of years constructing space Arks, for what reason?"

The image shifted to show Spascia.

"I believe they intend on putting these things in orbit around each of the Helion worlds. From there, they will conduct an assault of the like never seen before. They will hit the Doomsday weapon systems and then attack the Black Rift directly."

"And then the rest will come through," Gun added.

"Worse than that. Once the Black Rift is opened and uncontested, they will unleash whatever terrors they've been mobilizing since their banishment. Helios will go, and then so will every single race that has helped them."

Gun grasped his right fist and squeezed.

"Well, Admiral, if they were looking for a fight, they've come to just the right place."

Admiral Lewis tried to smile, but the magnitude of the threat facing them made that impossible. He looked again at the motley selection of ships and wondered how many of them would stand when the enemy Arks were in range.

Will they fight to the last man, or will they surrender or retreat at the first sign of battle?

* * *

Jack's head shuddered as the Mauler smashed through the upper atmosphere with a thump. The descent was a lot rougher than he'd expected, and it felt as though he'd been struck on the side of the head. He looked to his right and watched the lines of other marines as they shook about on the way down. The couplings holding them in place were firm and reliable, but that never seemed to stop the feeling something bad was going to happen. Riku saw him looking about and tapped the top of her helmet to get his attention.

"Jack, don't fall out!"

She wasn't serious, but Jack had heard the horror stories of when magnetic couplings failed, and marines had been thrown from the safety of their harnessed seating. There were rumors that during the assault on the Titan Naval Station, an entire platoon had been smashed to a pulp when a landing craft had been hit by gunfire. Power had apparently been lost, and the marines had slammed into each other and even the metal framing of the craft itself, instantly killing dozens of them. Jack swallowed and felt his throat drying up. Images of Hunn and the others returned from Helios Prime, and that first major battle with the robotic killing machine.

Get a grip, Jack. You've been in much worse since then.

Adrenalin began to pump through his body, giving him a feeling of excitement, dread, and fatigue all at the same time. He could feel something almost like sickness in his stomach and resorted to striking his head with his right hand. It was an odd gesture, but seemed to do the job for now.

"Jack?" Riku asked.

He ignored her and concentrated on his routine. There were a number of checks to be performed before a combat drop, even if they weren't expecting trouble. It was every marine's responsibility to ensure that once they hit the ground, everyone was ready for whatever needed to be done. A flicker of movement caught his eye through the tiny flank portholes in the craft, and he was convinced he could see the burning shape of another Mauler coming down alongside them.

Not long now.

The craft joined the many other Maulers and Hammerheads that had been dropped while the fleet remained in orbit. From this far down, there was no chance of seeing the tiny dots that were the fleet, but the small windows and the video feeds inside Jack's helmet still gave him a detailed view of what was going on. Icons moved around the distant ships, and he could see that a number of them, including ANS Conqueror, were already turning back to the Rift.

This is a critical front, my ass. The real fight will be wherever

Lewis goes.

It really shouldn't have mattered to him what the fleet was up to, or even what their posting on this unusual planet was all about. A frontline was much like any other. They would dig in and prepare, and if things worked in their favor, they might live. It wasn't that, it was more that Jack knew this fight was going to be unlike any they had seen before. This comet looked like it had been converted into a number of orbital bases the size of small moons, and each one had the capacity to carry numbers of ships and soldiers more than equal of anything the Alliance could throw at them. If Jack was going to be in a fight, he wanted it to be in the one that counted.

Just my luck to get posted to this backwater, when the real fight is over there.

He looked to the icons showing the leaving ships, wishing he were still on board one of them. It was quite clear to him the savaged marine battalions were being taken away from the real frontline. Gun had said otherwise, but Jack failed to see why such a combat proven unit would not be placed right where it could do the most good.

Hell, even General Daniels has left us for Helios Prime.

As he sat there considering his situation, an image of Lieutenant Elvidge appeared. It would be the same for every other marine in his platoon, and a much better way of passing on orders than via a communal video display. Jack was very surprised to see the man. It was the first time he'd seen his face since their fighting withdrawal from Eos. He recalled the gunshot wounds, and it surprised him even more to see him on the visor.

He must be fit and ready for action. Weird, I thought he was being sent back to Terra Nova for some R&R.

"3rd Platoon, we have a job to do, and it ain't a pretty one."

An image of the surface of the planet popped up and rotated about to show a desolate region in the north. It zoomed in until finally reaching the shattered ruins of Spascia city.

"Spascia is the largest of the seven cities on this continent, and it is built on both sides of the deep valley here."

The imagery blurred as it zoomed in closely, showing the valley that split the city into two main areas.

"Ninety-five percent of the city is based on this side of the valley. The remainder is built on the eastern side and is protected by substantial artificial and natural defenses. The base of the valley leads into the mountain fortress used for the Doomsday weapon. 3rd Platoon will be assisting with the defense of the southwest perimeter of the city, and this valley is the only way into the facility."

The image changed again to show the northern continent of Spascia.

"The cities are spread out over a wide area, with waterways, woodland, and mountains blocking multiple routes. Defense of the other six will come down on the NHA. Alliance and Khreenk forces are taking the lead at Spascia. We will be linking up with two more battalions from the Marine Corps 22nd Regiment; that gives us near to six thousand marines plus change."

Yeah, and what were our numbers on Eos? Jack wondered.

"Sergeant Stone, I want the entire platoon deployed at this point."

The Mauler shuddered once more, and Jack almost twisted his neck with the impact. Only the thick padding around his head and upper body stopped him sustaining a serious injury, and his vision blurred for a moment.

"Our battalion is joining the Khreenk to establish a defensive line along the western front of the city. Spascia volunteers manning weapon platforms will assist us. Good luck, people, I will see you on the ground shortly."

His image vanished, and Jack found himself staring directly into the visor of the marine sitting opposite him. The man didn't seem to notice, and Jack found it almost impossible to make out much in the way of detail on the man's face.

So, we're on the frontline again. This had better work better than last time.

"Three minutes to the landing zone. Get yourselves ready, marines!" growled Sergeant Stone.

Jack twisted his head about to spot the man standing at the end of the Mauler. His body was being held in place by two vertical clamps and gave him the perfect view of the rest of the marines in the Mauler.

"When we land, you will move out to the designated position to assist in the defenses. I want a clean deployment and quick work. The enemy is coming, and we need this city ready for the second coming!"

He looked from left to right before saying his last words.

"You get me?"

"Yes, Sergeant!" came back the chorus from the entire platoon of thirty-six marines, most of whom Jack had never even seen before. He selected the forward view from the Mauler, and his visor filled with a wide panoramic view of the horizon and the approach to the city. The first thing he could see was the vast tear in the ground that was the valley. They moved along it until in the distance he could see the shape of a low mountain peak. The valley ran almost directly to the mountain and then split a short distance in front. It was at that split where the bulk of Spascia City lay. Although it covered hundreds of square kilometers, it was the sectors nearest the valley that included the tallest and most well developed buildings. On one side the city covered it as far as the eye could see, while on the other bank it was almost completely devoid of buildings. What stood out the most was that this section was made up of jagged rocks and mountains that from a distance looked like a saw blade.

"Jack, can you see it?" Riku asked.

Jack nodded. He wanted to speak, but his throat was still dry and rough, and he doubted he was capable of much in the way of decent conversation right now. Instead, he turned his attention back to the display. They were now directly over the entrance to the mountain, and he could see large numbers of vehicles and equipment moving around it. The entire approach and entrance to the mountain were surrounded by tall structures covered in guns.

"Marines, what you are seeing below is what our engineers have been working on for the last four days in a row. They are called the Three Sisters."

Jack looked at the odd structures and wondered who could have come up with something so large and so ugly. They were massive, and by his estimates at least forty meters tall and almost square in shape. He counted to himself and found it was actually a sixteen-sided building. Small platforms extended from the flank from which batteries of railguns had been installed, but it was the guns fitted to the top of the Sisters that surprised him the most. Sergeant Stone spotted him shaking his head.

"What is it, Private?"

Jack looked up and continued shaking his head.

"The guns on top of those things, aren't they naval weapons?"

The Sergeant smiled.

"You bet your ass they are. One of the first tranche of

Crusaders gave up her guns while she'd being upgraded. Some wise guy engineer by the name of Sanlav suggested they could be installed on the ground."

The engines blasted at a different angle, and the large Mauler slowed down and began its final descent. Its nose lifted slightly, and it dropped several hundred meters toward the city. The Mauler's cameras angled downward to show the city in even greater detail.

"What you're looking at here is the pinnacle of military engineering. Three fortresses, each built with four-meter thick walls and four twin-mounted 128mm railguns that are powerful enough to damage a frigate. Each tower carries additional eight quad-mounted 20mm coilguns for short to medium ranges. If anybody thinks they can land troops within a kilometer of this part of the city, they will pay with body parts."

The Mauler banked sharply, and the view changed to show a vast open area running alongside the east flank of the city. There were dozens of landing strips and platforms cut directly into the rock. Massive road bridges connected the landing areas to the main parts of the city.

"Here we go, marines, thirty seconds!"

Jack's body tensed, and every meter they traveled brought them closer and closer to their ultimate objective. It seemed to take an eternity, but finally the Mauler touched down on one of the many landing strips. The doors hissed open, revealing the bright daylight of the ruins of Spascia

City.

"Everybody out, now!"

Riku was on her feet at the same time as him. Without even thinking, the unit was out of the doors, down the ramps, and onto hard rock. The sensors on his suit confirmed the temperature, humidity, and composition of the air around them.

All breathable, apparently!

He was no fool though and kept his visor in position. Long columns of marines marched from many more craft and toward large groups of Bulldog armored vehicles. Six pulled up in a small column, and right behind them came two of the mobile gun variants. Jack almost stopped upon seeing so much hardware in one place. No matter where he looked, he could see hundreds, if not thousands of marines, and all of them had somewhere to go and something to do.

"Marine, watch your step," said somebody to his right.

Jack twisted about and found himself looking up at the shape of five Jötnar, all wearing their heavy JAS armor that gave them a look more like metal giants than of artificially created men. The sergeant of the Jötnar unit stared at Jack, but there was no sign of recognition. He shook his head, and the group then moved away to be replaced by Sergeant Stone.

"Private, get your ass into the Bulldogs, ASAP!"

"Yes, Sergeant."

He followed the rest of the column, and they moved two-by-two to the Bulldogs. Three filled up and moved away to make space for the next few vehicles. As he waited for the doors to open, another vehicle drove up and stopped nearby. This one was tracked and slightly longer than the Bulldog. It appeared to be unarmed and lacked any discernible markings. The side doors slid open and out came a pair of Khreenk warriors. Both carried two-handed blades on their flanks and carbines hung in slings along their chests.

"Private, let me introduce you to my kin," said a familiar voice.

Jack looked to his right and then his left before spotting Jae Jaan. The Khreenk commander must have arrived on one of the other Maulers before they had. Jack nodded but had no idea what to say. Jae Jaan noticed his confusion and signaled for the two to approach Jack. They stopped and extended their hands in the common sign of friendship in the Alliance. Jack shook them both and noted how like all the Khreenk, their bodies and armor were modified and customized to the individual.

"I'm Private Jack Morato, 8th Marine Corps Battalion."

The first of the two new Khreenk released his hand.

"I am Tessuk, commander of the First Fist."

Jack looked to Jae Jaan for an explanation.

"Ah, I see. First Fist. It is the name we use for the standard combat unit on board one of our Corsairs. Your equivalent would be…uh…"

"A Captain," said a gruff voice.

Jack noticed the shadow across Jae Jaan's torso and moved his eyes to the shape of Colonel Gun. A bodyguard unit of Jötnar, as well as a handful of heavily armed Vanguards flanked him. Jack felt like a child in comparison to them. Gun extended his armored fist to the Khreenk commander and shook his hand.

"Commander Gun, your reputation is well known to us."

Gun didn't seem overly impressed by that.

"Yours will be determined very soon."

He then looked to Jae Jaan.

"Do your warriors have everything you need?"

Jae Jaan nodded.

"Yes. Our positions have been marked out alongside your own. All we need is somebody to shoot."

This finally brought a different look to Gun. He struck Jack on his shoulder.

"Yes, we will all get a chance to kill a few of our friends very soon. Just make sure your positions are ready, and remember, watch the skies!"

CHAPTER FOUR

The arrival of the comet in the Helios system surprised everybody, including those members of the Narau defending the Black Rift. Promises had been made to the Alliance that the area of space around the defunct Rift could be rendered useless; just months after the arrival of the comet, this promise proved to have been misleading. The Black Rift Stronghold, as it was known, contained both the generator equipment to create a new, super-long Rift to the enemy's homeworld, and also the ancient weapon used by the T'Kari and the Helions to collapse Rifts. The promised weapon to stop a Rift even being formed proved to have been a promise too far, and one that would cause much enmity leading up to the comet's approach to Helios Prime.

Accounts of the Prophecy of Fire

The journey to the designated zone for 2nd Squad took nearly thirty minutes through the city. By air it could have been done in less than a minute, but following lessons learned on Eos, the marines had made some changes; that meant it would be almost impossible for them to make the trip by air. Jack spotted some of these as they made their way down one of the busier streets. Large metal and concrete spikes extended upward in all of the main open spaces, and more were being erected even as they passed.

"Sergeant, who came up with that idea?" Riku asked.

Sergeant Stone had been watching from his command cupola atop the Bulldog and had to drop down to see her.

"The spikes?"

Riku nodded. "Yes, Sergeant."

He rested his arms on the brackets below the cupola and looked at the small group of marines, each jammed tight inside the Bulldog. There was little free space, and if there had been anymore, it would have been filled with even more marines or equipment.

"That is what is known as an air defense spike. They are quick, cheap, and perfect for causing trouble for rapid air assaults."

The Bulldog hit a bump, and the Sergeant moved up into the cupola and narrowly avoided hitting his head on the metal frame. The Bulldog slowed down, and he looked back at the marines as if nothing had happened.

"We have substantial air defenses manned by Helion soldiers, the majority positioned on both sides of the chasm. If they are stupid enough to attack there, they will suffer massive losses. If we're lucky, then that is exactly what they will do."

He looked to the left, looking at something as they moved past. His cold, hard eyes watched for several seconds and then turned his attention back to his unit, as if the focus of his attention had never been there in the first place.

"Check your gear again. We arrive in thirty seconds."

They made their way through the last of the recently cleared streets and past the lines of Helion civilians being evacuated to the other side of the chasm. It seemed to take much longer than thirty seconds, but finally they were there and on the furthest section of the city that was still occupied. The Bulldog slid to a stop, and the door opened before the dust even cleared.

"Go, go, go!" Sergeant Stone shouted.

Jack was first out of his Bulldog and stopped upon reaching the ground. The city was in an even worse state of repair here and the number of civilians reduced substantially. Wherever he spotted an open space, there were at least five of the vertical poles pushing up into the air. This world was very different to the design of Helios Prime or Eos. The buildings were lower and the streets narrow. It had more in common with a human world, and that surprised him.

"I don't think those things will stop a Biomech lander," he said quietly.

Riku tapped him on the shoulder and pointed to another group of marines moving about a command Bulldog. It was markedly different to the other vehicles by the amount of antenna and extra equipment fitted to it. Dozens of robotic mules, known as Rams, moved at the speed of a quick walk, carrying supplies and equipment to the dozens of squads preparing their positions. Colonel Gun had beaten them to it and was marching about issuing orders to the waiting Alliance officers while a group of Khreenk commanders watched on. Jack and the others moved closer until they could hear his voice. Jack spotted the man furthest to the right was Lieutenant Elvidge, his platoon's commanding officer.

"Look, the LT," said Callahan before Jack could say a word.

"This is the first line of defense," continued Colonel Gun.

The others watched intently as he showed them a view of Spascia City. Jack stopped and watched from a short distance but was quickly spotted by Sergeant Stone.

"Private, that's none of your concern. Leave planning this operation to the officers. I have some work for you that is just up your street."

He fell in with the rest of the platoon as a column of marines filed past the officers. Jack only managed to hear one last piece about the marines in this sector would be assisting in the defense of the outer perimeter. They moved to the other side of the street where the buildings had been smashed down to no more than two stories in height. Nestled amongst the ruins were trailer mounted anti-aircraft guns. Jack peered at the first and noticed Helion civilians were operating it. He looked back and found Sergeant Stone right next to him.

"Problem, Private?"

"Uh, no, Sergeant."

"Come on, Lad, if you have something to say, spit it out, or don't waste my time to start with."

Jack considered keeping his mouth shut, but the question just kept bouncing about in his head.

"Sergeant. If we leave our marines out on this perimeter, won't we lose the mobility advantage that the Marine Corps has?"

The Sergeant nodded in agreement.

"That is not a bad point, Son. Luckily for us, Command has decided to keep all Bulldogs in reserve for just that. If we hit trouble, then there will be armor to extract us. Hammerheads are being armed and fueled at the landing platforms all over the mountain fortress. This isn't Eos. This time we'll be ready."

Jack kept on moving, but no matter how hard he thought he couldn't shake the images of yet another bloodbath. Even as he looked about at the ground they would be defending, he could see images of death before the fight even started. He shook his head, but the shattered bodies of marines appeared as if ghosts in his visor.

Man, you need to snap out of this, now!

He looked to his left at the Sergeant looking right back at him.

"Good. Now, all of you get to work with the defenses around these flak guns. CES engineers will be here within the hour, and you will assist them with constructing lines of defense around the designated positions showing on your heads up displays."

Jack's comrades had now reached him, and each waited as the Sergeant pointed out the key points of their defense. Lieutenant Elvidge walked over to them, along with Jae Jaan and Tessuk.

"Sergeant Stone. What is our status?"

The Sergeant saluted smartly, and the rest of the marines straightened up at the sight of their officer. All three squads merged together into a substantial block that was two deep and packed with fully armored marines.

"Lieutenant, the entire platoon is present and accounted for. We've been fully reinforced and rearmed as per orders."

"Excellent work, Sergeant."

The Lieutenant grimaced for a second, as he turned from the Sergeant and looked at the marines and checked the first few in turn. A good number he recognized from their brief but violent action on Eos, but over half had come from other units, and there were many fresh faces he hadn't even seen on the ship prior to their latest operation. There was not one among them who hadn't seen combat though, and as was traditional, the marines never hid the scars and marks of war from their armor. The Marine Corps artificers would tidy up the paintwork and repair damage, but they were ever present, each one a reminder of the struggles taken in the past.

"We've been given an important mission, Sergeant. 2nd Squad has been chosen to defend this section of the line."

He pointed out to his left and right.

"Now, we have three companies of marines along this entire front, plus a company of Khreenk warriors under the command of Tessuk here. Colonel Gun has sent us a platoon of Jötnar, all of them packing some of the newest kit we have available. I am stationing a four-man fireteam of them with you to bolster this section of the line."

Tessuk nodded in agreement.

"My unit will be two hundred meters back and in cover. If you need assistance, just call us. We will be ready."

Jack spotted a dozen or so of the alien warriors in the distance. They wore dark clothing with the usual assortment of mixed armor and edged weapons. They would normally have made him nervous, but today he was just thankful they would have a reserve of some kind. Even so, Jack's first thought was that it sounded like a lot of combat units for such a small area, but at second glance, he could see they would need an entire company to fully defend just this one block. Instead, they had enough to hold only a fraction of the ground. The Lieutenant could see the worry on his face and varying levels of confusion amongst some of the other marines, but especially with Corporal Frewyn.

"What is it?"

"Well, Sir. After what happened on Eos, why would they land outside the city? Surely they will either bombard the mountain fortress itself, or just directly assault the city by dropping troops in the middle."

"Or just land on the other side of the chasm where they can directly access the entrance to the mountain," Private Jenkell added.

Sergeant Stone made to cut them off, but the Lieutenant waved him back.

"No, it's okay. They are all good questions, the same ones I've been making to Command."

Jack felt his heart sink for a moment. He had no problem fighting, but the thought of another Alliance debacle left a sick feeling in his stomach that he wished he could drown with something, anything. Lieutenant Elvidge must have spotted him because he moved closer, doing his best to hide the pain as he walked.

"Luckily for us, the eastern approach to the city is mainly rough terrain and mountains, and they have kept it that way deliberately. Two hundred meters below the surface of that sector are support facilities, living quarters, and enough space to house almost twenty thousand soldiers."

Even Jack was surprised at this. Riku turned her head just a few degrees to look at him.

"Is it me, or have they been expecting this attack?"

Jack shrugged, but he had to admit, her logic was sound.

"The NHA is putting ninety percent of their air defense units to cover the approaches to the mountain, and that's right where the weapon system is stationed. Alliance air units are spread out over two-dozen temporary air bases that we've established within a hundred kilometer range of the city. The only viable approach to attack in numbers is to strike from the west, right over there, while keeping us busy with aerial assaults."

He pointed away from the city and out toward the flat country that extended as far as the eye could see. The surface was full of jagged remains of buildings that had been abandoned long ago.

"The rest of the city has been divided up into segments, each of which is based around a fortified zone. This time it will be different to Eos. Instead of holding a line, we will be holding a small fortress, with overlapping fire coming from the next two along and one behind us."

He pointed to the north, east, and then finally to the south.

"There is a single platoon stationed at each of these redoubts, and I want you to make sure ours is strong, and I mean impregnable. We are not planning on holding the entire perimeter by ourselves. All we have to do is defend this block of sixteen ruined buildings surrounded by what's left of these old streets, and we have only a day to prepare. Intel has the Biomechs making landfall here first, and in approximately twenty-nine hours. We have to be ready for whatever they throw at us. We will need heavy weapons at every point, and make sure we have plenty of cover."

He looked to Sergeant Stone.

"Get markers out there to designate ranges in all directions. I want accurate, targeted firepower in this fight. Also, I we need a covered trench to the rear."

"Yes, Sir."

"And those, Sir?" Jack asked.

He pointed at the shape of the mobile Helion anti-aircraft mount that was moving to fit itself directly in the middle of a smashed room. It was a tight fit, but with low walls that provided protection on three sides, it was obvious why the crew were so keen to place it there.

"Yes, a good point, Private. The Helion 10thAnti-air Unit has spread thirty-seven of these mobile units around the outer perimeter of the city limits. That mean one for most of the redoubts, and that one is for us."

Jack looked back at the equipment, and only then did he spot the long hair on the Helions. There was a crew of six, and all wore cloaks covering them from their shoulders downwards. Most had their hair tied back or pulled under the cloaks but one, the tallest of the group, had hers running down over her shoulders.

"They're all women," he said, louder than he intended.

Riku saw him watching and bashed him on the forehead.

"You've never seen female soldiers before, Jack?"

He looked back to her, and at this distance, it was impossible to avoid the scorn showing on her face. Lieutenant Elvidge ignored their discussion and pointed back to the shattered block they'd been chosen to defend.

"If this goes to plan, the Biomechs will be forced away from the canyon and will land out of range of our main guns. That's if they want to live and that's when we can expect trouble. The perimeter flak guns will be there for air defense and also as improvised heavy weapon emplacements."

He paused for a moment while checking details on his helmet visor and then looked to Sergeant Stone.

"News from the fleet. The enemy's Ark is coming into range. All assessments suggest they will be engaging it very soon."

The Sergeant nodded grimly and then twisted his head back to look at the thirty-six marines, each of them waiting patiently.

"Right, corporals get here now. I want this place bottled up in under six hours. Whether the fleet is victorious or not, we have to make sure we're ready. They are busy doing their job, and if it comes to us, and the Biomechs get here…"

He gave a grim smile to them all.

"Well, we're going to give them hell to pay!"

* * *

The Spascia Fleet flagship, ANS Victory moved slightly ahead of the battle line and turned five degrees to the right. The massive engines of the Crusader class warship burned hot in the cold vacuum of space, and added to the scores of other lights that marked out the engines of the Alliance fleet. There were now thirty-four ships spread out along the front, the seven Narau advanced cruisers mixed in amongst them. Their number had been reinforced with the addition of four more third tranche ships to boost the number of Crusader class ships up to twenty. Four Hunter class frigates and ten of the new Liberty class destroyers under the command of Commodore Hampel provided the fighter and missile defense screen for the entire fleet.

"Are we ready?" asked the acting Admiral of the fleet, Jose Pezal.

"As ready as we could ever be, Admiral," replied Commander Keegan.

The Admiral had only been given his command in the last ten hours, and he was already finding the strains of commanding a force of seventy-one ships almost impossible.

"Good. This is going to be a complex operation, and if it's anything like Eos, the entire thing will turn into a massive mess in seconds."

"I agree. The splitting of the fleet will make it easier to respond to problems, just as long as the squadron commanders do their jobs."

Admiral Pezal nodded.

"True. Still, a single third tranche Crusader leading a six-ship squadron should prove more than manageable."

It was a minor change that he'd decided to make since his involvement in Admiral Lewis' management of the battle for Eos. His simple idea was that when the fleets were engaged, it was easy to lose control of the fight and more importantly, to lose the concentrated firepower of large numbers of ships. This one minor change meant that a single officer could direct the firepower of six ships against a single target. It was a slower, more time-consuming approach to battle, but in his opinion, it would give them the best chance at targeting and breaking down the Biomechs ships or systems. The XO, Commander Keegan pointed to the small groups of Khreenk ships that had been positioned above and below the Alliance force in two groups of fifteen ships.

"What about them?"

"The Khreenk? I'm not sure about their ships yet. Their own reports say they are armored with a mixture of plating and reactive systems and are heavily armed. They are also very small and apparently maneuverable, though quite how that is of use in a space battle with weapons that can hit at the speed of light, I can't imagine. We've never had to rely on Khreenk ships before, but we have to make use of them. I have a plan for them, but they won't like it, not one bit."

Commander Keegan creased his brow.

"A skirmish screen?"

It was a simple question, but the implication raised was, did the Admiral intend on throwing the Khreenk away as nothing more than cannon fodder for the opening phase of the battle?

"No, not at all. If what they say is true, then the Khreenk believe their own ships are enough to take on Biomech vessels, one for one."

The XO looked surprised but decided to move past that line of inquiry for now.

"And our newest ships?"

Admiral Pezal tapped the image of the nearest and looked at it carefully. At first glance it looked more like a civilian ship than the crude looking Crusader class. The ten Liberty Class ships were the first of their kind to be posted in this part of space and had been fitted for combat, rather than transport in their triple mission bays. They comprised a mixed unit of air defense and guided missile destroyers. Though between the size of the Hunter Class frigates and a conventional cruiser, they were modular and capable of carrying out various missions, depending on their configuration.

"Admiral Anderson swears by this new design. According to him, they can match an Uprising era cruiser, or you can just swap out the mission bays and use them as heavy transports. If we ever get the time to deploy more of them, I will be very interested to see how they perform."

"Admiral, incoming message from High Command," said the communications officer, "It's General Rivers."

"Put him on the mainscreen."

The seasoned face of the old General appeared in the center of the CIC, and most of the officers looked up from what they were doing to see what the man had to say. General Rivers was more than just the senior military officer in the Alliance. He was something of a legend and had fought numerous campaigns in the Uprising.

"Men and women of the Alliance Armed Forces, I bring news of a great victory against the machines."

A video stream appeared alongside him showing a fiery red world. Flashes of what looked like electricity flickered about slowly in the background, giving the scene a hellish look like something from a person's deranged mind.

"Prometheus," muttered somebody in the background.

The rest of the CIC was silent as they watched the footage. Admiral Pezal nodded to his communications officer, who was busily checking incoming message streams.

"Put that out on all screens, for the record."

There was no change inside the CIC, but now every single crewmember on the ship, and also those Alliance ships in the fleet, could see the broadcast coming from Terra Nova. He sensed this was going to be one of those critical moments, one where good news of a major victory could push his own crew on to greater things in the coming battle.

"Just hours ago the entire Biomech fleet operating in Alliance space was engaged in battle. Using skill, training, and a good deal of planning, Admiral Anderson managed to draw the enemy's forces in from a dozen worlds and a multitude of hiding places to attack Prometheus. This attack inflicted heavy casualties, but the defenders under the command of Admiral Churchill and Colonel Morato held firm. They beat off multiple attacks, with the Jötnar Red Watch earning special commendation for their heroic defense of the underground facilities."

Images of Prometheus showed the carnage in corridors and wide passageways that were filled with smashed machines and the bodies of hundreds of enemy warriors. Admiral Pezal even smiled at the sight of three Jötnar bashing their heads together and laughing. The three wore advanced Marine Corps armor that was tinted crimson and now covered in dirt, dents, and blood.

Those crazed fools.

"With the Biomech forces fully engaged, Admiral

Anderson baited their fleet and engaged their forces as they entered T'Karan space in pursuit."

Now the imagery shifted to the whirlpool exit of the Prometheus-T'Karan Spacebridge. An Alliance ship of some kind came through first of all, but its details were fuzzy, as though there were some basic digital artifacts present. He looked around it and noticed it was only around the ship.

So, they redacted that part. Who was it that was the bait?

Just a moment later came the first of the Biomech ships, and then one by one the rest came in right behind it. Admiral Pezal found himself holding his breath as the first massive volley of railguns and particle beams tore the Biomech ships to chunks of molten slag. One after another was destroyed, and finally the camera panned to show the vast Alliance fleet. He lost count as he moved past thirty ships, noting how every single vessel was concentrating its fire on one Biomech ship at a time as they came through. A cheer spread through the CIC, and he could only imagine how excited the rest of the crew must have been feeling.

"This entire Biomech force has been smashed, and only small groups of Biomech infiltrators and war machines remain on Alliance soil. We will not stop until their taint is removed from our territory. Today marks the greatest victory over the machines by our forces, but it is only the first."

The General continued, but Admiral Pezal found his attention drawn to new information coming in about the Biomech orbital station. Even as the cheering finally died, and the imagery from General Rivers vanished, he was still looking at the object.

"I cannot believe the size of this thing. Is the information from the Khreenk scouting screen accurate?"

The XO nodded quickly.

"It is just over eight kilometers in length and constructed from a large hollowed out section of the comet itself. If it wasn't for the transmissions and the change in course, this would be an irregularly-shaped comet fragment, nothing more."

"Wait, I've got something," said Lieutenant Jesse Powalk, the ship's tactical officer

The tactical board currently showed a single red object in the distance and an assortment of green and blue icons that showed the allied squadrons assembled to defend Spascia. Three more lights appeared, and then the display filled with scores of new shapes.

"I've got contacts. Multiple warships are moving out from the station."

"Numbers, assessment?"

"Uh, locking it down now, Sir."

More and more shapes appeared on the screen. There were numerous sizes, with the majority showing up as cruiser size or smaller. Admiral Pezal tried to count them again, but for every one he added, another two appeared.

"Sixty Biomanta class light attack cruisers, five Ravager class carriers, and a single Cephalon class command ship."

Admiral Pezal swallowed as he digested the figures. The data from the Battle of Prometheus, as it was being known, had given them new information on the ships, but much of it was still arriving, and it would take time for a full assessment to be made by his own intelligence units and those of High Command.

"Fighters?"

"Oh, yes," Lieutenant Powalk replied.

"The Ravagers are launching fighters, eighteen from each vessel, that makes ninety, and they are spreading out in the fleet."

He looked up from his bank of screens with a questioning expression on his face.

"It's a substantial force, Sir, much larger than the numbers we encountered at Eos."

"And their course?"

Lieutenant Powalk brought up a quadrant map on the mainscreen.

"Sir, this attack force is heading directly for Spascia, and the armored Ark is right behind them. The computers say we will be in range in seven minutes."

"Very well."

The Admiral paused and considered his strategy one last time.

I have to protect the planet, but I can't do that if this fleet is able to break through.

He nodded to his XO and then tapped the option on his tactical display to contact the commanders of the squadrons.

"This is the Admiral. As you all know, this approaching enemy force is not here for us. It is here to take control of Spascia. Destruction of the enemy fleet is second to stopping the attack on Spascia itself."

Even as he said the words, he knew it was a risky strategy. Deep down he wanted to take on this fleet head on, but he also knew this enemy Ark was an unknown, and so far no landers or transports had been detected. He started to speak, but the images from the long-range optical scopes had just arrived on his screens. This was the first detailed image of the Ark, and it was nothing like he expected. With a single button press, he muted the audio to the fleet and looked back to Lieutenant Powalk.

"What kind of assessment do you have on that thing?"

The Lieutenant's face tightened as he was forced to run through pages of data to give a quick and simple summary of the Ark specifications and capability, with just seconds to spare.

"Admiral, the vessel is massive. I detect..."

"Wait, the rest of our captains need to hear this."

He pressed the button on his intercom again.

"All commanders, bring your main guns to bear on

the approaching target. Ready fighters but do not launch. I repeat, do not launch fighters. I have a short tactical assessment of the Ark."

He nodded to Lieutenant Powalk.

"Proceed."

"Yes, Admiral."

The young man opened his mouth, coughed, and then began.

"Multiple scans confirm the Biomech Ark is actually a large section of the comet that has been carved out and modified into a massive fortress or super-battleship. It is roughly oval in shape, but irregular and covered in gantries, structures, and many weapon systems. Toward the rear are dock areas with several partially assembled vessels. There are engines fitted on one side, and at least five large-scale direct energy weapon emitters fitted at different points."

He took a breath and wiped his forehead.

"There are eight main launch bays, each one large enough to release a single cruiser class vessel at a time from inside the Ark itself. The front is almost entirely untouched, comprised largely from the original comet, and is massively thick. The middle and rear sections are completely artificial, and are more in common with a starbase and super-battleship than a satellite, though parts of the original comet are retained. There is enough space for upward of..."

He ran his hand through his hair as he double-checked

the numbers.

"...a hundred medium-sized ships and up to half million crew and troops."

Admiral Pezal looked at him with a raised eyebrow.

"How in the name of all that is holy, can you tell that? Are you telling me they fitted that entire fleet inside their Ark?"

The Lieutenant pointed to a smaller screen to the right of the mainscreen. The image showed a cross-section of the massive Ark, along with colored segments that showed the comet structure as well as the artificial compartments, power plants, troops, crew, and weapon systems.

"This is from the Khreenk. One of their scout drones made it to within six hundred kilometers before being detected. They have a full ultrasonic, infrared, and radar analysis of the Ark. It confirms the approximate layout and configuration."

Well, I'll be damned! Admiral Pezal thought. *They aren't completely useless after all.*

"The hull is approximately eight kilometers long and five kilometers high. Structure penetrating radar measures it at twelve meters thick in the thinnest sections of the armor, and a total mass is estimated well in excess of two and a half million tons."

Admiral Pezal shook his head in total amazement. The sheer numbers and specifications completely flabbergasted him. Just a quick calculation in his head showed him that this Ark could hold scores of ships.

"It is big, but not so big that we cannot beat it."

He spoke to no one in particular, and Commander Keegan looked lost. Admiral Pezal noted his confusion and pointed to the massive structure.

"This Biomech Ark is the primary target. So far, we have only seen ships of war being launched. I suspect their Sawfish assault transports are being held inside for safety, and they must have already released over half of their ships, based on our tactical assessment, right?"

The tactical officer checked his data for what must have been the fifth time before agreeing.

"Very well, then."

Admiral Pezal clicked the toggle button and continued speaking with the fleet.

"All Alliance and Helion ships are to bring your main guns to bear on the Ark. The priority is its launch bays and crew areas."

Even though it was an audio only transmission, he still pointed to the section of the Ark showing on his mainscreen.

"It is imperative that we whittle down their numbers as fast as possible. If we fail, we have to do what we can for those fighting on the ground. Prepare your fighters, but do not launch. I repeat, do not launch them."

The acknowledgements were quickly and efficiently received, and in less than thirty seconds, the combined

Alliance, Helion, and Khreenk force was ready to open fire on the Biomech fleet.

"Fire!"

The Battle for Spascia began with the largest opening bombardment seen so far. The sheer quantity of gunfire from the combined Alliance and Helion warships was massive. The first tranche Crusaders unleashed volley after volley of railgun projectiles, while the third tranche loosed invisible blasts from their particle beam emitters. It was easily enough firepower to devastate a single ship in one go, but this time the firepower hit the Biomech Ark in a hundred different locations. Explosions and flashes covered the front and flanks of the station, with many chunks of rock and ice being torn off and cast into space.

"Admiral, the enemy ships are altering their course," said the XO.

Admiral Pezal shook his head in mock annoyance.

"Let me guess, toward us?"

The XO smiled.

"How did you guess?"

Lieutenant Powalk looked less than excited though as multiple displays flashed up warnings. His face visibly paled at the sight of the latest information.

"Energy signatures detected. They are preparing to fire."

"Brace for impact!" barked the XO.

Most of the crew was already buckled in, but even the

XO only just managed to activate his clamp unit as they were hit. The impact of the first particle beams shook ANS Victory as though a heavy warship had just rammed her. Two ensigns were hurled through the CIC and struck the front bulkhead with a sickening crunch sound. Admiral Pezal was experienced enough to know there was little point in checking on them right now. They were certainly dead. More impacts slammed into the ship, and the view of the forward video displays showed ripples and flashes across the bows of almost every ship in the fleet.

"Damage report?"

"All ships in action and returning fire. Damage reported throughout, no losses...so far."

"And us?"

"Breaches on three decks, multiple turrets offline, and a damaged forward escape deck."

We got off lightly, he thought.

"All ships advance on the Ark."

He twisted about and tapped the icon for the Khreenk contingent.

"We'll deal with the Ark. Keep their combat ships busy. I repeat, engage their warships."

The commander of the Khreenk force sent back a coded response that had to be translated by the computer. It took less than two seconds to come through in an intelligible form. Even the XO seemed surprised at the plan of attack for the Khreenk.

"Only the Khreenk are attacking the fleet? How can we expect to survive with a force of that size?"

Admiral Pezal rubbed his cheek as if even he was uncertain as to his plan.

"You saw the numbers, Commander Keegan. This Ark is a mobile base for the attack and conquest of Spascia. This isn't a battle to decide who controls this section of space; this is to whittle down the number of warriors they will have for the invasion."

Commander Keegan looked stunned at this news.

"Invasion? You don't believe we can win this battle?"

One of the Helion advanced cruisers exploded in a bright white flash on the left flank of the fleet. As the light faded, its shattered hull broke into three sections, each of them spinning slowing out of control. Admiral Pezal shook his head.

"No, Commander. We will do the best we can, for as long as we can. Now, all power to engines, and bring us in close to that station. I want to see it burning before this battle is done."

"Aye, Sir!" came the sharp response from Lieutenant Glinda Scookins, the ship's helmsman.

With a mighty shudder, the immense bulk of the Alliance warship increased its forward speed on an intercept vector for the Biomech Ark. The remaining Helion ships fired large batteries of hypersonic atomic warheads, and as they moved in alongside their Alliance comrades, every one of them pushed their engines as hard as they could.

CHAPTER FIVE

The original plans for a reduced sized fleet, following the massive losses sustained in the Uprising is now considered flawed. Exploration into the New Charon system, now to be called T'Karan, proved a need for cheap, flexible ships to be extended. The Crusader class was the first part of this transition to twelve-ship battle groups based around a Conqueror class Battlecruiser. Optimistic plans for five of these groups were already vastly under capacity for an Alliance of six home star systems, plus T'Karan, and new duties in Helios. Only mass production in the Alliance shipyards, and the design of the new and cheap class of Liberty destroyers, would allow useful levels of ship coverage.

Naval Cadet's Handbook

The small group of officers waited patiently in the briefing room of ANS Endurance. There was a palpable feeling of nerves and tension as they waited. Lieutenant Commander

Sanlav Erdeniz watched each of the Alliance officers and the two civilian scientists with interest. All of them looked at the projected image of Admiral Anderson busy chairing the meeting from the other side of the Rift, and they were not enjoying what they heard.

"So after over a year of field tests, this is all we have to show for it? I was promised the ability to move my ships using this technology within a nine-month timeframe of launching this expedition. In the last three months, you've received help from some of our finest scientists."

He extended his hand to point to a number of those men and women in uniform. The mood shifted at those few words. Dr. Banner, the leader of project interrupted him.

"Admiral, with all due respect. This is a science operation, and these military personnel are not what we need to complete the project. Additional support vessels and a secondary team will speed up the testing phase immeasurably."

Admiral Anderson didn't look impressed. As the man responsible for the defense of Alliance holdings in the Orion Nebula, he had been granted complete control over Alliance facilities and its personnel. He was impatient, that was clear, though few realized the actual strain he was under prosecuting the war against the machines. Even so, he signaled for the man to continue.

"The development of ANS Beagle was based upon

the findings from Hyperion that proved workable. Every single Rift system we have created since has been based on this technology. Rift generation stations are massive affairs, something that cost the Alliance trillions of adjusted credits. Our research has proven that miniaturization is possible, and it will lead to smaller, more advanced systems in the future."

"Just not yet," Anderson snapped back.

He wiped at his eyes, his attention evidently somewhere else.

"I know you and your crew have work hard at this, but these results…well…they are too little for the resources we've put in. Even with additional power siphoned from Beagle, your ship can open a Rift barely big enough for a single cruiser, and it's unstable."

He brought up a video recording that showed the last test where an entire derelict transport entered a Rift, only to emerge as ruptured slag on the other side.

"I've read all your results, and they are troubling. One time in three it collapses in less than fifteen microseconds. The best you've managed is a temporary tunnel for three seconds, after which the system suffered a catastrophic feedback loop and killed three researchers, not to mention destroying half the power system on the ship and putting the project back by two months."

Erdeniz watched as the Admiral spoke. He'd been working on the system for six weeks now, and although disliked by most of those on board, he was convinced he had a better idea. Every time he'd brought it up, the research teams had knocked him down. He was beginning to doubt the timing, but deep down he knew the science worked.

This is your chance, your only chance. Speak now or forget this entire project.

Lieutenant Commander Erdeniz raised his hand to speak.

"Admiral, I have something…"

Dr. Banner shook his head with irritation.

"No, Commander, I am getting tired with your side-projects. You know our policy on the use of this technology for anything other than the original project. Your plans would destroy this ship, and likely anything within a thousand kilometers. It is dangerous and reckless speculation, nothing more. Please keep your ideas at the simulation phase…"

Admiral Anderson listened to them with interest before eventually interrupting the Doctor.

"Dr. Banner, what exactly are you talking about? What side-projects is your crew working on?"

The officers exchanged angry looks, but finally the Doctor answered him.

"Admiral, we have been sent a number of military scientists to assist in this project. Commander Erdeniz is part of the weapons research program and has been here, along with two others to examine the use of this complex and dangerous technology for military applications. I specifically asked for this to…"

Lieutenant Commander Erdeniz spoke.

"Admiral. I was sent here at the request of Terra Nova High Command."

The looks from the other scientists ranged from shocked to horrified at what they were hearing.

"The results from the previous tests proved one thing, to me at least. That this ship and this project had the potential for other uses."

He looked to Dr. Banner who was still shaking his head in disapproval.

"The funding for the project was pulled two months ago. This research is now being covered by the Alliance Navy only."

That did seem to get some attention.

"I was sent here because my analysis of the project showed it could be as useful as a weapon as it could as a method of transportation. In many ways, this system might have more to offer us than any of you have dreamed possible."

He stepped out from his position and moved toward the front of the room, not far from the virtual presence of the Admiral.

"My team has been experimenting with the idea of using the failure of this transport technology to produce something else entirely. Something that might actually be useful to the Alliance, to the Navy, and perhaps in this coming war."

Dr. Banner jumped from his seat.

"War? Why does everything we do have to come back to this damned fight with the machines? Our fleet is more than capable of the task, without resorting to genocidal weaponry."

He pointed to those around the table.

"We, the people behind this project have created something that could transform space travel, and with it our ability to explore, build, and expand our influence in every direction. We could…"

Admiral Anderson stopped him right in the middle of his rant.

"I understand your concerns, Dr. Really I do, but the project has proven something of a failure. The technology is just not mature enough for the role we envisioned for it."

He nodded toward Sanlav.

"Let the man speak, Dr. Banner. Sanlav Erdeniz, you're the man that designed the Sanlav projectile, are you not?"

"Yes, Sir, but that was a long time ago. We've moved on from railguns since then."

Anderson smiled.

"Very true, but there are still plenty of ships in the fleet using them. I remember using those rounds for the first time. Short-ranged, but they didn't cause considerable damage. We used one once on Crusader to stop a suicide attack on the ship. Your projectiles tore the vessel to pieces instead of punching it with holes."

He tugged on his tunic and nodded to the Commander.

"We need that kind of outside of the box thinking, Commander."

He shook his head in frustration at the rest of them.

"I know you are all focused on your primary fields of research, but let me be clear here. I needed this technology to move my ships in and out of combat as quickly as possible. Trade, exploration, and the rest is wonderful, but in peacetime. Right now we're facing the greatest threat to our survival in our history, and if we can use this offensively, then it at the very least warrants investigation."

Then he looked to the Erdeniz.

"So, you've been thinking of a way to use a failed Rift generator science ship in some kind of offensive capacity? Engineers on Prometheus tried something similar two years ago. It just lost us an entire frigate and to no benefit. You think you can do better?"

The Commander nodded.

"Yes, Admiral, I think I can. If my calculations are correct, with some fine-tuning a ship like this one could create a transitional Rift for a fraction of a second by focusing our emitters. It would allow us to position a Rift within a short distance of the ship for a small moment of time."

"What? This is nonsense," said one of the civilian doctors.

The man in the traditional lab coat moved from his chair and approached the spectral form of Anderson.

"We discussed the use of this technology over a decade ago. Our technology is barely able to create a Rift in the first place. That, coupled with the equipment to collapse one as quickly as we build it, makes the system useless."

He turned and looked at Lieutenant Commander Erdeniz.

"Our research brief was to test this equipment's ability to move a ship through space using nothing but Rift technology and maneuvering thrusters. You want to bastardize it into some form of genocidal weapon?"

Erdeniz shook his head furiously.

"There are no genocidal weapons."

He then looked to the Admiral.

"Only the people who use them against the wrong targets."

That seemed to pique the interest of Admiral Anderson.

"I see. Send me the latest on your research, Commander. In the meantime, I want this project put on hold. We have bigger problems, and this ship is on the wrong side of the border. Return to this station for debriefing."

He made to turn away but then stopped.

"You are dismissed."

The officers and scientists stood up and made for the door.

"Not you, Commander. Stay where you are."

The rest left the room, and the last to go was Dr. Banner. He threw Erdeniz a withering glace and then yanked the door shut firmly behind him. Admiral Anderson waited a little longer before speaking.

"Tell me more about this idea of yours. How quickly could it be put into use?"

* * *

The strengths and weaknesses of the ships on all sides became apparent as the space battle continued. Most of the ships stayed at long-range to make better use of their powerful ranged guns and missile systems, whereas the agile ships of the Khreenk moved in amongst the Biomanta attack cruisers. Crusader capital ships blasted the Ark while Liberty class destroyers provided air and missile defense, or bombarded the enemy with volleys of gunfire and missiles.

"The Cardiff and Plymouth are abandoning ship. ANS Valor has sustained heavy damage, but she's still in action. The Crusaders are taking one hell of a beating, but the destroyers are holding back most of the anti-ship gunfire, Sir," said Commander Keegan.

He pointed at the imagery around the Biomech forces.

"That Ark is putting out fire like I've never seen before. It's more like attacking an Alliance naval station than a mobile station or ship."

Admiral Pezal nodded but said nothing. The reports of damage and losses had stunned him to silence, yet he was still as calm and collected as when he'd ordered the initial attack. Imagery on the mainscreen confirmed that the two Liberty class destroyers were now burning from within. Small flashes of different colors indicated the massive internal damage they had sustained during the massed rush toward the Biomech Ark.

"Status of their forces?"

"The Ark has sustained substantial damage to its dorsal superstructure. Multiple breaches and two of the launch decks are out of action. Those destroyers are impressive. I just wish we had a few more. Commodore Hampel is doing good work with them. His escorts have managed to hold down most of the fire from the Ark, as well as strafing the gun positions on its hull."

Admiral Pezal tried to smile, to offer something positive and encouraging, but he failed. He had to agree about the Liberty ships though, much to his surprise. On paper, he'd been less than impressed. They had been constructed mainly in civilian shipyards and built using their equipment and methodologies. The hulls seemed well built, but the crews were small, and the modular weapon systems barely out of testing and antiquated by the standards of the day.

Prior to the battle, he'd had doubts they would be able to stand up to much punishment, or even to add much to the battle.

The evidence before him was exactly the opposite of what he'd expected. The Liberty class destroyers were putting out almost as much power as a fully-fledged cruiser from fifty years earlier, but all in a package that was only fifty percent larger than a frigate.

"Good, that is something. The damage inflicted by the missile destroyers is especially impressive. What about the Khreenk fleet?"

"All their ships are deployed and fully operational."

Admiral Pezal looked at the tactical display and the list of forces on both sides. The Biomech numbers still outnumbered his own, and so far, the only ships lost on his side were Helion and Alliance. He brought down his fist onto the side of his seat. The damage indicators on the Ark certainly suggested they were doing something right, yet the enemy's entire battle fleet remained in action, and the Khreenk seemed to have avoided the worst of it so far.

"They need to do something. What in the name of hell is going on out there? We need those Biomantas brought down, and fast."

The tactical officer caught his eye and pointed to the map on the right of the mainscreen.

"Admiral. The Khreenk ships have split up and are

attacking them ship-to-ship."

He looked at the screen and watched as a pair of Khreenk Corsairs separated and moved in close to two of the Biomanta assault cruisers. Although smaller than the Biomechanical ships, they were faster, and their bewildering array and variety of weaponry bombarded the enemy with a constant shower of explosions. Even so, there were few in the way of losses on either side, and that worried him.

"I see."

He watched as the computer system overlaid the beams from the particle emitters as bright blue lines traveling at the speed of light toward the Khreenk ships, yet somehow missed. Three of the attack cruisers actually broke off their pursuit of an Alliance Liberty class destroyer to try and turn their gunfire on the Khreenk instead. One beam struck the engines of a stray Corsair, but the collective fire of two Alliance destroyers then hit the Biomanta.

"How are the Khreenk not being hit?" he demanded, after watching five separate ships move directly past the Khreenk.

Commander Keegan shrugged.

"They refused to divulge information on their specific capabilities or defenses. They are doing an excellent job at distracting the Biomech ships though. By hitting them and avoiding damage, they must have had their threat level raised by their commanders," he replied.

"Perhaps. That would mean their ships would task more resources on their destruction. This could give us a chance. I just wish we had some of that technology on our own ships."

He made a mental note to push that idea up the chain of command, assuming they managed to come out of this fight in something like one piece.

"Admiral, I might have some ideas on that," said Commander D'Vani, the ship's engineer.

He brought up a series of images that showed the beam attacks on the Corsairs and froze two of them.

"Our sensors are picking up distortions around the ships, Sir, right at the time of the impact."

"I don't follow," said Admiral Pezal.

There was irritation in his stressed tone, and he turned his eyes back to the tactical display. The Alliance and Helion ships had now moved into position on three sides of the Ark. More data was flooding in, but most of it was unnecessary now. He knew the vessel's capabilities, and so far had been unable to identify any substantial weaknesses.

"I want every ounce of firepower kept on that thing!"

More fire from the fleet pounded the Ark, and even more of its outer structure was torn off. After so much bombardment, the Ark looked heavily damaged, but Admiral Pezal knew that what counted was what they had done to its interior.

"What is their status now?"

"Massive breaches in the hull. They are venting substantial gasses toward the rear," replied Lieutenant Powalk.

"Gases? Interesting, have we ruptured a fuel or power unit?"

"Perhaps, Sir. It isn't easy to tell."

He started to speak and then stopped himself as one of the Crusader warships vanished in a bright fireball. A shattered Biomanta appeared as it smashed through its hull and then also exploded in a terrifying blast that must have vaporized any living thing in range.

"Who was that?" said the Admiral, barely able to speak.

"ANS Leopard, Sir. She took a direct impact to her flank."

He shook his head and noticed that both his executive officer and chief engineer were trying to get his attention.

"What?"

"The Khreenk, Sir," started Commander D'Vani.

"They are using some kind of shifting technology to project a copy of themselves within a short distance. It looks like a kind of jamming system, and it is making hitting them with the particle beams almost impossible."

"Fair enough. That should keep them busy, for now. I suggest..."

Commander Keegan pointed to the mainscreen.

"Admiral, she's launching more ships."

All three of them looked at the dozens of light cruiser

sized vessels being pushed out of the Ark. One by one they launched from the many hangars and launch bays built deep inside the fortress.

"Three-dozen Sawfish class assault transports. Plus fighters!" said Lieutenant Powalk.

The ships showed up as multi-colored vessels, each brightly colored and carrying the iconography of something resembling Echidna, but with this design adopting a fusion of creature and machine. Thick plating and studs ran down the undersides and flanks, and they bristled with weapon turrets.

"Intel from Admiral Anderson says these are transports for Bioray landers. This must be the ground assault component."

The warship shuddered as she sustained a triple burst of energy from two of the Biomantas, and they swept overhead, each pursued by a Khreenk Corsair and a flight of Alliance Hammerhead gunships. Admiral Pezal grabbed his harness as he selected the Alliance squadrons in turn and allocated general targets. He avoided specifics, so as to give his junior captains the chance to use their initiative. Half of the Alliance squadrons turned their attacks to the Sawfish and their escort fighters, the other half he split, one group to help the Khreenk in their fight against the Biomantas, and the remainder with him to continue their attack on the Ark. He connected verbally to the other ships in this smaller formation.

"Target this location and fire on my mark!"

The eleven ships moved in from their different positions, with their selection of missile systems, guns, and particle beam emitters focused directly on the small target area. Warning sirens sang their song as the ships from both sides mingled together in a vast dogfight that included over a hundred capital ships and three times as many fighters. Admiral Pezal would not be distracted though. He could see the other ships were busy, and his job was to limit the opportunities the Biomechs would have in assaulting Spascia.

"Fire!"

The target was just fifty meters from the venting on the Ark and directly above what Commander D'Vani suggested might be a primary power unit. One explosion followed the other until a series of arcs and flashes obliterated a section the size of a Battlecruiser from the Ark. A great chorus of excitement burst throughout the ship as the scanner detected debris, bodies, and machines drifting about the massive enemy vessel. The scanner quickly identified the form of what appeared to be a Ravager class warship as it tumbled amongst the wreckage.

"Major damage, Admiral. That power plant took over ten percent of the entire Ark with it. It must have been a major auxiliary system," said Lieutenant Powalk.

His look of excitement quickly vanished at that word. Admiral Pezal felt the blood drain from his face as he watched Lieutenant Powalk.

I thought that would have ended the damned Ark. Now it's just an auxiliary unit?

"So the thing is still operational?"

Lieutenant Powalk nodded.

"Yes, Sir. Just give me a second..."

He pressed multiple buttons as though he'd just made a terrible mistake. Screen after screen of data moved about on his displays, but none calmed him. He reached one showing the center of the Ark. He stopped as if it was exactly what he'd been looking for. Finally, he looked up and directly into Admiral Pezal's face and gulped.

"What?"

The man swallowed and then looked to the mainscreen. Nothing else followed, as the entire forward section of ANS Victory vanished in a fireball and sent shredded metal through the rest of the crippled hull. The last thing Admiral Pezal saw, was the screen in front of him vanish into a thousand pieces, before he turned to dust.

* * *

Captain Jim 'The Hammer' Evans spun his Lightning fighter about on its axis so that he was facing backwards and tried to do his favorite maneuver. These Biomech fighters had either been programmed against it, or had learned since their last encounter. Both targets had moved sideways in a strafing movement that moved them away from the nose-mounted guns on the fighter. One of the small craft jumped up in relation to his fighter while the other moved directly below.

"Dammit!" he muttered, removing his finger from the trigger.

The Biomech fighters were pure Biomech machines, a fusion of a biological computer and a mechanical machine. The basic shape was of a single powerful engine surrounded by vent outlets, giving it the incredible speed to change attitude in the middle of a fight. It was fitted with small but powerful automatic cannons that could shred a fighter in seconds, and that was exactly what they tried to do.

"Alert! Alert! Alert!" wailed the threat computer.

Captain Evans almost choked at seeing the position he was in, just as the gunfire ripped through his left wing. Damage alerts activated instantly as system after system failed.

"I know we're hit dammit!" he snapped.

For a brief moment, he found himself angrier at the fighter's computer system than at the Biomech fighters still shooting at him. Another few rounds struck the tail, but nothing major seemed to fail.

Hey, you're still breathing. Remember your training!

He looked at the figures coming in on his visor and identified the damaged and working systems.

"Okay, good. We have power, one engine, and weapons. That's enough."

He stamped down on the foot pedals that simulated what would be rudder control on a conventional airplane, but in this case they were managed by the computer to power the thrusters that altered the yaw of the fighter. Now that he was facing in the same direction as his attackers, he slammed the emergency retro button. The straps pulled in tightly, and it felt as if he'd hit a wall. The Biomech fighters raced past him and did the same, but they had already moved past him.

Now, bring them down!

A quick squeeze sent a stream of cannon rounds into the rear of the nearest fighter. It sparked and flashed before exploding in a spectacular explosion.

One down.

His scanners picked up the shape of the other fighter altering its course to join a formation of three others to his right. It gave him just a few seconds to check on the position of the rest of his wing.

"Form up on my six. We have work to do!"

The other Lightnings did their best to get back into position, but most were still engaged in vicious dogfights, even his wingman was busy with his own troubles.

This isn't going well.

The fight was such a mess that he didn't even see the shape of ANS New Carlos until the last moment. Using his thruster control override, he screamed over the top of its hull, watching with glee as the massive warship unleashed a hail of round from its multiple turrets at the Biomech fighters. Where there had been four Biomechs, there were none, and the others that had been chasing his comrades were suffering a similar dilemma. Captain Evans adjusted his course and moved in to help two of his officers.

We can do this.

* * *

The Spascia Fleet had now split into separate divisions to deliver their attacks against the Biomech Ark. Even the larger capital ships looked like minnows alongside a large shark as they did their best to destroy it. The invisible pulsed particle beams from the more advanced ships caused damage almost instantly, whereas the massed gunfire from the older warships smashed holes through rock, ice, and metal with ease. It wasn't enough though.

Even as explosions began to rock the target, the massive Ark activated its guns. Like the particle beam emitters on the Crusader class ships, the pulsed particle beams could strike a target at the speed of light, and strike with an energy output well in excess of a gigajoule of kinetic energy. The Ark was able to put out ten times as much energy, its only restriction being a charge time of almost a full minute, and it used this to devastating effect. It wasn't just the particle emitters that were causing trouble. The Ark's turret defenses had activated in the last minute, and the entire facility was surrounded in a massive cloud of flak. A short burst raked the dorsal sections of three destroyers as they past directly beneath the Ark.

"Rotate and present our belly. We can't take another volley topside," said Commodore Hampel.

The Liberty class destroyer twisted about on its axis just as another barrage swept past the ship. Most of the small chunks of metal whooshed past, but at least three struck the hull plating, one tearing a hole almost a meter wide that breached the outer seals.

"This is insanity. Fire on her with everything we have, and get us the hell out of range of those flak guns."

The ship shuddered as its powerful engines activated and sent it hurtling away from the turrets. Even as they moved, explosions marked the total destruction of a number of ships.

"Sir, I'm detecting something massive. It's the Ark."

Commodore Hampel felt sick as he watched the shattered hulk of ANS Victory sustaining a continuous bombardment from the Ark. The emitters from the Biomech fortress activated and fire simultaneously at a single point. Each time they made contact, another massive section of the capital ship would vanish and explode into tiny fragments.

"We cannot fight that kind of firepower. The entire fleet

will be gone in thirty minutes," he said more to himself than anybody else.

Either we destroy the fortress and disable its weapons, or we get the hell out of here.

His gut instinct told him that with the range of particle beams being effectively infinite, there would be little chance of escape. Yet the idea of closing with the station filled him with dread. Even its defensive flak guns were capable of annihilating the Spascia Fleet.

Another ship, this time a Helion advanced cruiser, succumbed to the overwhelming firepower of the Ark. The first barrage exploded the ship as though it had been blown apart by a massive explosive charge fitted directly at the heart of the vessel. As the blast cleared, there was little left other than chunks of warship no bigger than a fighter.

"Sir, the Helions are withdrawing."

Commodore Hampel, the Captain of ANS New Carlos, and the man in charge of the defensive screen for the fleet, looked around at his small cadre of officers. It was a vastly smaller group than he was used to, even on the smaller Hunter class frigate, ANS Spearfish that he had transferred from only a week earlier. He looked for the tactical display and then remembered that to reduce the amount of crew and displays, the single holographic unit directly behind the frontline of officers presented information for most of them. It was a new design feature on board the brand new Liberty class destroyers, and it was taking him a while to adjust.

"So, the Khreenk are holding their own, the Helions are gone, and our ships are bearing the brunt of the enemy firepower. How are we doing with their transports?"

"Three down, Sir, the rest have formed a convoy and are moving at speed toward..." said Lieutenant Morgan.

"Spascia, I assume?"

The ships executive officer, who also doubled as the tactical officer, nodded slowly.

"Well, who is in charge now that Admiral Pezal is gone?"

It was a pointless question, and one he already knew the answer to. The chain of command had been well established before the battle began, but that didn't make the decision to act any more comfortable.

"Very well."

He activated the earpiece and connected directly to every captain in the fleet.

"This is Commodore Hampel, ANS New Carlos. I am taking command of the Spascia Fleet. All Alliance and Helion ships are to move into contact with the Sawfish convoy. Deploy fighters and move in close."

A ripple of gunfire clattered along the port flank of ship, but the armor deflected or absorbed the worst of it. He shuddered a little as his eyes ran down the damage reports.

Nothing devastating...yet!

He selected the icons for the Khreenk squadrons made up of the agile and surprisingly versatile warships.

"Corsairs, I need you to split up and run interference. I want ten Corsairs to assist the convoy assault; the rest will keep the Ark busy. Don't try and destroy it. Just get those damned guns off my ships."

There was no argument from any of the officers, and the formations of ships moved apart and changed course in a slow motion ballet. The entire arrangement might have even been beautiful to watch, apart from the continuous exchanges of gunfire and exploding ships. The combat around Spascia was no longer a stand-up fight to try and destroy the Biomechs. This was now a hit and run operation, pure and simple.

"All Alliance ships, stay away from the Ark, and do as much damage as you can. We need every one of these ships."

He glanced over to his XO.

"I need a withdrawal location ASAP. This fleet has to be retained, no matter the cost. We can keep this fight up for a short time, but at some point that Ark will turn its attention on our easier to hit ships. That is the moment we're in trouble."

He noticed the look on his tactical officer's face and immediately felt the blood drain from his face.

"What?"

"Uh, tactical reports from Helios Prime itself. It

says another Ark has detached from the comet and is decelerating. Ground forces on Helios Prime are bracing themselves for a major assault when it makes contact."

Commodore Hampel raised an eyebrow.

"So? That's not unexpected."

"It's the size, Sir. The estimates put it at something like five times the size of this one, perhaps even larger."

He shrugged in reply.

"Son, we have our own worries, right now. The Helion Fleet is substantial. I'm sure they can deal with this situation. If not, well, we'll get to that when it becomes necessary."

Still, if they are sending a larger Ark to Helios Prime, it's easy to see where their real effort is being focused, all the more reason to preserve this fleet for what's to come.

He looked to the mainscreen and noted with satisfaction the bulk of the Alliance-Helion fleet had carried out his wishes. Those that could had now moved in amongst the enemy ships as they made their way to Spascia, while the Biomech Ark followed on its longer route to take it into a high orbit around Spascia, like some foul marauding moon. A beam flashed on the mainscreen as the computer overlaid the invisible particle beam from the Ark. It struck the corner of a Khreenk vessel but also managed to strike a Biomech Ravager astern. Both ships exploded in a flash of light. Commodore Hampel felt a pang of guilt at the loss of the Khreenk ship, but the shattered remains of the

Ravager more than made up for it.

Every ship we can bring down is one less landing party for our boys on the ground to deal with.

He looked at the countdown and the list of potential paths his ships could take. There was one that would require a great degree of fine control, finesse, and more than a little guile.

"Helm, double-check this for me."

The imagery showed the standard parabolic orbit the fleet would be expected to follow around Spascia. The modified version he had entered into the system would taken them lower than even the course they had taken at Eos.

"Really, Sir?" asked the officer incredulously.

"Yes, I want to know if it is doable."

The man still seemed almost unable to comprehend the plan.

"Sir, you realize this will put us inside Spascia's atmosphere? The Crusaders are unable to do that, not without taking a serious risk of catastrophic damage."

He nodded slowly.

"That's right. I want to put the fleet in the upper atmosphere and then accelerate out into a position on the other side of the planet. The lower we go, the more the particle beams of that Ark will dissipate."

The helmsman looked back to his screen while shaking his head. Something caught his eye and he looked back.

"Sir, there's one other option."

"Which is?"

"The Rift, Sir. It would take us back to Helios Prime."

The Commodore looked at the tactical display and realized it was something he'd missed. The ship shuddered as it loosed more gunfire at the enemy, but it failed to distract him from the situation. The display showed Spascia, the intertwined ships from both sides, and the menacing shape of the Ark. The icon showing the orbiting Rift station and its minor defenses flickered green. He watched it and for a second felt a moment of doubt. The Helios Rift would take them away from the violence of Spascia and right into whatever was heading for the homeworld of the Helions. He considered it only for a few seconds and then looked back at the man and shook his head.

"No, our job is here. If we abandon Spascia, we will leave our ground forces with no air or space cover. The enemy will be able to attack at will."

He pointed to the outline of Spascia.

"This is what we're going to do…"

* * *

Jack wiped away the sweat and looked over to the line of soldiers, marines, and civilians. Riku was a short distance away with a pair of NHA soldiers, and he could see so many more working on their defenses. Since arriving, they'd achieved far more than he would ever had expected. The air defense unit was a meter lower than when it had been first wheeled in, and the Combat Engineer Suit marines had actually dug a pit for the machine to operate inside. Jack and the others had spent the time improving the walls for the fitment of heavy weapons at every conceivable point. With the basics completed, it was now time to work on something that was proving backbreaking. Jack looked down at the zigzagging trench they had been working on. Sergeant Stone spotted him stopping and called out to him.

"Private, we've got work to do."

"I know, Sergeant. I just don't get it."

The seasoned marine marched over to him as fresh as he'd been since their landing. Hours seemed like weeks to Jack's bones, and he could see that Callahan, Riku, and the others were also feeling the same.

"What is your problem, Son? You object to the hard work and grind? Back in the twentieth century they spent five years slogging it out in trenches just like this."

That did even less to persuade him, and now he straightened out his back and looked back at the building on this alien world they had decided to use as a blockhouse.

"This city is a ruin. Our marines are fast, tough, and can make a difference, if we use them right. So why the hell are we digging in, like this?"

Lieutenant Elvidge overheard the last part from his position two floor up, where he was assisting in siteing a series of surface-to-air missile batteries.

"Private, you causing trouble down there?"

Jack looked up and shook his head.

"No, Sir, no problems here."

Sergeant Stone pointed at the trench works.

"Our boy here is not convinced about digging in to the ground."

Elvidge smiled.

"It's certainly not the kind of work we're used to, but in the past the marines made use of trenches, when and if they were needed. These are different though, have you seen the pattern?"

Jack looked down at the trenches still being scraped out by the CES teams. The machines moved very much like the Biomech robotic warriors, but they allowed substantial amounts of work to be done and in a short period of time. The trench works were long and changed direction as they worked back into the city. He looked back up to his officer.

"No, Sir, not really."

Sergeant Stone shook his head.

"That is why he's the officer and you're the private, Son."

He looked back and pointed to the building being established as the next strongpoint. It was barely visible in the distance but did have perfect line of sight to their position.

"These trenches are not for our combat forces to fight from."

Jack looked confused, but Callahan had heard what Sergeant Stone was saying.

"Supply?"

Sergeant Stone grinned.

"Give that man a cigar. Exactly."

He looked back to Jack.

"The Private is right. When this fight starts, we're going to need a way to get supplies and reinforcements into position. After Eos, we've learned how to do things differently. They might command the skies, but they can't hit what they can't see."

Jack watched as a CES engineer lowered a plate over a section of one of the trenches, instantly turning it into a lightly armored tunnel. Jack might have been impressed, perhaps even excited at this change in tactics. In reality, he knew it was something very different.

They aren't expecting a quick fight, not even a battle.

He watched as Riku and Corporal Frewyn helped lifted a twin-mounted gun system onto a lower window frame. They grunted with the effort as they clamped it down onto the mounting bracket.

This is going to be a long fight, and we're gearing up for it.

He could feel his heart pounding and try as he might,

Jack couldn't shake the images of Helios Prime and Eos from his head, the waves of enemy soldiers and the shattered bodies of his comrades. The voices began to slow down and soften, and his vision began to blur.

No, not now! Get a grip, you fool.

He tried, but his legs felt weak, and he found the walls beginning to spin about. He hit his knee on the ground and then vomited on the floor. The force of the retching knocked him down to both of his knees, and then there was nothing but darkness. As his vision faded, he could hear slow, monotone voices calling out. The last one he heard was the raspy growl of Sergeant Stone.

"Medic!"

CHAPTER SIX

The assortment of ground units assembled to defend Spascia included robotic ground troops. These were not simply just the Rams as used by the marines. The modular SAAR robotic system was deployed into combat for the first time. This vehicle joined the Ram to offer a semi-autonomous tracked machine to remotely position sensors and weapons systems for the defense of forwards bases and outposts. SAAR robots outfitted with 40mm grenade launchers and a single L56 Mark III support weapon were the first models into action, with more variants following shortly afterwards.

Robots in Space

The crackle of rifle fire reverberated throughout the interior of the four access shafts in the habitation zone for the underground facility. Each one was large enough to drive a Bulldog armored vehicle through, and it gave the

Alliance forces quick access to the center of the complex. There were signs of battle and bloodshed at almost every turn now as the Alliance marines and Jötnar of the Red Watch hacked and blasted their way through. It was the larger of the two refinery sites serving the greater City One area, and also included a substantial habitation and retail complex that was the largest on the Mars Colony, outside of the city itself. The marines moved cautiously, but they held nothing back upon reaching any signs of the Biomechs and their dreaded soldiers. They were taking no prisoners.

"Hostiles, behind you!" shouted one of the Jötnar.

Three Thegn warriors leapt out with their guns blazing. A fourth dropped from a hiding place in an air duct above them and landed directly on Khan's head. A metal arachnid machine scuttled from the shadows to join in with the ambush. The Thegn falling from the ceiling hit Khan with such force, that the two of them crashed into the wall. Khan dropped to his left knee and instantly twisted, so as to land directly on the creature. The heavy impact broke several of its bones, but that wasn't enough for Khan. He lifted himself up and then used the carbine in his right hand like a club to smash down on the warrior.

"To the right," came the familiar voice of Spartan.

Khan had fought alongside Spartan long enough to know when he was being serious. There was no need for Khan to even check, and he just lifted his right arm to take aim with the second TEK40.

Got them.

He squeezed the trigger, but it was too late. The two Thegns dropped down with holes in their skulls where Spartan shot them with perfect precision. The final one tried to embed its blade into Khan's face, but he grabbed it about the neck and snapped it like a piece of rotten wood. The lifeless corpse fell to the ground, and Khan found himself unable to move properly.

"Dammed armor, I thought this was the latest gear?"

"It is!" muttered another.

Only the metal arachnid machine remained, but the column of marines had been expecting trouble and was ready. A barrage of coilguns did what the TEK40s could not. High power blasts of magnetic ammunition tore holes through its arms and body until it dropped to the ground, a lump of wrecked and smoking metal. Khan laughed happily at their destruction.

"It's about time we got some decent weaponry!"

He felt an impact and lifted his arms to defend himself as a pair of Jötnar warriors struck him. He spun about and deflected one of the strikes with his shoulder, and then pulled back his fist to hit back, only to find them hammering down a bent section of metal. He lowered his eyes and watched as they hit it again to force the Jötnar armor back into shape around Khan's immense frame. With a final kick from the shorter one of the pair it clicked into place, and Khan could finally lift himself back to his feet. He twisted about from left to right and tensed his chest to make sure every part of the unit moved as it should.

"Yeah, that's better. Good to see Jötnar engineering hasn't changed."

The armor was a special version of the standard marine issue equipment but enlarged and reinforced as befitted its wearers. Unlike the JAS armor used by most Jötnar, this design allowed them full mobility and movement, without making them much larger than they normally were.

"I'm missing one thing, though," he said almost jokingly.

He bent down to pull the modified TEK40 carbines he'd embedded in the skull of a Thegn soldier. A massive mechanical weapon system moved in front of him and blocked his path. He almost struck it aside before spotting the hands of the Jötnar holding it.

"Can I recommend this fine vintage instead?" said the shorter Jötnar sarcastically.

He handed the short multi-barreled weapon and dropped it into Khan's outstretched arms. Even with his strength, the weight made him adjust his stance.

"Welcome to the L56 Mark III, the latest toy for our armory."

Another Jötnar lifted a combined power pack that included the double battery system and ammunition packs for the main weapon. It clipped directly onto Khan's back with a dull clunk sound. The first Jötnar then dragged two metal feeds to the gun's body and tapped a lever on the side.

"There, you're good to go."

He moved about at the waist, testing the flexibility of the feeds. He was able to move it further than expected before the feeds pushed tightly to his body.

"Yeah, this is much better."

That was when he spotted the Jötnar warrior from the original landing. This one bore a number of markings, insignia of a kind directly onto his chest and helmet. It was both unfamiliar and also vaguely recognizable, yet he couldn't put a finger on it. Khan watched the Jötnar marine move around him, eyeing up the battered Khan carefully. His armor was dull, but the crimson paintwork still showed through like a layer of fresh blood. In fact, as he looked more closely, he realized half of the red actually was blood, with some of it even covering his visor. The warrior wiped it with the back of his left arm, and the visor opened with a gentle hiss.

"Olik?"

The Jötnar opened his mouth and beamed with his set of crooked teeth.

"Khan, old friend, about time!"

He threw himself at Khan, and they crashed together like a pair of Biomech machines engaged in some kind of titanic death struggle. Khan struck Olik in the chest and pushed him back so hard, he had to stagger and then lock his foot to the ground to stop him from hitting the wall.

"What the hell are you doing here? And who are these Jötnar?"

Olik pointed upwards.

"I'm with Colonel Morato, commanding her Jötnar contingent. We've just come from Prometheus to save your asses!"

Khan's eyes narrowed and he looked intently at his old friend.

"These are from the garrison on Prometheus. They are called the Red Watch."

"Because of the color of their armor, right?"

Olik sniggered.

"Maybe. They are a good unit, Khan, an entire marine force that is one hundred percent Jötnar. They've been kitted out with the best armor and weapons."

Khan looked at Olik and several of the other Jötnar as they continued to file past toward the sound of battle.

"I can see that."

He turned his attention back to Olik.

"What happened on Prometheus?"

Any other marine might have looked worried, but Olik couldn't hide his pleasure. He stepped closer, crashed his hand onto Khan's shoulder, and they moved on to follow the others inside the structure.

"You missed one hell of a fight, Brother. The Biomechs

assaulted the entire planet, and we crushed them. Colonel Teresa Morato, Admiral Churchill, and Osk were all there, and we cut them down in the hundreds and thousands. It was like…poetry or something. There were dead and dying everywhere, rivers of Biomech blood."

Spartan and Teresa followed a short distance behind the Jötnar, but close enough that they could hear the discussion between Khan and Olik.

"Is that true?" Spartan asked.

"Which part?" Teresa replied.

"Prometheus. Did the Biomechs really hit the planet that hard?"

He looked at her face, and her facial muscles alone answered his question. Spartan shook his head.

"Why Prometheus? Surely High Command could have intercepted them before they landed?"

Teresa stepped over the body of two Thegns and then stopped. She lifted her hand and waited for a moment. Spartan kept his weapon trained off into the distance, ready the instant a target might appear. Her body language softened and then they continued onwards.

"Spartan, things have become a little complicated since you left. We've met many races and forged a long-term Alliance with the Helions."

Spartan had already found most of this out during his time aboard Dauntless, but he let her continue as they carried on through the underground facility. It was a slow, monotonous slog as it was anyway, and he found himself more than happy at just hearing her voice.

"The Biomechs have arrived in Helios in substantial numbers."

She looked at him with a serious expression on her face.

"They intend on controlling the Nexus to all of our worlds, and one by one they will control or destroy them all. Jack's out there."

She looked away quickly.

"...and Ingo and Matius."

Spartan didn't worry too much about the other two, but the news of Jack felt like a knife in the stomach. He knew his son was now in the Corps and involved in the fighting, but from what he'd heard, the battle for Helios was going to be one of those monumental events. In his experience, that went hand-in-hand with massive loss of life. He knew there was nothing to be done right now, so he moved the subject back.

"So, what's all this about Prometheus? I still don't understand what happened."

Teresa knew he'd changed the subject, but she was more than happy to brush that aside for now. Not being able to help the fighting around Helios was one thing, but spending excessive time worrying about it was another.

"It was a trap, plain and simple. A plan put into motion by General Rivers and Admiral Anderson, and mainly coordinated by Admiral Churchill to purge the last remaining elements of the enemy. They have been popping up all over the place, and if we're going to pull our weight in Helios, we needed to make sure the last of them were gone. It worked too. Even the last of the Sons of the League showed up, and they died with the rest."

That last part really seemed to choke her up a little. Spartan reached out to her, but something up ahead forced them all to their knees. A dozen coilguns targeted the shape in the distance as it changed into the shape of humanoid figures.

"Hold your fire," said Olik.

They became even clearer and then changed to that of three human workers, all filthy and each looking equally terrified. They moved up to them and continued past with a single marine staying with them as escort.

Spartan looked down at the entrance to the secondary habitation wing. It was only a short distance away and exactly where the reconnaissance robots had already reported signs of hostages and of the enemy. Teresa looked back at Spartan, still shocked that he really was there.

"Are you up for this?" she asked.

Spartan sighed slowly.

"Really, do you need to ask?"

Teresa smiled but said no more and simply looked at him. It seemed like a decade since they'd last met. She felt older, but Spartan had definitely been through the worst of it. His face was lined and weary, and he was now sporting a short beard that covered his chin and lower cheeks. Teresa could also see from the way his body moved; he was in pain. It was only then she remembered the news on his arm. Teresa glanced down, and Spartan spotted her eyes. He lifted the left arm and to her surprise it looked normal.

"You won't see any difference while I've got the armor on."

She winced a little as he explained. Teresa's mind was far more creative, and she imagined all kind of terrible horrors when it came to the maiming of Spartan. The reports had mentioned the breaking of so many bones, but it was the severing of his lower left arm that still stunned her. She shook her head and concentrated on what she could see, Spartan and a full working set of PDS Alpha armor.

Both of them were fitted out in the same armor, and it was definitely the best the Alliance could make. It wasn't as tough as the heavy suits worn by the Vanguards and CES units, but it was much tougher than the earlier PDS armor she'd used for so long in the Uprising. Her suit was still battered and scarred from the fighting on Prometheus, though the artificers on board had at least given it a clean and hammered out some of the more obvious dents.

Spartan's armor was the same design, but other than that it looked like it had just come fresh from the factory. His was a brand new unit that had been carefully fitted around him just minutes after the landing of the reinforcements.

In their hands, they carried the reliable L52 Mark II carbines, the standard issue for a generation now.

"This is something I never thought I would see again," said Khan.

Olik looked confused and paused to look back at the marines. He could see Spartan, Teresa, and the entire host of marines moving carefully behind them. Unlike the Earthsec operatives, these warriors were careful and well equipped. They checked their angles and moved surprisingly quiet through the facility.

"What do you mean?"

Khan nodded toward Spartan.

"The two of them."

Olik hadn't really given it much thought, but as he looked at them, the memories of the past mixed with the stories they had all shared for so many years. For anybody else, it might have just been two marines in regular equipment, but to Khan and Olik it was like seeing something from a painting. The two of them were a legend in the Corps, and Khan had never truly believed he would see the day when the two would be together in battle once again. Spartan noticed them looking first.

"Yeah?"

Khan cleared his voice and looked back to Olik.

"What's the situation?" Teresa asked.

Olik moved a little closer, as usual forgetting to make use of the ranged digital communications channels that every single one of them was connected to. He knew how to use the technology, but at such short-range, he preferred the old fashioned way more.

"Combat drones are inside and have done a sweep. The site is on two floors and comprises one hundred and sixty-five separate apartment complexes, shops, and facilities. The site is in an L shape, with entrances to the public transportation system at both ends and in the central plaza that connects the two wings. We're positioned at the entrance to this end."

Spartan nodded as the imagery came through on his visor. It had been some time since he'd had access to such technology, yet it felt second nature to him already. Teresa started to speak, but Spartan got there first.

"We are on the lower level here, not far from the access to the mass transit system, right?"

Olik nodded. "That's right."

He pointed to the wide space in front of them. It was a hundred meters ahead and very wide. There were a number of stores facing them, and the main passage turned ninety degrees to the right and disappeared. There were displays and windows from shows and businesses on the next floor up, along with a wide walkway running directly above their heads.

"This is more like a shopping mall than a city," grumbled Khan.

"True," answered Olik.

"This place is home to tens of thousands of people in the attached apartment blocks. The center section is more like a city center, like downtown Terra Nova but buried under the ground."

Captain Cobb now arrived, along with two of his operatives. His confident air had long vanished, but being back in familiar territory had at least improved his demeanor.

"You're right. This place is a den of black market dealings, crimes, and blasphemy."

Teresa raised her eyebrows and tried to hide a smile. Spartan was much less diplomatic.

"Maybe we can forget the religious piety for one day and save these people?"

Khan chuckled loudly at his friend's intervention, and Teresa had to turn away to avoid being seen.

"I...uh...you need to know that this place is not as it seems. A store may be a front for a criminal enterprise, that is all," said Captain Cobb defensively.

Spartan watched him carefully, his mouth not moving, but his face telling the man everything. Unlike the others in the facility, Spartan had a way of exuding authority, even to those that had never met him. Captain Cobb pointed into the compound and the flickering lights.

"The bulk of the rooms and facilities at this end of the complex were the sites of a major department store plus luxury apartments."

Teresa checked the details coming in from the scouting teams. The marines had moved a good way inside but were under orders to not push too far. As soon as they had taken fire, the teams had reported back and then consolidated the immediate area for signs of the enemy.

"Yes, the rooms and structure on the lower floor appear to be abandoned. Our marines are already clearing them closer to the lower plaza. The raised walkways and facilities above us are an unknown though. Reports from the advance teams say they took heavy fire trying to move through them."

"What's their plan?" Teresa asked.

Spartan looked to Olik as well, both expecting a response.

"Same as it always is," said a calm voice.

Spartan looked back at Captain Rivers and another squad of marines as they moved their way back toward them from inside the facility.

"Captain," he said with an outreached hand.

The man saluted to him instead, much to Spartan's surprise.

"Sir, you might be officially retired, but out here that means nothing. Once a marine, always a marine."

He then looked to Captain Cobb.

"We need your skills and local knowledge for this one. It's pretty messy in there."

"Rivers, did you say?" Spartan asked.

Teresa nodded and leaned in.

"He's the General's boy."

The Captain did not seem impressed and chose to point back to the direction he'd arrived from and then continued to speak.

"The Earthsec operatives say there are four sets of escalators that move between the levels. There are two on each side of the two floors of the plaza. Power has failed on all four, but they take less than ten seconds to move up."

"That is correct, Captain," said Cobb.

"There are other ways to the next level up. Are you sure that is where the enemy is hidden?"

"Hidden?" said a gruff metallic voice.

All of them looked to the shape of Z'Kanthu, the rebel warlord of The Twelve, and the only known Biomech to now be working alongside Alliance warriors.

"You've got something to add?" Spartan asked, as if talking to a child.

The great machine turned about on its waist to look at him and then to Teresa.

"Yes. Dersna landed here with her fourteen bandon; her aim to destroy or recover me, and then turn this world into a base of operations to assist in their war effort. With her gone, her remaining warriors will proceed with their last orders or until they are given new ones by a Core. Something I think we might be able to achieve."

Khan stepped toward Z'Kanthu and pointed his hand angrily at the machine.

"Wait. Are you saying we could have just reprogrammed these days ago?"

Z'Kanthu lifted himself up straight and struck his upper body on the ceiling. Chunks of masonry dropped down, and Spartan had to activate his visor just before a handful of sharp stones hit his helmet.

"Thanks for that."

The machine seemed unimpressed at what he was seeing.

"No. You misunderstand. Designated leaders, the same as your generals and commanders, command our armies. With this leadership gone, they are forced to rely…"

"On their last orders. Yes, we get that," finished Khan impatiently.

He looked to Spartan and the others.

"You remember Terra Nova."

Spartan didn't need to answer. For those of them who were there, it had been the bloody last battle to end the Uprising. It was hardly an event he might be able to forget, even if he wanted to.

"The AI Core sent out an override signal that spread through the entire Biomech force. Can we do that again?"

He looked to Z'Kanthu who stood motionless like a statue.

"No, that is not how it works," he said.

"The Cores are keys to the minds of the long lost. The oldest and most venerated might contain a mind that is a thousand years old. Some are politicians, other engineers, but most are soldiers. They provide the leadership of the Steersmen. The signal cannot be modified or duplicated without the involvement of the minds."

Captain Rivers checked the magazine on his carbine and walked past Z'Kanthu. He looked ahead for signs of trouble and then turned back to face them all.

"So what exactly are you suggesting, then? If we can't use the signal, we might as well hunt down and finish off these things, right?"

Z'Kanthu lowered himself almost a meter.

"Not quite. There is one thing even I can do."

He pointed back inside the large mall shaped facility.

"I am detecting the evacuation pods of Dersna's command ship, approximately twelve hundred meters in that direction."

Captain Rivers was already cross matching the details with his mapping, but Captain Cobb, with his local knowledge got their first.

"That's on the other side of this site, and above the mass transit station. We'd have to work our way up to the next floor, across the entire length, and then cut through the apartment complex near the opposite end."

Rivers withdrew a secpad from its clipped mount on his thigh and showed it to Captain Cobb.

"This location is where the enemy is strongest."

"Yes, that is correct," said Z'Kanthu, "The Core must be intact. With their attack failing, they are regrouping to defend their commander."

Cobb started to move, but Spartan grabbed him.

"Hey, slow down."

He then looked to Z'Kanthu.

"So what? We broke their attack and they have regrouped. That doesn't mean some Core has magically appeared. What happens next? We already have marines in position to block a withdrawal from this site and further toward City One. We have them trapped."

The machine shuddered and said something unintelligible.

"What?" Khan said impatiently.

"They will protect the Core and consolidate this area. The Core is more valuable than ten normal Biomechs. It is the equivalent of your…generals."

The machine bent down lower to face Spartan.

"My race can survive in harsher conditions than yours, and my kin will know this. With Dersna destroyed, the only leadership remaining is with this Core. Without it, her bandon will continue to fight until they are victorious, or all your people are dead."

Captain Rivers nodded ever so slowly as he started to realize what was happening.

"I see. The fact they are not just throwing their last

warriors at us tells us one thing."

Khan agreed. "Yes, they have leadership."

A small amount of gunfire clattered far into the distance, followed shortly after by the thump of a single small explosive or grenade being activated. The gunfire ceased, for a few more seconds at least. Z'Kanthu continued.

"I would offer only two choices if the Core is intact."

Spartan glanced at Teresa and back at the machine as he waited for its revelations.

"The first is to establish a defensive position by using the civilians as hostages to stop us from attacking. The second is to exterminate every living thing in this facility, but this would leave them with no way to exploit this planet other than to remove it as an asset to your own forces."

Spartan indicated for Z'Kanthu to lower himself down to his head. It took an odd series of movements for the machine to come down that low, but Spartan refused to move until he'd completed the maneuver.

"What can you do if we get to this Core?"

The machine looked about at the others as though wary of exchanging some great secret. Finally he spoke.

"I can transfer my mind into the Core temporarily. If successful, I will be able to command the genetically coded bandon of Dersna. I cannot do this on my own though. It will be defended by her most powerful guardians, and they will destroy the Core rather than let it fall into our hands."

"And you have a plan, right?" Spartan asked.

Again the machine made an odd series of sounds.

"The guardians of Dersna are not sophisticated, and there is one thing their masters want more than any one world of yours. The capture of the remaining rebels of The Twelve is worth the loss of a hundred bandon."

"You want to be bait?" Teresa asked him.

Spartan looked to her and was surprised to see genuine concern on her face for the alien machine.

"No, I do not, but the survival of The Twelve and our revenge against our betrayers will never happen if your race is defeated. Your Alliance is confused, violent, and weak. But you have still managed to fight and defeat an enemy that even we could not. This planet and its Core can offer us insight into the enemy's plans. It is a big risk."

Khan scratched his head as he listened, but he'd been quiet far too long now. He paced to the side of Spartan and then stopped, resting his arm on his friend's shoulder.

"If this works, we could control the bandon of this Biomech...Dersna? That could be hundreds of warriors, some we might even be able to reprogram."

Spartan very much doubted the last part, but he couldn't disappoint Khan, not just yet. Since the freeing of the first generation of his people, Khan, Gun, and the others had made it their mission to seek out the Biomech creatures, no matter where they were or what they did. Thousands had been sent to Hyperion, the new homeworld of the Jötnar, deep inside Alliance territory. Those few synthetics that could be turned would join their ranks; the remainder would be executed or freed on the surface. Spartan had visited Hyperion many times, and the great Jötnar hunts were now infamous for their danger and violence.

"Right, it's time to make a decision, then," said Spartan.

His voice was cool and calm, and as usual he cut right through the conversation.

"We have a major hostage situation, plus an enemy that needs crushing. But that's not all, is it? What's the status on Helios and the rest?"

Teresa spoke over her suit's communications system, and Captain Rivers joined in. It gave Spartan a moment to consider his thoughts. He looked to Khan and Olik, both of whom looked impatient to get on with the fight.

"So, the plan?" Khan asked.

"We're getting to that."

Teresa took a step toward Captain Rivers and spoke quietly. They discussed specifics for almost half a minute before she finally she turned to the rest. Captain Rivers moved back to speak with the junior officers of the marines that had now arrived, along with additional platoons of marines. Teresa looked extremely serious, perhaps even a little nervous as she spoke.

"Our fleet has engaged the Biomechs at Spascia. Major Terson is coordinating our units from inside Tamarisk, and he has been collating the reports coming through the Terra-Nova Rift. It would appear that Comet C34 is less than a day away from reaching a high orbit around Helios Prime, and High Command is expecting a major attack. All military units are active and waiting for their postings, but most are being assembled either at Terra Nova, Prometheus, or T'Karan. It's all about to hit off."

"The goddamn Biomech War is about to start, and we're out here on the ass end of the Alliance," grumbled Olik.

Captain Cobb looked up at the angry looking Jötnar. He opened his mouth, but Khan reached out and placed his hand over the man's face.

"I wouldn't if I were you."

"How is the fight at Spascia?"

Both Khan and Teresa detected a minuscule hint of nerves with the question from Spartan.

"The Biomechs have deployed an Ark to command their attack from. The first assault wave is heading for the surface at this very moment. Our fleet is trying to stop them, but it doesn't look good."

Spartan nodded as she spoke, finding himself not in the slightest surprised at what he was hearing.

"So the Biomechs are hitting the Helions and hitting them hard. Once they fail, they will move onto the others, probably us. I say we smash these machines right here on Mars, take back the world, and use whatever we can get out of them to help this war effort."

Khan seemed to positively glow at this suggestion.

"You want to rescue the hostages and capture the Core?" Captain Cobb asked quietly.

The doubt in his voice came across as almost being insolent, and he quickly realized that.

"That isn't quite what I meant. This kind of operation will be…well, it will be…"

"Tough," finished Spartan.

He looked to his comrades and rubbed at one of the many scars on his cheek.

"I say we take this Core, free our people, and get these bandon on our side. They could be a handy weapon, and if this war goes the way I think it will, we will need every asset, including planets, people, and soldiers."

He looked back to Teresa.

"We're gonna need soldiers for this war, a lot of soldiers."

Captain Rivers stepped past them and indicated for two squads to spread out ahead, slightly inside the facility. He looked back to Spartan.

"We don't have soldiers here, Spartan, but we do have marines."

Spartan laughed at that.

"I know. It's time we used them."

CHAPTER SEVEN

The commitment to the defense of the Helios Nexus marked the official recognition of the importance of the Orion Nebula. Some had argued for independence from the alien domains of Orion, but the riches in trade, communication, medicine, and technology were nothing next to simple human curiosity. Once man had stepped onto alien worlds, there was no going back. Who would have even considered establishing a trading post on the Helion homeworld, just six weeks after making first contact, would be possible?

Musings on the Alliance

The low grinding vibrations of ammunition crates being moved by the robotic loaders into position could barely be felt inside the ship. What could be were from conveyor belts fitted between the weapon units on both sides. The ammunition itself was kept in armored shelters deep inside the mission modules to avoid them being struck in a firefight. One by one they clunked into position, and the status indicators inside the destroyer flashed from amber to green.

"Fire all weapons!" said the XO in a calm but firm voice.

He ran his fingers along the firing sequences that would send the entire stock of loaded ordnance directly into the path of the enemy ships. The response was instantaneous as the guns fed in one round after another. Even the missile tubes launched their ordnance in a blind salvo with there being almost no need to even identify a target. The destroyer shuddered as the weapon systems in the three mission modules unleashed a powerful broadside into the passing Biomanta. The gun turrets raked the Biomechanical ship and tore off small sections of plating and armor, while at point-blank range the missiles looked more like cannon broadsides that exploded entire sections of the ship.

"She's breaking up, Sir!" said the chief engineer.

Unlike the rest of the Liberty class ships, ANS New Carlos had been fitted out with two air-defense modules and a single guided missile module. Each of these was actually pairs like panniers that were slung under the spine of the ship and provided the bulk of its center mass. All Liberty ships were equipped with a pair of quad 20mm coilgun turrets, one fore and one aft, plus a pair of hull-mounted torpedo tubes fitted just below the chin of the nose of the vessel. The mission modules provided two additional quad-gun mounts plus stowage space, ammunition, and armor or a motorized missile unit with twenty spare anti-ship missiles and launch tubes. This arsenal provided a total of six quad-gun turrets and four missile tubes, the perfect compromise for the new flagship of the Spascia Fleet.

"Good work, Lieutenant. One down and a few more to go," said Commodore Hampel.

He groaned and twisted as the medic applied the warm feeling glue to his forehead. It immediately stung, and he winced involuntarily. The XO continued issuing orders directly to the crews managing the weapon systems. Even from their position inside the ship, it was possible to feel the almost continuous vibrations as the 20mm coilgun turrets firing without pause. The massive ammunition hoppers allowed the weapons almost limitless firing, and the gunners were taking full advantage of that.

"You really should get a full scan in the medical bay," said Dr. Jones.

His tone was concerned but also more than a little frustrated. Commodore Hampel lifted himself to his feet just at the moment another series of impacts thudded along the starboard flank of the destroyer. He shook his head angrily and walked back to his seat.

"Thank you, Doctor. If we survive this, you can be sure

I will get myself checked in."

Commodore Hampel watched the scores of tracer trails on the holographic display. The moving shapes were almost mesmerizing, and he had to admit the firepower being put out by just six quad-gun turrets was impressive.

"Very well, Sir. I will return to my duties."

He watched the officer head for the door.

"Do that."

As the Doctor left, he immediately regretted his outburst to the chief medical officer. He was tempted to call him back, but the explosions and flashes on the mainscreen instantly turned his attention back to what was happening aboard his own ship. The large shared holographic unit showed the entire ship, as well as the status of each section. There were yellow flashpoints in a hundred places but only a few minor red sections showing system failures or major breaches. Lieutenant Morgan pointed to the shapes representing their other vessels.

"Sir, we've knocked out three more of their ships, but we're getting awfully close to Spascia. Our ships are intermixed, and it's turning into a fight of attrition. Our destroyers are putting up one hell of a fight, but the particle beams of their Biomantas are impossible to avoid. Nearly every ship in the forward squadron has been damaged."

Commodore Hampel didn't like that at all. Exchanging one of his ships for one of the enemy's was a tactic that would lose him the entire fleet, and in his experience, the

Biomechs always seemed to find more ships.

"And the Khreenk?"

The XO moved the model about with his hands to show the Biomech Ark. It looked more like a massive bug with great swarms of fighters and gunboats circling in a bloody and deadly battle. Clouds of flak covered it, and beams from the emitters flashed out every few seconds to vaporize fighters or to destroy missiles and torpedoes.

"The Biomechs have launched fighters to try and keep the Khreenk ships busy, as well as another squadron of Biomantas. The Cephalon command ship has also altered course to help protect their Ark. So far they've disabled five Corsairs, and some of the Biomantas are moving back to deal with the rest. The Ark has stopped focusing on capital ships and has split the fire from its primary emitters to attack any ship it can reach."

Give it another thirty minutes and the Khreenk will be on the ropes, and for what? To buy me time to reduce these ground forces before they can make planetfall.

A new alert flashed up, showing a breach in the armor-plated mission module toward the rear of the destroyer. Lieutenant Morgan sent orders to the damage teams while continuing to check the status of the battle.

"That was the Ark. It hit ANS Crusader, but the damage was minimal. We got the tail end of the strike, but it still tore open a hole big enough to land a Hammerhead inside."

"Contact!" said the computer system in a loud alert.

A number of red diamonds appeared on the holographic display around the flanks of the Biomech Ark. First there were two, and then they multiplied and morphed into something completely different. The computer system attempted to reclassify the new targets, but even the Ark came up as unrecognized on the scanners.

"What in the name of..." muttered Commodore Hampel.

Lieutenant Morgan tapped the shapes and crosschecked them with their own databases. Image after image flicked past, but only a small number matched the details already contained in the Alliance databases.

"The Ark, it's partially disassembling itself. It looks like large sections of the rear are actually additional warships. I'm detecting eight more Sawfish and at least another Cephalon command ship."

He moved about nervously and then looked back to his commander.

"Scratch that. There are more than two-dozen Sawfish, another Cephalon, and two Ravager class Battlecruisers. The Ark has reduced in size by almost twenty percent."

Both of them watched the imagery with an odd mixture of surprise and fascination. Never before had an enemy shown such advancements in technology and robotics. For any officer it would have been almost exciting, but to them it was an enemy with almost super-human technology and resources.

"Incredible. Just incredible," said Commodore Hampel.

There was a sense of awe to his voice that made Lieutenant Morgan a little nervous.

"True. But they die just like everybody else."

"Indeed so. Nonetheless, we need to understand them if we are to beat them. They must have constructed the ships directly into the apparatus of the Ark. So for the last centuries they have been harvesting the comet itself to construct a new fleet and a myriad of weapons for this war."

"That makes sense," said the Lieutenant, "The record states that only a modest number of the Biomechs escaped at the end of the war. According to the Helion account, the majority was pushed back through the Black Rift in their final battle."

Commodore Hampel smiled.

"Well, if we believe what their accounts have to say, we'd think the Helions defeated them man for man and scattered them to the wind. We know better than that though, don't we?"

He looked about the CIC and at the officers as they went about their job of fighting the devastating battle of Spascia.

"These Biomechs are not stupid. They knew their end was coming, so they put plans into action. I suspect the truth is more like they withdrew their main force to their homeworld, and then shut themselves away to rebuild."

He then pointed to the icons of the ships in the current battle.

"The remainder were scattered to prepare the ground for their return. Some traveled to different worlds like ours to ferment revolts and potentially rebuild their armies. The rest, perhaps even their leadership made for C34 as it left the system. It was a long-term plan, but now it's coming to fruition."

He looked at the model of the Ark once more. There was something else changing with its structure, and for a moment he couldn't tell what it was. Only when the small spikes pushing out from its outer surface did it become clearer.

"Look, the station is deploying something."

Lieutenant Morgan's attention was taken to a set of new targets off to the right.

"Sir, Biomech fighters are closing on our stern. Give me a moment."

There was need to intervene as his executive officer directed two nearby Lightning squadrons to intercept. It was fast, efficient, and deadly. They unleashed missiles in salvos and quickly cleared a path toward the destroyer. Commodore Hampel tried to hide a smile as the destroyer guns blasted the last three fighters just as they opened fire themselves. A sound like the patter of rain on metal ran along the flank of the ship but set off no sensors. He looked back at the display, squinting as he tried to assess the capabilities of the ever-changing Biomech weapon systems.

"What about that Ark? Tell me we're bringing it down."

Lieutenant Morgan rotated the Ark model and pointed to its frontal area.

"It is still operational, though we have inflicted substantial superficial damage to its outer structure. Particle beams are causing considerable damage to the armor, but most of our ordnance is being detonated before it can penetrate inside."

He pressed two buttons and then stopped as if he'd just seen some terrifying demon. Commodore Hampel looked carefully at the shape of the Ark and picked out movement around its rear. The Lieutenant shook his head in disbelief.

"It would appear additional transports are being unloaded. Wait, scanners are detecting ports opening all around the Ark."

He turned around.

"I think they're preparing for the next stage."

Commodore Hampel tapped the button that connected him to the entire fleet.

"All ships, the Biomech Ark is about to act. This could be a prelude to a major attack. Get closer to the enemy and keep them busy. You have to give them minimal opportunity to intercept your ships."

He looked back at the battle closer to Spascia. The forces of both sides were heavily intertwined with Sawfish, Biomantas, Crusader, and Liberty class ships engaged in a battle more reminiscent of the line battles of ancient Earth. Gunnery exchanges took place at close range, while fighters from both sides tangled in a dogfight that included hundreds of small craft.

So they have reinforcements, and this Ark is changing form and function. It's time to let the ground pounders to some work. We'll use these ships where they can do the most good.

He glanced to the XO, his grim expression clear and obvious.

"Okay, it's time to turn this around. I want my secondary plan put into effect immediately. This fleet must be maintained for the coming fight."

Lieutenant Morgan looked surprised.

"Sir? We can hold for at least another ten minutes."

"Perhaps, but this battle will not be decided in ten minutes. We're outnumbered, and Spascia needs our help. We must get our ships away from those particle beams."

He tried to look less nervous, but it wasn't working.

"Prepare the ship for atmospheric combat. Things are about to get very interesting."

The XO raised an eyebrow, but he'd already made his thoughts known.

"Aye, Sir."

Commodore Hampel selected the commanders of

every squadron remaining and brought up the video feeds for each of them.

"It is time. All ships capable of atmospheric combat will follow us to our rendezvous vector. From there, we will establish a mobile reserve to support the ground troops under Colonel Gun while inside the atmosphere. Ground-based fighters will provide us with additional cover."

The XO watched him as he checked the positions around Spascia.

"All other ships will execute order Beta Six, skim the upper atmosphere, and meet out of line of sight of the enemy. I want a secure orbital position in less than an hour."

He licked his lips as he visualized their positions over the next hour. The larger or more heavily damaged ships would be forced to engage in a cat and mouse game in orbit around Spascia. It wouldn't be easy, but as long as they avoided the Ark, they would be free to operate independently.

Unless the Biomechs send their remaining ships after them.

That wasn't necessarily a bad thing though, and he wondered if the Biomechs would be stupid enough to leave their transports and ground forces vulnerable for so long. In his mind, he could see groups of Alliance ships launching swift strikes against transports as they made their way down to the surface.

We can only hope.

"We are in this fight for the long haul, and I want this fleet kept intact. Bring in your fighters and get to safety. There will be no heroics, just the calm professionalism expected of all Alliance officers. Good hunting."

* * *

Jack leaned back and looked up to the alien sky. He'd spent time on many worlds from Hyperion and Kerberos, through to Helios Prime, and now this rock. Each of those worlds had something unusual about them. With Hyperion it was the jungles and creatures, both of which were as likely to kill you as the atmosphere. Terra Nova was the home to the greatest wealth and decadence in the entire Alliance. Kerberos was a hive of industry, engineering, and some of the most suspiciously black market dealers and smugglers he'd ever known. Even Helios Prime, with its stunning skylines and massive structures had at least been the pinnacle of alien engineering and success.

But not here!

Of all the planets he'd visited, he never expected he would face the largest battle in his life on a planet famous for just one thing.

"Bloody ruins, nothing but bloody ruins. This entire place is ridiculous."

He hadn't meant to blurt it out, but he was finding the place less inspiring by the minute. Corporal Frewyn laughed at yet another complaint from Jack and stopped what he was doing for a moment. He looked from the robot container and back to Jack. There were a number of containers strewn about, and a technical unit was busy testing two of the SAAR combat robots. Both sat motionless, like a pair of tracked metal statues, yet taking up no more space than a Vanguard marine. They were short, barely taller than a man's waist, yet looked deadly in both design and construction. The paired weapons mounted centrally on a rotating mount topped off the killer machines.

"What are you complaining about now, marine?"

Jack stayed flat on his back and took in a long, deep breath of air. It felt slightly damp to him, like the feeling you got when in a place below sea level where it was warm. It wasn't a feeling he particularly liked. He twisted a little to look at the Corporal, and the outer section of his armor groaned and creaked on the stone as he moved.

"I can understand Helios Prime. It's the capital of an entire race and this supposed Orion Nexus. What I don't get is, why we've put so much down on this planet? Isn't the only thing worth controlling here that thing?"

He looked back and pointed at the barely visible peak, now covered in low cloud mixed with dust. Dull yellow beams tried to punch through the mist, but even the most powerful proved unsuited to the task. The massive ground based weapon was impossible to see right now, yet everybody on Spascia knew the importance of such a powerful weapon to the coming war.

"Private Morato, are you causing trouble again?" Sergeant Stone asked.

Jack looked about but was unable to find the Sergeant. He finally moved out from where he'd been talking with an Alliance officer next to the wall. The nearest SAAR robot powered up and drove off, all under its own power and control before vanishing off down the street. Jack watched it move away and then turned his attention to the annoyed looking Sergeant.

"Uh...no, Sergeant. Not at all."

The sound of chattering people and excitement caught all their attention. A pair of Jötnar in full JAS armor stormed past, along with a dozen or more Helion soldiers. Jack sat up and found himself speechless at seeing lightly armored Helion synthetics moving out in the open. It reminded him of Vadi, one of this odd race that was effectively the Helion equivalent of the Jötnar. Not as big but still strong and bulky, they had been ostracized on Helion worlds, but now it seemed some of them had been given a role to play in the coming fight. The gear they wore looked as though it had been hastily cobbled together, and Jack very much doubted it would do any more than keep them warm.

Still, it's better than keeping them locked away and hidden from the state.

"What's going on?" Corporal Frewyn asked.

"Well, for starters, it looks like the Helions are getting more pragmatic every day."

A flight of Hammerheads screamed overhead, leaving a vapor trail that ran off into the distance. Right behind them moved a Marine Mauler, the heady, square shaped landing craft with engines at each corner and bristling with turrets.

"Have you heard the news?" Riku shouted.

The young marine balanced precariously a floor up and on what remained of the smashed floor to the higher level. Riku leaned out and waved over to Jack to get his attention and lost her footing. She slid but caught an exposed girder just before she would have dropped to the ground. Jack looked up to her and shook his head, half with amusement and half with thanks that she hadn't been hurt.

"What news? What's happening?"

She began to speak, but with their visors open, the barrage of sonic booms and screeching engines blocked out everything she said. Something like a thunderclap echoed through the ruins of the city, and reverberated so many times, it actually shook the foundations. Jack spotted others pointing up, and he followed their hands to see the colored shapes appearing in the sky. His pulse instantly quickened, and he could feel the adrenalin start to course through his veins. Sergeant Stone shouted something at him, but he still couldn't hear. With the tap of a button, his visor locked into position and drowned out the booming sounds. It was replaced by the shouts of the Sergeant.

"Marines, to your positions!"

Riku vanished from her position, and Frewyn, Callahan, and Jenkell appeared from where they had been resting and ran toward the outer wall on the lower floor of the building. There were clear paths for them to follow, and Callahan grabbed Jack's shoulder and forcibly yanked him in the same direction.

"This is Colonel Gun. Admiral Pezal has been killed. The Spascia Fleet is falling back to regroup. They've done their part, for now. Now it's up to us. We have to weaken them before they can bring in more troops. We can expect planetary assault shortly. Be ready!"

It was short and exactly as Jack would have expected an order to be from his old friend. More marines ran to their allocated places while armored vehicles moved from the streets and into their prepared positions they had hidden from immediate view. Incredibly, the ruins of the city looked almost deserted in less than sixty seconds. Even Jack was impressed.

"Here they come!" Jenkell shouted.

The unit's medic had been hiding, hunched down behind the window frame where her carbine rested against the old, smashed stonework. Jack looked at her, but she quickly pointed with her left hand to the sky. It was lower than before, and Jack could see the dark shape, wreathed in flames and trailing smoke as it traveled through the thick planet atmosphere.

Another planet, another attack.

A moment of panic shocked his system, and he felt as though he couldn't breathe. That one feeling immediately froze his chest seemed to create the condition he feared so much.

Breathe, damn you!

He closed his eyes and forced himself to calm down. It took a superhuman effort, but when he opened his eyes, he could feel the air moving through his lungs and saw the dark shape of a warship as it thundered overhead.

"What in God's balls is that?" Corporal Frewyn asked.

As the flames began to subside, the huge shape became clearer and easier to see. It was hard to gage size without other ships in the vicinity, but the basic components were clearly not alien.

"It's one of ours!" Sergeant Stone called out.

There was certainty in his voice, and even Jack found himself busy looking at the shape to try and determine the type and status of the vessel. Sergeant Stone was standing out in the open with his hands on his hips, looking directly up at the shape of the starship. Jack could see flashes of light on his face as additional ships dropped in through the atmosphere, each wreathed in flame from the high-speed reentry.

"What are they doing here?" Frewyn asked.

A bat shaped vessel appeared next, its form completely

black due to the silhouette and the smoke that trailed behind it. Arcs of light flashed about it as it tried to make use of its particle beams. The Alliance ship leading it fired back with traditional light auto cannons of some type and instantly blew chunks of its body. The marines waved their weapons in the air in delight as the pursuing Biomanta twisted and then plummeted from the sky. Three Hammerheads followed it down and strafed the machine as it tried desperately to recover. Even though it dwarfed the size of the Alliance fighters, it had sustained too much damage to put up much of a fight.

"They're going down," said Jack quietly.

He and the others watched with sickening curiosity as it shook under the weight of heavy gunfire. Pieces broke off from its hull, yet it refused to drop out of the sky. The fighter pilots must have smelt blood because they moved in even closer to try and finish it. The Biomanta then managed to fire a short burst of kinetic gunfire at one of the Hammerheads.

"Whoa!" yelled a marine.

The gunfire chased along the wing and struck one of the engines. The small blast ripped a chunk off the wing, and the fighter spun out of control toward the ground. Only moments before impact, the cockpit burst open, and the crew module blasted up into the sky, well away from the wrecked fighter. Two more moved in to take its place and continued firing at the almost indestructible warship.

Jack looked to his left and right, wondering what was going on. He spotted the massive gun mounts of the hidden anti-air system that had been buried inside the ruins of the city block his unit were defending. The mount itself was moving, and he could see it tracking the Biomech ship as it moved across the sky.

Why aren't they firing?

He didn't have to wait long before the gun mounts of the Helion 10th anti-air ground forces opened fire. The tracer fire reached up into the dusty clouds as they did their utmost to pick out the attacking Biomechs. Three streams of cannon rounds battered away at the nearest Biomanta as it dropped to below a thousand meters. The ship leveled off, trailing three separate streams of thick black smoke. It shuddered as the ground units hit it hard, and then as quickly as it had arrived, the warship tilted over on its side.

"Yes!" shouted a marine on the next floor up.

Jack couldn't take his eyes away from the burning wreck. The ship was the size of an assault cruiser and big enough to devastate a large swathe of city. It continued to tilt until it was upside down. More gunfire hit it repeatedly, and finally the fighters pulled back just as it crashed into one of the nearby mountains. The impact shook the very ground the marines were waiting to defend, and small layers of dust shifted from the powerful crash.

"That is how you deal with Biomech scum!" Callahan

murmured.

Jack noticed more than a little malice to his voice.

"Get your heads down, now!"

The voice of Sergeant Stone boomed over their intercoms, and as one they dropped down into their positions. Jack moved forward to the lower level window that looked out to the west. He slid down and dropped a meter into the slit the CES team had dug just inside the smashed wall. Riku and Callahan were already there and activating the rangefinder on the bipod mounted L56 Mark III. A box lay on the ground containing a power unit and two spare ammunition feeder cases.

"Jack?" Riku asked.

She stared into his visor, but his expression seemed lifeless. The glasslike material glowed orange and red, and she turned to speak with Callahan.

"What's wrong with…"

The other marine put his hand on her head and pushed both her and Jack down as low as they could go in the slit. At almost the same time, a blast of heat ran over the building and would have burned them if they hadn't been protected inside their armor. The soundproofing in the helmets cut out most of the noise, but Jack could hear the screaming of somebody outside. Callahan tried to stop him, but he scrambled up and looked backwards into the ruins of the block. The anti-air unit was still firing, but only two Helions remained and both wore NHA armor under their smoking robes. Three of their comrades ran into the street screaming, surrounded in flames as their clothes burned.

"Somebody help them!" he shouted.

Jack took one step, and then a great impact shook him so violently he slipped and fell to his side. His point of view shifted, and he found himself looking up at the shape of a Bioray, one of the Biomech landers that could put an entire company onto the surface. It hovered a hundred meters above the ground, and only a quarter of a kilometer off to the west. Shapes dropped from its flanks as it deposited warriors to the surface. More movement caught his attention, and he rolled back to the slit on the ground. Additional Biorays appeared from much higher as they left the fuselage of a cruiser-sized warship. This one was long, darkly colored, and bristling with studs on its flanks and underside. Then he spotted the small black shapes on its superstructure.

Guns!

A hundred flashes went off at the same time, and then the rain of metal fell. Thousands of the deadly projectiles came down to the surface in such a dense pattern it could have been hail.

"Stay here, you fool!" Riku shouted.

She grabbed Jack's arm and yanked him back down. She tapped his visor and looked inside. He was breathing, but the rate was increasing, and she sensed he was close to an attack of some kind.

"He's in trouble," she said nervously.

Callahan bent down, checked the information on the tiny display to the side of his helmet, and then looked back at Riku.

"He's having another panic attack. Talk to him, calm him down, and get ready. They'll be here soon."

Another massive salvo of gunfire smashed into the ground and then a great vibration as the cruiser-sized ship moved toward the city.

"Look!" Callahan shouted.

Streaks of light moved at impossible speeds from the triple towers near the mountain on the other side of the city. One impacted with such energy that the cruiser shuddered with the impact. Then came shot after shot before the vessel turned to try and move away. The Alliance ship from earlier moved around it, taking full advantage of its greater maneuverability.

"That's a Liberty destroyer," said Callahan with satisfaction.

Jack had heard of them and tried to concentrate on it as the Alliance vessel unleashed a monstrous fusillade at the Biomech ship. Two more Alliance ships joined in, and as quickly as they had arrived, the Sawfish was losing height and trying to escape off to the west. The capital ships moved quickly and were soon replaced by the arrival of dozens of smaller Biorays, each one heading for the surface as quickly as they could.

"Here it comes," muttered Riku.

Gunfire from the city now reached up to the sky like yellow and white fingers. Rifles, machineguns, and automatic cannon anti-air weapons opened fire with an intensity that could have almost blotted out the sun. Two Biorays were sent spinning to the ground, and those trying to reach the city were forced back by the fury of the guns.

"It's working," Riku said, shaking her head.

Callahan grabbed both her and Jack and lifted them to the edge of the window frame so they could see far off to the west. Smoke trails marked the course of so many of the Biorays, but more importantly, they could make out the shapes of dozens of them as they dropped down and hit the ground; well out of range of the guns of the city. Jack closed his eyes and slowed his breathing as best as he could. It took a while, and he could feel Riku squeezing his hand as he tried to calm down. When he opened them, she was looking right into his eyes.

"Jack…Jack, come on, get ready!"

She let go and moved to the window frame. Callahan grabbed the back of the gun mount and Riku took aim. The weapon shuddered as they unleashed a number of short bursts off into the distance. Jack pulled himself up and reached out to Riku. There was a bright flash, and then both Riku and Callahan vanished. A hole the size of an armored vehicle was all that remained of the gun platform and the barricade they'd spent so long preparing. Blood splattered against the walls, but there was no sign of either of them.

"No!" he shouted hysterically.

Jack lifted himself up and looked out at what seemed to be a wall of monsters. The tallest were the Eques heavy walkers, the mighty six-legged walking tanks that he'd seen before. Out in front of these were hundreds, upon hundreds of the Decurion assault machines, and they were moving quickly.

Riku!

He left his position and scrambled about, but he could find nothing but blood and pieces of armor. Finally, he came to a section of the front of her helmet. He recognized the markings she'd made less than an hour earlier as they had waited.

"Private, get here, now!"

He looked up at the face of Sergeant Stone. The man leaned over the broken wall to the side of the room the three of them had been tasked with defending. Jack reached out, and the seasoned marine yanked him from the scene of death of destruction to the next room.

"Son, we're in trouble. Now get your ass on the firing line and do some damage."

Jack could barely breathe, but the Sergeant looked down, grabbed the carbine still slung about Jack's chest, and pushed it firmly into the marine's hands. He pointed to the low wall that looked much the same as the one he'd just left.

"Get on the firing line and open fire!"

Jack stumbled and fell down amongst a pair of marines he'd never met before. Neither even bothered to look at him. He lifted his carbine and placed it on the low wall. A tap flipped open the optical sight, and he looked down it and saw the wall of advancing Biomech war machines.

We can't hold them back, not this number.

Explosions shook the terrain behind them, and then a dark shape rushed overhead and crashed into the ground spikes a hundred meters to the north. Jack watched the door open like petals to reveal the shattered interior where so many of the passengers had been embedded on the hardened metal. The small number of survivors tried to jump down, but a group of three Jötnar covered the access points of the Bioray with such a devastating fire that nothing but bodies hit the ground.

Yes, you bastards!

He turned back around and took aim at the approaching horde. One squeeze sent a single shot out that hit a Thegn foot soldier directly in the face. As it crumpled to the ground, he held down the trigger and began to howl. Sergeant Stone watched him and then moved his attention to those defending the northern and southern approaches.

"Keep up your fire, marines. We have plenty of ammunition. Use it!"

CHAPTER EIGHT

As the Helios Nexus faced its greatest crisis since the Great Biomech War, one question continued to be asked. Where were the great races of the Orion Nebula? Of the two hundred and thirty-one ships preparing to defend Helios Prime, the majority were Alliance and Helion. Only a small number of Klithi, Byotai, and some Khreenk mercenary ships had managed to arrive. It was true that other ships were assembling over Micaya, but their reliability was questionable, as was their quality. There were some on Terra Nova that even suspected the alien ships arriving at Micaya were there for nothing more than show. Even fewer suspected they might be waiting to show their allegiance to the enemy.

The Path to the Apocalypse

The three squadrons of Alliance fighters moved at high altitude with their engines on full burn. Every fifteen seconds their flare launchers released special sequences of countermeasures to protect them from the missile fire still coming from the Bioray landers. Captain Jim 'The Hammer' Evans checked the computer one last time and then found what he was looking for. He selected the shapes with his eyes and designated them as their next target.

"Target spotted, two Biorays heading for the mountain. Bring them down."

He'd been given specific orders since launching over the city. The enemy had already landed a good portion of their ground forces, and the Alliance fighters were tasked with thinning out the rest coming down from space.

"Captain! Fighters, four o'clock!" yelled his wingman.

Captain Evans knew the position of the fighters from memory, and without thinking flipped the fighter about. The rear-facing cameras already showed him the pair of enemy fighters, and as he moved, a dozen projectiles ran directly beneath his craft.

That was close.

The fighters further back tore the Biomechs apart with short bursts of gunfire, dispatching them as quickly as they had arrived. He moved back into his lead position and hit the boost button. The Lightning fighters were much more sluggish in atmospheric flight, but even here their engines could accelerate them to greater speeds. The dark shapes of more Biomech ships were visible like black moons in the sky, as the enemy continued to send all that they had down to the surface. Streaks from their lower gun positions marked where their weapons were firing, and he could see the explosions as far as the eye could see.

This is like something from hell.

There were columns of smoke rising up to the sky in every direction, and at least a dozen Biorays had crashed around the city, most being damaged or broken up on the hastily prepared defensive towers and spikes built by the defenders. The mountain was something else again though. Its defensive guns fired without pause against anything moving within five kilometers. Missiles and tracer fire surrounded it, while a small group of destroyers circled in low orbit just under two hundred kilometers from the surface. At this distance their guns were ineffective against aircraft, but they were still able to lay down devastating wide area bombardment of the Biomech landing sites. Captain Evans checked the status of his missile bays and set them for long-range fire. The other fighters followed his lead.

"Target their engine systems and put them on the ground."

He checked the area one last time and then gave the order.

"Fire!"

Each of the Lightning fighters launched a brace of Sea Skua anti-ship missiles. The weapons rushed away, leaving a gentle trail of gray behind as they moved through the sky.

"Attack pattern Charlie for target two...now."

The fighters broke apart to change their attack approach on the second of the Biorays. By the time the missiles reached the first, they were ready to initiate an attack from three directions. Captain Evans found the super-heated exterior of the Biomech vessels almost mesmerizing. The extreme heat from their descent was something his pilots had been spared. These Lightning fighters were capable of atmospheric flight, but the perils of reentry were much too risky to undertake without significant preparation. Instead, they had mitigated the problem by landing on board the descending destroyers just minutes before entering the upper levels of the atmosphere. Although not designed as carriers, each was capable of carrying a small number of fighters or shuttles in a transport capacity. It had given his pilots time to fix minor problems and rearm on those ships that carried suitable ammunition.

"Ten seconds and counting, hold your fire."

The fifteen fighters moved in like a pack of wolves closing in on a wounded bison. Closer they came, each jinking just a fraction around the withering defensive fire. Two were hit, but both shrugged off the damage and powered on even though they now trailed smoke. The two Biorays used all their remaining power to head toward the center of Spascia City when the missiles hit the lower of the two. Half of the missiles were shot down, but at least thirteen of them struck the rear and exploded with such force the Bioray tipped over on its side in a death roll, yet continued forward.

"Get ready," said Captain Evans while watching the range indicator running down.

"Now!"

Each of the Lightning fighters unleashed a blistering bombardment from their cannons that hit the engines and support equipment on the Bioray's stern. That, coupled with the ground-based fire, sealed the fate of the vessel. Explosions raked along the ship, and two of the engines cut out, instantly depriving the ship of the forward momentum needed to keep it airborne. As it tipped forward, the first Bioray tried to tilt away, but it was too little and much too late.

"Get away, now!"

Captain Evans hit the boost button, and the others quickly did the same. There was no time to discuss plans or tactics, just the basic desire to get out of harm's way before their fighters could be damaged. As one, the fighters activated the emergency afterburners that were rarely used in combat. Almost all the combat the Lightning fighters had ever seen was in deep space, but occasionally they would be called upon to assist in planetary combat sorties. This is where the fuel ejectors fitted to the outlets of their engines proved useful. The pumps dumped a quantity of fuel directly into the stream to give an instant boost of power. The short-term blast of power pushed them out of danger just as the two Biorays collided. The impact occurred slowly, and there were no major explosions, just a long series of small flashes before both vessels broke in two and dropped out of the sky.

Great work!

Captain Evans looked to his left and then back to his right. Even though they'd just struck another blow against the invaders, he could still see the signs of their planetary assault. The IFF system tagged hundreds of landers and fighters, as well as a seemingly infinite number of warriors on the ground.

"There must be over a hundred thousand of them down there now."

He spoke quietly and found himself surprised to hear his own voice. New orders came in from the ground with requests for attacks against a myriad of targets. The fighters computer system crosschecked the targets, along with the positions of the other aircraft and allocated targets in seconds.

What do we have now?

* * *

A missile streaked overhead and narrowly missed Gun as he watched the battle going on all around him. He laughed as it crashed into the building to his left and exploded, sending chunks of masonry off in all directions. A smattering of NHA soldiers scattered as the material collapsed around them. Gun and his small entourage of Jötnar had taken over a long derelict factory building for a temporary headquarters. A flyover had collapsed alongside it, and that gave it a reinforced section to the rear, as well as partial protection from the air. Even better, the entire site was situated in a raised part of the city that gave him good views in all directions. Vehicles moved along the debris-strewn streets to drop off new soldiers or supplies, while others helped fill out the bunkers and breastworks all around the site. It was more a citadel now than a command post.

"Colonel, the mountain," said one of his Jötnar guards.

The Jötnar pointed through the gaps in the shattered walls toward the chasm just a few hundred meters away. To the right and at the end of the chasm was the lowest level of the mountain that shielded the weapon systems contained deep inside. A Bioray had moved directly over the site, but the gunfire from the Three Sisters tore it apart and sent the ruined vessel down into the chasm where it vanished in a bright flash. He looked back and pointed to the kilometers of devastated city.

"If they want this city, they will have to come up through the ruins. There's no way they can land anywhere near it. "

CES teams had erected air defenses and bunkers

to cover all approaches to the mountain, but the only routes leading actually inside its thick exterior were either through the underground shafts or via the gunports that were currently closed. Gun watched more landers moving in around the fringes of the city and smiled as the streaks of anti-aircraft gunnery tore at them.

Less than half must have made it to the ground. We'll get the rest.

He could see the odd body here and there where his defenders had beaten off a number of attacks. Very few of the enemy had made it this far into the city, but some still made it through. The Thegns, in particular, were masters at infiltration, and a ten-strong unit had actually made it to the chasm before being spotted and hunted down by the Khreenk. In the last hour, they had been hit by the remnants of multiple landers, but each time the pillboxes, machine gun nests, and hidden NHA soldiers had stopped them. Gun stepped back to the three Bulldogs that had been positioned together to form a small compound. Panels were pulled out with multiple displays, and a holographic model of the city projected between them.

"How are we doing then?" he asked, not expecting a reply.

He checked the positions of his company commanders, noting the bulk of the fighting was taking place out in the suburbs. Reports continued to stream in of wave attacks led by the Thegns and supported by the terrifying war machines. Biomech landing sites had been established in a number of the outlying urban areas, and reports were already arriving of them taking prisoners to use as human shields.

They have no honor.

Gun's bodyguard waited patiently, no one wanting to interrupt their commander's thinking. Mixed in with them was a handful of Vanguards, each of them a veteran of Eos, and almost the equal of the Jötnar themselves inside their powerful armored units. Gun ran his hand through the holographic model and stopped upon reaching the chasm. It was a wide and incredibly deep fissure that had been covered with a dozen sprawling bridges over the centuries. Now it marked the rear of his position and the area he could not let fall.

If they reach the chasm, they will have direct access to the mountain and the weapon.

The side of the city running next to the chasm was just behind where his command post was situated. Each of the tall buildings nearby was filled with Khreenk sharpshooters and Alliance marines, while the more open ground was defended by dug in NHA soldiers. He looked at a pair of soldiers dressed in the dull yellow uniforms of one of the many NHA units. The army itself was largely dependent on the leftover resources used for the Narau Army. Gun shook his head, as the two seemed more interested in the column of Bulldogs rolling past than watching their designated zones.

"Fools, if they want to die, they are going about this in the right way."

The crunch of metal on stone caught his attention. He tilted just a fraction to watch as an older looking Major from 22nd Marine Regiment approach, along with four of his officers.

"General," he started.

Gun looked down at the Major with wry amusement. He was the Colonel of his own battalion, but technically he was the general in charge of defending Spascia. He quite liked the name, even though it wasn't something he'd given much thought to.

"General Gun," he said and then laughed.

The Major looked to his officers and then back to Gun, offering an almost apologetic look.

"General Gun. My battalion has moved to cover the mountain approaches as ordered. One company is deployed here to cover the approach to the chasm, and we have machines from the Khreenk assisting there. I have also sent a platoon to the other side to assist with the guns on the blocked approach."

"Good...good," said Gun.

He looked back and beckoned for the man to stand alongside him to look at the display. He examined the plan and moved the map about to check every point where Biomechs had landed troops. The red markings now surrounded Spascia City on three sides, making the remaining territory look more like an island. He rotated the model until reaching the chasm.

"The approach from the other side of the chasm. My reports say it is all but impossible to land troops there. Do you agree?"

"That is true, General. We have scouting teams watching from the high ground. The weapons fitted to the mountain are impressive. It has enough firepower to hold back several warships on its own. If the Biomechs try to take it from the air, they will lose their entire army. The air defenses are...well...impregnable."

Gun didn't seem impressed.

"Yes, that is why they are landing out of range of its guns. Either they surround the city and then take it, the chasm, and then the mountain from this level or..."

A quick movement of the wrist changed to the rocky terrain on the approaches from the other side of the mountain.

"They will need to work through the mountains and take the chasm from the other side."

The Major shook his head firmly.

"I don't see how, Sir. The mountain guns cover the landing pads in that position. Any attempt to drop in ground troops would be fatal."

Gun looked at the mountain and then to the Major.

"You're forgetting one thing. What if they decide to

simply reduce the mountain to slag? A coordinated assault could break through eventually."

It was clear the idea was not one the Major had even contemplated. Gun watched as the blood seemed to drain from his face. Gun might have found it amusing if it hadn't been for the gravity of the situation.

"What is it, Major? You do understand they are not here to destroy the thing?"

The man still appeared confused, but Gun was more interested in the shape of a Biomech warship high in the sky. Its shape was hard to determine, but there were dozens of black shapes dropping from it.

Bombs?

They moved down fast, and the first crashed into the ground almost a kilometer to the south.

"What the hell are those things?"

"Colonel!" shouted one of his guards.

A pair of the shapes hurtled toward his command post, but both exploded from the streams of gunfire coming from the Three Sisters. The shattered wreckage crashed down with such an impact they almost hid the shape of a landing craft following them down. A Bulldog reversed and then vanished as a large object smashed into it and destroyed half the building. It was too small to be a Bioray but certainly large enough to be a landing craft or assault shuttle of some kind. The entire crash site quickly disappeared behind a thick cloud. The dust and debris obscured the remains of the buildings a hundred meters back into the city. Three NHA soldiers ran from the dust, only to be cut down by gunfire. There was more movement, and his suit quickly flagged it as a potential hostile. Three bullets glanced off his shoulder and he looked to his right.

"Thegns!"

A score of the humanoid soldiers rushed from the cover of their hidden lander and made directly for Gun. All of them were armed with firearms, and they blasted the Alliance warriors as they moved ever closer.

"You didn't tell me your name," said Gun accusingly.

He looked for the man but couldn't find him. Several more rounds struck about him, and as he tilted his head, he spotted the group of marines, each of them on the ground and riddled with bullet holes. A Captain lifted his hand. Gun grabbed it and yanked him from the ground. Another volley of shots struck Gun's leg, and he winced more in annoyance than pain.

"Ah, well, now I don't need to know."

He looked right at the Captain.

"Son, you're in charge of your battalion now. What's your name?"

"Captain Bale, Sir. My unit is..."

Gun grabbed him about the shoulder.

"No, your battalion is here. Get back to your officers and prepare for their attack."

The man looked stunned and Gun pointed to the sky.

"They're throwing assault units at us. Look!"

More of the shapes crashed down, and finally they were able to see one of the six-legged machines falling like a fireball to the ground. Yellow flames underneath marked the use of some form of retro-engine, but it still struck the ground with an almighty bang. More shapes followed its course, quickly confirming it must have been ejected from one of the ships in low orbit. Another one smashed into an Alliance Mauler on the other side of the chasm and vanished inside a crater. Gun pointed at it.

"Take command of your forces around the chasm. Don't let a single one get anywhere near the mountain."

He then grabbed the Captain by the collar.

"Understood?"

The man nodded and then stumbled back. He glanced down to the body of his commander, but the roaring coming from Gun took immediate precedence.

"He's dead. His fight is over. Get back there and help those still alive."

He looked in the direction of the crashed landing craft. The computer detected gunfire and triangulated the position instantly. Gun selected the targets with his retina and opened fire. The multi-barreled shoulder mounted L56 shredded the enemy as one popped up from cover.

"Defend the Commander!" called out his guards.

The heavily armored warriors ran into position like the

oathesworn warriors of ancient Earth. Bullets clattered about them while they returned gunfire in equal measure. One of the Jötnar took multiple rounds to the leg and dropped down. Another took his place and then they all returned fire. The heavy weapons fitted to the JAS armor proved devastating. So many were killed that it distracted them from the thirty more that had climbed over the wrecked walls on the other side.

"Commander!" shouted one of his guards.

Gun twisted about, surprised to hear one of them using his honorary title, as opposed to his official rank of Colonel. He started to berate the Jötnar to find his comrade being dragged to the ground by five Thegns. They stabbed at him with edged weapons and then blasted open his armor with their firearms.

"No!" roared Gun and then he was on them.

As Gun stabbed his right fist into a Thegn's body, he didn't even notice the massive shape of the Biomech Eques heavy walker. It scuttled over the rubble and headed right for him with a company of Thegns swarming around it like bugs.

* * *

Jack slammed in another clip and lifted himself back up to the firing line. Unlike the start of the battle, the enemy was now making effective use of the rubble, shattered buildings, and the bodies of both sides to shield themselves from view.

"Get on the northern wall, now!" Sergeant Stone ordered.

Two of the marines next to Jack lifted themselves up, and a third appeared from behind the next wall and moved to the left of their defensive position. Three yellow streaks ripped through the terrain, and one of the marines was struck in the back of the head. He slumped forward and landed face down in the dirt.

"Medic!" screamed the nearest marine.

Sergeant Stone stepped closer, shook his head, and pointed to the north wall.

"He's gone, now get on the damn line."

He then turned to Jack.

"Go with them. The enemy is up to something. I can tell."

Jack didn't bother thinking; his mind was too shattered from the last hour of combat. Instead, he moved as quickly as he could while keeping his head down. He moved past the fortified area they'd created for the Helion anti-air unit, and on to what remained of the broken building at the end of their city block. It was the most intact section of this area, and when he arrived, he found a dozen marines, three Khreenk warriors, and one of the SAAR robots all entrenched and watching the north.

"Private, over here!" said a Corporal.

Jack nodded, ran to the space, and slid down into cover. The wall provided decent cover. It had been covered with additional material, raising its height to nearly two meters. Behind it was more rubble, both to thicken the wall and also to give the marines something to stand on. Jack stepped up to take a look, but an armored hand grabbed him and pulled him back. Under the thin cloak was the dull gold of his breastplate. Jack noticed more of them huddled down along the wall.

"No, Jack, stay down."

He instantly recognized the sound of Jae Jaan. He hadn't seen the Khreenk warrior since the start of the fight, assuming he had joined the remainder of his forces that were operating as a mobile reserve.

"How is the west wall?"

Jack's mind flashed back to the bloody firing line he had been on for so long. The images stunned him for a moment.

"Not good." It was the best he could manage.

Warning indicators flagged his blood pressure. The suit automatically pumped in chemicals to try and calm his system, and it took the edge off. He could feel sweat running down his temple and shook his head angrily.

Get a grip, Jack. Get a grip!

"We held off the first attack, but since then they have been trying to infiltrate through the rubble. The last attack was made with just the Thegns on their own. Three got inside before the Helions turned the AA gun on them."

"Impressive."

Jack recalled the exploding Thegns in the middle of the defenses and found the imagery too much to bear. Their position was the most remote of the western defenses, and there was nothing further out from where they waited, other than the enemy. It was enough to send a man away screaming, yet every marine had stayed at their posts. Jack looked up to Jae Jaan.

"Why are you here? I thought you were our reserve?"

Jae Jaan laughed in reply.

"We are. Orders from your commanders, they want us to assist in a withdrawal of all but the key strongholds. The Biomechs are close."

He pointed to the east, a place where black smoke almost obscured the mountains far into the distance. Streaks from rockets and missiles moved continually up in the sky and dropped back down, as the forces on both sides fought over the small number of positions where the Biomech had made landfall.

"The enemy has tried a different tactic. Look."

He pointed at three dark objects that fell from the sky and toward the city. Two Alliance destroyers blasted them, but they were soon well out of range. The Biorays were heavily damaged, yet they came on. The ground shook as the Helion anti-aircraft gun unit opened fire and added its firepower to the remaining positions around the city.

"Ninety percent of their ground forces are blockading the city. The rest are launching suicidal attacks from orbit to try and break our chain of command. My people have seen this before. It is a terror campaign."

Jack watched as the wrecked Bioray tried to slow down but lost control and spiraled downwards. Once it was less than five thousand meters from the surface, a dozen shapes burst from its flanks and scattered outwards. They fell far more slowly while the Bioray ploughed nose first into a tower building. A massive explosion engulfed the entire city block.

"Those are Eques walkers. They are the only machines that can stand the fall. If they can secure a landing site in the city, they will be able to bring in their forces right in the middle of your defenses."

The ground began to shake, and the loose sections of the building shuddered and broke. One floor quickly collapsed, and two marines vanished in the rubble. A CES unit moved in and began clearing the rubble to find them.

"What the hell is going on?" asked the Marine Corporal.

Jae Jaan moved to the wall and looked out before looking back to his people. He spoke quickly, and they moved back from the wall and prepared their weapons. Each carried a different gun, but all of them looked deadly. Jack was particularly interested in the double-barreled carbine carried by the shortest of the group. The barrels were punctured with holes along their sides, and an ammunition hopper on his flank connected via two tubes to the base of the gun. The Khreenk warrior noticed him looking and laughed.

"You like?"

The accent was thick, yet the Khreenk warrior was able to speak those few words with little trouble. Jack looked to his own carbine, but compared to the bulk of dull metal and tubing it looked puny. He began to speak just as the inner wall collapsed.

"Quake!" shouted somebody that vanished in the cloud of dust.

The ground shook and rumbled, and that was when Jack spotted the crumbling ground. He stood up and jumped away just as a large chunk of stonework vanished behind him. Jae Jaan stumbled and tipped backwards, but Jack leaned back and reached out. Jae Jaan spotted his hand and grabbed on. Two of his comrades dropped into the hole as they staggered into the shattered stonework. Dust scattered all around them, followed immediately by a massive blast that threw them to the ground. Small fires burned throughout the improvised citadel, and medics ran about helping the wounded. Jack could follow them via the IFF scanner built into his armor, but he could see little other than thermal signatures.

What's going on?

Jack lifted himself back to his feet and wiped his visor. It took three attempts to clear enough to let him see, but there was still nothing but dust. A marine barged into him, almost knocking him down.

"Private?" asked a familiar voice.

Jack twisted his head about, but he knew the sound of Sergeant Stone without needing to see his face. More of the unit arrived and grabbed at him as they passed. A Vanguard marine ripped open a chunk of wall to let in light. Another pair of hands turned him about; this time is was Private Jenkell.

"Jack, are you hurt?"

He shook his head without even thinking to check his status indicators. Adrenaline was an excellent way of hiding injury, if it was never its intention.

"No, no, I'm fine."

Shapes moved up from the massive hole in the ground. Jack bent down to help them, assuming it must be fallen marines. Instead, the form of a Thegn warrior pushed a gun out through the dust and opened fire. Jack stumbled back and managed to avoid all but a glancing hit as he tripped over a Khreenk warrior. Luckily, more marines were running past, and two held him up and stopped him falling on his face.

"Stop them!" shouted somebody.

Every one of them trained their firearms onto the Thegns trying to climb up out of the shattered floor. Jack was sure he could see at least thirteen of them, perhaps many more. Gunfire flashed back and forth, and at least three marines were hit and one killed. For every Thegn killed, another appeared to take its place.

Grenades!

Jack grabbed at his thigh and pulled out a proximity grenade. The small cylindrical device simply required a quick twist, and he dropped it inside the pit and stepped back. Two others spotted him and did the same. The blast occurred deep within the crater, but the updraft of debris struck Jack and would have hurt him if he hadn't been wearing the reinforced PDS Alpha armor.

"Fall back!" another marine shouted.

As one unit they slowly gave ground while continually checking for the enemy. A few tried to attack from the outside, but the marines and Khreenk were ready. A dozen Thegns were gunned down by the time they reached the broken outer walls. Light finally burned through the dust and was replaced by three Bulldogs skidding to a halt. Their powerful lamps cut through the dust and created a dull yellow hue. Lieutenant Elvidge appeared next to Private Jenkell. The Khreenk and marines looked to him for advice. Unlike the first time Jack had seen him, the Lieutenant seemed calm and collected, even in the middle of something as violent and traumatic as this.

"The machines are making use of the sewer system. We're sending teams down there to slow them down."

He then pointed to the breached wall.

"We have orders to fall back to the General's compound.

Grab what you can, and get out of here, fast!"

He moved out through the gap and headed directly for the first Bulldog. The ground continued to shake, and Jack increased his speed to reach the doorway. Hands reached out for him and dragged him inside while the vehicle's top mounted gun turret swiveled about. Even as Jack found himself being manhandled inside, the gun opened fire. As he struggled to maintain his balance, Jack looked back and the door slid shut. The last image he had of the battle was a line of Thegns blasting away with rifles.

"Get us out of here, now!" Sergeant Stone hollered.

Jack looked about inside the darkened interior at the faces of Jenkell, Sergeant Stone, and others he knew. All of them were filthy from the mixture of dust, smoke, and blood. Worse though, Jack could see the look of resignation on them.

That wasn't a win. We only held for hours, not days.

He pulled down one of the ceiling mounted displays that showed the exterior of the Bulldog. Street after street flashed past, but that wasn't what really got his attention. It was the long columns of black smoke filling the city, and the never-ending streaks of flame and smoke marking the arrival of yet more machines.

"Sergeant. What happened up there?"

He pointed up in the air.

Sergeant Stone looked as impassive as ever.

"The fleet, Son. It's lost space superiority. They're

preserving the fleet for hit and run attacks. The fight's gonna be decided down here now…not up there."

Jack looked up as though he could see through the armor of the Bulldog. He'd seen the reports coming in, of the fighting in space and more recently, the struggle for dominance of the sky between fighters and light warships capable of atmospheric flight.

"We've not got long. When we reach the compound, we need to get ready for the next one."

Private Jenkell looked surprised.

"For what, Sergeant?"

The seasoned warrior deactivated his visor, and it slid up into the armor. His sweaty, slightly pale face peered out at her. Before he answered, he looked about at the motley collection that had escaped.

"We took fifteen percent casualties on the line, mainly injuries, but some deaths too. The AA gun is down, and the NHA is regrouping with those at the next compound back."

He lifted his hand to wipe his face and then thought better of it. For some bizarre reason, Jack recalled trying to do the same. A scarred and rough armored fist was the last thing you wanted touching your face. He started to speak, but the sound of Lieutenant Elvidge's voice entered the helmets of all those inside. He shrugged and said no more.

"The initial attack has been halted, but Biomech forces

have infiltrated multiple points and established heavily defended landing zones on the western approach to the city."

A simple two-dimensional image of the city appeared above his right eye. It showed the defenders' positions in green and the enemy in red. Just as had been explained, the city was now engulfed in red, and a chunk of territory on the perimeter had already been lost.

"Our forces are withdrawing to our secondary lines of defense. We have nine hours before the Ark will be in a position to launch the next ground assault. The fleet will do what it can, and so must we. Our platoon is being moved to plug a gap at this point."

The map spun about and moved further into the city before stopping between the ruins of two tower structures.

"CES teams have erected a breastwork at this point to guard the approach to the center of the city. The Khreenk have sent a ten-man unit to assist plus our SAAR robots. We have to slow them down. Time is on our side, not theirs. Their forces dwindle in size every hour; ours will increase when our reinforcements arrive."

He continued speaking, but Jack's mind was already wandering. Unlike most of the marines, he'd been following the campaign and force dispositions prior to Spascia. He knew where the ships were waiting, and he also knew that every one that could be used was already on the line. The bulk of the Allied fleet waited around Helios Prime, and a myriad of forces were positioned on the ground, ready for the inevitable carnage.

Reinforcement? What reinforcements?

CHAPTER NINE

The Echidna Union was the tortured child of that shadowy organization known as the Sons of the League. Following the armistice in the last days of the Great War, a number of high-level assassinations and suicide bombings destroyed the archives of the League. Many Generals, officers, and politicians vanished along with these records, only for them to reappear in the service of the Biomechs half a century later. This led many to speculate that these humans were the emissaries of the machines, perhaps even clones of long dead statesmen, and a way of preparing humanity for the rise of the machines. One group of scientists even proposed that they might actually have volunteered to join a Biomech program, as a way to seek revenge in return for their indentured servitude.

A Brief History of the Zealots

A Biomech fighter flew past with a single Hammerhead in close pursuit. The rumble of its guns was barely audible over the sounds of heavy weapons throughout the city. They vanished as quickly as they'd arrived, merging into one of the hundred columns of black smoke rising into the sky. Behind it came a battle damaged Bioray that crashed into the city block and slid over two hundred meters before hitting an NHA barricade. Some of the soldiers broke cover and ran, but the majority stood their ground and opened fire with everything they had left. The hatches hissed open, but less than a dozen Thegns clambered out, only to be shot down by thermal rifle fire.

"Order your soldiers to surrender!" said a mechanical voice that dripped with anger.

Gun tried to move, but after the third attempt, he gave up and grunted. All he could see was the smoke filled sky, and his limbs felt as though they had been pinned down under the weight of a Bulldog vehicle. He forced himself to twist to the right and managed a brief look at the heap of bodies all around him. The majority were the mangled remains of the Biomech foot soldiers, but there was also a smattering of Jötnar.

Wait, who's talking to me?

It hadn't even occurred to him that it must have been the enemy. He shook his head and coughed.

"Help me up. Then we can talk."

His view changed almost immediately, and he found himself facing a machine twice his size and heavily armored. It was bipedal yet carried no obvious weapons.

Its torso was shaped like a plated egg, but there were no eyes or head to speak of. Gun raised his eyebrows and laughed.

"What the hell are you?"

Just ten meters behind it, a Jötnar and a Vanguard were engaged in a brutal melee with an Eques walker. Though outmatched, the two dodged its attacks and continued to fight, even as the thing tore at their armor, leaving holes and gashes.

That's my boys!

The machine lowered itself on its legs, bringing it to only slightly above the height of Gun. As it did so, Gun moved his eyes slowly and scanned the area around the battleground. There were still NHA soldiers fighting with Thegns in something more akin to a medieval battlefield. He watched as a trio of Thegns with the sickening blades butchered one alive. His blood pumped faster, and he could feel adrenaline screaming through his body. Further back, the shapes of several of the massive Eques walkers marched about and hacked at or blasted any of his warriors still left. Then he spotted them, a small line of black Jötnar. They were at the bottom of the mountain and in a small circle, each back to back with his comrades. There were just six of them, and Thegns surrounded them.

"Order your humans to surrender," it hissed.

Gun turned his attention back to the machine in front of him. The Thegns holding his arms relaxed, and he dropped to his knees in front of it. Gun tensed his muscles, preparing for what was to come, but instead another group of Thegns approached with two prisoners. One was a female Helion soldier, the other an Alliance gunner from one of the artillery units. Gun looked at them and back at the Biomech.

"Obey us, or they...die!"

Gun didn't hesitate. He lurched ahead even as he spotted the Thegns thrust their blades into the hostages' chests. He ignored them, sacrificing them for the kill and leapt directly at the Biomech. It lurched back, but it was too little, too late. Gun was on its torso and forcing the machine backwards even as the hostages fell to the ground, spurting their last few breaths. The Helion said something in her alien tongue, but as Gun smashed at the machine with his fists, he heard the dying gunner shout out just one thing.

"Kill the bastard!"

Gun tore open the metal housing on the Biomech, and it emitted a piercing shriek from some hidden speakers. Anybody else might have stepped back, stunned from the sound, but not him. The two fell to the ground, and Gun ripped it away to reveal the protective sphere inside that was surrounded by pipes, cabling, and wires. Its robotic arms flailed at him, but a Vanguard staggered alongside him and fell onto the machine. The marine's armor was covered in marks, and at least a dozen holes indicated where the armor had already been penetrated.

"Do it," said a female voice from inside the suit.

Gun punched at the machine three more times to clear his way past the protective plating inside its body.

"I am not..."

He grabbed the pipes feeding some kind of nutrients into the body and ripped it out. A foul collection of fluids rushed out like the blood of a ruined beast. Most of it ran down the Biomech's body, but a large part spurted over Gun's shoulder and down his flanks.

"Human!" he finished with a scream.

He reached inside and ripped out the Biomech's core, raising it over his head like some hunting trophy. The Eques walkers and Thegns fighting in the streets turned back like a switch had just been flicked inside them. Every single one in sight moved directly toward him, each ignoring their foes and intent on protecting their master. He was alone, with a non-functioning firearm, and a small army heading toward him. Gun lifted the object in front of him and staggered over the bodies toward them.

"Brothers, to me," he said quietly over his intercom.

The survivors of Gun's elite bodyguard needed no further encouragement though, and even the NHA soldiers emerged from cover and ran out to charge down the Biomech soldiers. A Bulldog, partially ablaze, rushed out from the right and crashed into the leg of the first Eques. It staggered and collapsed before trying to right itself; too late though, and the NHA soldiers swarmed over it like ants. The Thegns reached Gun first, and although some managed to wound him with gunfire, it was the melee that decided the fight. First came three, and then Gun was buried under the weight of all the remaining Thegns in that city block. He vanished for a moment until his six comrades arrived. They stopped and took aim at the mass of bodies.

There was no hesitation, just the need for the kill. One by one, they blasted the Thegns apart, and then ran into the bloody mess to hack and stab like demented demons. In seconds, the Thegns were dead, each one shot or butchered like cattle. Underneath the bodies was the still shape of Gun, his armor bent and crushed. Yet as one leaned down to check him, he pushed onto one knee and lifted himself upright.

"Colonel, are you hurt?" asked the first of the Jötnar.

Gun activated his visor, and it lifted halfway up before jamming. He breathed in the warm air and then began to laugh. Only a handful of Thegn foot soldiers remained, and the NHA contained them while the small group of Jötnar laughed and howled in amusement.

* * *

The five Red Watch Jötnar marines led the way, using their bulk and armor to shield those following from the odd stray round that hit near them. Spartan and Teresa inched along the upper-level, ten meters behind the small group of Jötnar. They kept as low as they could, though the Jötnar didn't bother. Their size and bulk made it almost impossible to hide. Broken glass and metal lay scattered across the floor from both the previous fighting and from when the Thegns had overrun the place. An entire platoon of marines followed right behind them, all with their carbines out and ready, each waiting for a sign of the dreaded enemy.

"How much further?" Teresa asked.

Captain Cobb and Captain Rivers were now alongside her. It was the Earthsec officer than answered first though.

"Another fifty meters and then into the apartment complex. Are you sure about this?"

They moved several more meters before Captain Rivers spoke.

"This is where the enemy is showing as the strongest."

A shape moved just a fraction ahead, and Spartan immediately dropped to his knee. A shot rang out and struck the wall near him. His response was fast and deadly. The L52 was a remarkable piece of equipment, and he found it hard not to smile as he struck the Thegn soldier in the forehead with a single burst. A dozen lights flickered across the windows of two shops, and two of the marines dropped to the ground.

"Now!" Spartan shouted.

The group of Jötnar exchanged gunfire with the Thegns. Two were killed instantly, but the others melted into the shadows. In their place appeared the horrific arachnid walkers, the machines that had proven so deadly in the past. Several bullets hit them before they too hid in the shadows. The Jötnar fanned out to present a firing line to the wide front of the apartment section. The marines spread out along the raised walkway to ensure all lines of attack were covered. Their return fire was impressive, but the enemy had now gone to ground. None of the Jötnar moved closer and instead held their position, each one waiting for the order to move in.

"How much longer?"

Spartan could sense her nerves, but it was barely discernible.

She's calmer than I am.

"Z'Kanthu should be making his way through the transit area now," replied Captain Rivers.

He then placed a hand on Spartan's shoulder. He knew the old marine by reputation, but until today he'd never actually met the man. Even so, he and the others had quickly deferred to him when it came to fighting the Biomechs, and with good reason. Few in the Alliance knew as much about the enemy, or how to fight them.

"Are you sure this is going to work?"

Spartan shrugged.

"Probably. Just remember, they are not stupid. We

might just be demonstrating on this front, but they have to believe it is the focus of our attack."

He pulled himself closer to the Captain.

"If they believe for even a second that this isn't the real deal, they'll fall back and Z'Kanthu will be trapped. Understood?"

Captain Rivers nodded.

"Now all we need is the word from Khan and we go on."

Now Captain Rivers looked very concerned. He reached out to Spartan.

"Wait, I thought we were the diversion?"

Spartan chuckled.

"Yes, we are."

"So why are we waiting?"

Spartan shook his head ever so slowly.

"If I know Khan, he'll be itching to do some killing."

The Captain still didn't understand. He looked back at the waiting marines and began to wonder if his trust in this almost mythical man had been wise. Teresa was something else. Her reputation was more than just old stories. It was based upon recent events, ones that he had even witnessed with his own eyes. The more he thought about it the more he began to doubt the plan. Finally, he tapped Spartan's shoulder.

"It's bait, a diversion, nothing more. One Biomech and four Jötnar will not be able to reach the Core on their own. He does know that, right? We have to give them the diversion they need."

Spartan began to laugh, and it took Teresa to answer the man.

"Khan is a firm believer in Spartan's approach to a feint."

She moved up toward where Spartan and the others had taken position. Her movement was fast and stealthy, almost too quiet as she slid over the rubble to join the others. The other marines did the same, and in seconds they were in position, waiting for the order. She glanced back at the confused look on the Captain's face.

"Uh, what exactly is Spartan's approach?"

Teresa smiled, and even Captain Rivers could make out her expression through the smoked glass of her visor.

"Just wait."

* * *

Khan and Olik moved first, with the next two Jötnar following behind. They moved at a fast walk, checking for signs of the enemy, especially for traps or sabotage of some kind. The journey through the underground tunnel had taken them several minutes longer than expected, and it was making Khan uncomfortable.

"Spartan, are you in position?"

The imagery of Spartan's face appeared inside the visor.

"Khan, get off your ass and get moving. We've been here for thirty seconds."

Khan grumbled and then stopped as they reached a dead end. He looked around him, striking the wall on his right in frustration. The panel fell down and revealed a loading entrance heading directly into a derelict and partially fired damaged department store.

"Stupid place to put it."

The entrance was wide enough for two of them side by side, but that was still something of a squeeze for Z'Kanthu. They moved into the darkness, emerging into the rear of the department store. The suits' sensors picked up more than a dozen body signatures as well as movement further inside.

"Looks like we have friends in here," said Khan.

Z'Kanthu stopped, moving back a little into the shadows.

"I am detecting the Core; it is within two hundred meters. I can go no further until we have a safe route through," said Z'Kanthu.

Khan nodded happily.

"Good. Now it's time for the diversionary diversion."

Z'Kanthu said nothing, and Khan almost looked disappointed that nobody had found his play on words amusing.

"A diversionary…ah, forget it."

He looked to Olik and the other two Jötnar.

"We need this to look like a diversion. We keep them busy, but nothing too excessive."

He then concentrated his attention on Olik.

"That goes especially for you. Understood? When Spartan attacks, they will think his attack is the main event."

"And then we move in and secure the Core," added Olik.

Khan looked back to Z'Kanthu.

"Stay back. If they find you, we'll be in trouble…fast!"

"I understand. I will wait until you return."

Khan activated his weapon and checked the ammunition feed. Satisfied he was ready for action, he threw a quick glance to his comrades.

"Now, let's show these machines what an attack looks like."

The four lurched ahead, giving little consideration to noise as they moved. It took less than thirty seconds to reach the center of this part of the structure, and they were nearing the central shaft that was surrounded by a pair of winding escalators. From here, they could look up and down the different levels of the store. That was when the gunfire started. Small lights flicked about, and Khan tagged them via the overlay in his helmet.

"Bring them down!"

The four Jötnar moved into a line with three meters between each of them. Khan fired first, and then all of them were shooting. Using the networked targeting platform, they were able to share tagged targets and quickly moved between them, spreading their fire effectively at scores of potential targets. Three Thegns dropped from a higher level and vanished beneath them. The more Khan fired, the more his shouting increased.

"Watch out!" Olik yelled.

Two Thegns appeared from the floor below them and clambered over the ledge, hurling themselves at Khan. The third Jötnar, a young warrior called Knaprig pushed out to take the impact. The two fell to the ground in a heap of metal and flesh. Another Thegn joined him to attack with what looked like two-handed hammers. Though primitive looking, they were fast and ripped chunks of metal from Knaprig. Olik moved to help him, but Khan waved him off. Another Thegn landed on the back of Tajt, but he twisted about and slammed his fist into its face.

"Stay back!" Khan snapped.

Tajt leaned to one side while Khan took aim and removed the head of the first Thegn with a short burst. A pair of Thegns moved from cover at just the same time and was cut apart by stray rounds from the burst. The second Thegn with the hammers rolled to the right and dodged his fire, and then struck Knaprig so hard he removed the Jötnar's right arm from the shoulder. Tajt charged it down and smashed his fist so powerfully through the Thegn's head that he crunched its skull against the armored hide of Knaprig. The wounded Jötnar grabbed the dying Thegn and tore its head from its shoulders, casting it aside like a ball in some violent sport.

"Bastard!" he howled.

Olik tried to step closer, but three more Thegns appeared from under the ledge and jumped at him. Two were armed like the earlier attacker while a third carried a weapon more akin to a thermal shotgun. Its wide muzzle glowed white, and then Olik found himself staggering back. He looked down and found a hole the size of a man's head through his armor and pushing into his chest. He felt a weakness in his body and dropped to a knee. Just as the metal of his armor touched the ground, Khan grabbed him and pulled him to his side.

"Put them down, all of them!"

Knaprig climbed to his feet, blood still dripping from his shoulder and continued shooting with his L56 Mark III. He was forced to rest his weapon on a nearby cabinet, but more attackers forced him back. He refused to relinquish his weapon and spun it about, using it as a club with his left hand.

"Give ground…slowly."

Khan helped Olik as they attempted to move back a few meters. More Thegns appeared, but they kept themselves well hidden and relied upon their ranged weapons. The Jötnar kept their cool and demonstrated superlative discipline as they went back one step at a time. The exchange of gunfire was devastating, and after a few more seconds, Khan had lost his weapon and sustained damage to his legs and chest armor. A normal human would have been unconscious about now, but not Khan; he seemed to be enjoying it.

"Spartan," he said calmly, "They've taken the bait. It's your turn."

* * *

The entrance itself was wide and marked out by a dozen double doors, half of which were shattered. Spartan lifted his boot, kicked one open, and stepped inside. The marines moved in around him and then the gunfire started. The first two rounds struck Spartan in the flank, but he kept moving forward and screamed at the Thegns as he fired. A platoon of Alliance marines was a force to be reckoned with, and in less than a minute, the entire front of the apartment block was secure. Half of the marines dug in behind cover while the others inched forward under their watchful eye. Teresa and the rest followed them in and moved close behind the ground Spartan had taken. A number of corridors ran off into the distance. At the fair end were scores of lights from the defenders.

"Marines, push on!" Spartan ordered.

The veteran warrior moved into the open, and a number of the enemy soldiers took the chance. As soon as they tried to shoot, they were cut down by precision fire from the small number of marine sharpshooters equipped with the classic L48 rifle. Spartan was right at the front and directing fire into the Biomech position. Even though they seemed to be keeping them busy, there was little ground being covered. Improvised barricades made from furniture, debris, and even bodies now blocked the access points to the rest of the complex at a dozen points. The Thegns kept down low in the cover, exposing themselves only long enough to shoot back. Spartan seemed almost impressed.

Interesting, the Biomechs are learning how to protect territory. Very interesting.

He looked back and signaled to Captain Rivers.

"Send them in."

The Captain looked to Teresa. She did nothing more than offer a quick nod. He sent the signal and was immediately answered by the crashing of glass. A tracked robotic vehicle not much bigger than a Ram moved in. It easily pushed over the broken glass and surged ahead toward the enemy. The motorized turret fixed into its chassis gave the mounted weapons plenty of movement. It made it to within ten meters of the Thegns before taking fire.

"Now!" Spartan said.

The machine was mainly designed to be operated remotely and still required a manual override to activate its guns. The vehicle slid to a stop, and the turret swiveled about to track a single Thegn that had moved slightly out of cover to watch. Three rounds struck its hull, and one managed to block off a section of one of its tracks. Then the guns opened fire. The first was the 40mm grenade launcher. It released a pulse grenade into the blackness and tore the Thegn apart with a burst from its L56 Mark III gun system. As the body slumped to the ground, the pulse grenade flashed and sent white and blue sparks in all directions. It was a non-lethal weapon and used for distraction and effect only.

"Forward!"

Spartan pushed on even further and now reached the last useful cover before the open ground. The Thegns put down considerable gunfire to keep the marines back. The SAAR robot limped forward, moved past him, and then accelerated toward the barricades. A fusillade of gunfire tore it apart just a meter from its objective, and it crashed into the defensive position with a crunch. Even with its tracks shredded and its body shattered, the gun mount continued to function on a single axis. It moved from left to right, sending bullets past the barricade until a metal machine reached out and ripped off the turret.

"Walkers!" Spartan called out.

"Yeah, we know," replied Teresa from further back.

The machine lashed out from its hiding place and dragged the wrecked SAAR robot into the blackness.

More Thegns popped up and returned fire on Spartan and his forward team. Two more squads fanned out to put pressure on the entry points to the apartment block. Like the one near Spartan, they were all very well protected. That was when Spartan spotted the first hostage. He lifted his hand and the gunfire slowed.

"Look," he said, extending a hand toward the barricades.

"I see them."

The glittering of razor-sharp blades marked the arms of at least one of the eight-legged machines. Between its powerful limbs lay a bloodied but still living woman.

"She must be one of the workers," said Captain Rivers.

Even though he and Teresa were further back, it wasn't hard to make out the shapes at the Biomech defenses.

"What now? It's pretty clear what happens next."

Spartan closed his eyes and sent the signal. Then he opened them and looked at Teresa.

"It's Z'Kanthu's turn."

* * *

Khan watched patiently from his hiding place. The four Jötnar should have been dead, especially after the pounding they had taken during the withdrawal. Khan had expected they would run into gunfire, but nothing quite like what they experienced. The fire assaulted them twice during their withdrawal, and he could count over twenty dead or dying Thegns, but against the costs or wounds to him and all his comrades. The attacks had abated in the last few minutes, and they'd given up enough ground before breaking ranks and retreating out of sensor range. Now they waited, trying their best to ignore the pain.

"Come on, Spartan, give us the word."

"I haven't seen one of their soldiers for nearly ten minutes now," said Olik.

"We cannot take chances," said Z'Kanthu, "If they suspect I am nearby, they will redirect all their efforts against me. This must happen at the right time. We can do this only once."

Khan nodded and glanced back to the position they'd abandoned. It looked like a killing ground from back here, and he knew if they still had numbers, then they would be badly punished for trying again.

"What about the reserve?"

Olik looked back and shook his head.

"Still not here. According to the scanner, they are less than a minute away."

Khan didn't like that part.

"Khan, can you hear me?" Spartan asked.

Khan felt a great weight suddenly lifting from his body. His pulse began to slow until he heard the pained breathing of his friend.

"We've got them pinned here. Send in Z'Kanthu. We can't hold them indefinitely."

"Understood, Spartan, enjoy the show."

He looked to Z'Kanthu who took one step away from his position.

"So, it is time."

Khan took one of the guns from his wounded comrades and tapped Olik on the shoulder.

"Are you ready, Brother?"

Olik laughed, though not as loudly as he might have earlier. The damage to his chest armor was substantial. Luckily for him, the damage to his body was minimal, but it had reduced his ability to sustain gunfire in a major fight.

"Then we shall go. Z'Kanthu, lead the way."

The massive metal machine lifted himself up to his normal height so that his head almost scraped the raised ceiling of the large department store. He moved with a grace that was disproportionate to his size. Khan and Olik followed a short distance behind, but they were forced to speed up to a jog to match his movement. They passed the area of the previous battle and turned sharply to take a connecting tunnel that would move them right behind the Biomech forces at the apartment complex. Khan spotted the icons popping up as his suit picked out heat signatures ahead. A handful of shots came down but easily missed them.

"Spartan, we're halfway there. Targets detected. We're engaging them."

A gantry five meters up filled with Thegns, and then

promptly vanished as Z'Kanthu vaporized them with his main weapon. He didn't even stop and crashed through one of the walls.

"Khan, can you hear that?" Olik asked.

Khan was almost running as they appeared inside a much wider and taller open space. Inside it was clearly some sort of foyer area, yet it was too heavily damaged to easily identify much of the material.

"There!" Khan said.

At the far end were dozens of shapes, as machines and warriors surged out to create a wall to protect whatever was behind them. Z'Kanthu took aim and fired. Four Thegns vanished in a blue fireball but more took their place. The skittering shapes of the arachnid warriors broke out from the line and climbed the walls and floor to cover the distance. Worse though was the screaming sound coming from further behind them. Z'Kanthu altered his stance to prepare for the onslaught and shouted to Khan.

"They are calling for help. This is what Spartan needs."

Khan took aim with his weapon and began to wonder if it was the best plan they could have come up with. He could see hundreds of enemy troops, and right now they were all heading toward them.

"Spartan, do it!"

There was no more time, and all three of them opened fire with everything they had. The massive multi-barreled cannons of the Jötnar did their work, but it was the guns of Z'Kanthu that killed the enemy in great numbers. Khan glanced back in the direction they'd arrived from and could only think of his two wounded comrades and the marines that still hadn't arrived.

They'd better be ready, or this is going to be one hell of a bloodbath!

Z'Kanthu continued firing, but the Thegn and arachnid warriors were now halfway across the floor and ceiling and heading right for them. Khan could see they were already taking a big risk. Anymore and they would never get back in time.

"Olik, we have..."

Two metal blades punched through the chest of the Jötnar from behind and then wrenched apart, attempting to tear Olik in half. He spotted the blades extended out from his body and grabbed the tip in his armored hands and threw himself to the ground, forcing the blades from his body. He groaned in pain but continued to punch and kick at the Thegns and machines moving around him.

"Olik!" Khan howled.

He spun about and threw himself at the shape of a Biomech that had been lurking inside the shattered foyer. The machine smashed him aside like a toy and moved in on Z'Kanthu, who was now at risk of being completely encircled by the approaching Biomech warriors.

"Khan, I believe my plan has suffered a setback."

They were the last words he said as scores of Thegns ran at him with all manner of edged weapons. Z'Kanthu had no intention of surrendering and cut a swathe through them until the other Biomech reached him and hissed something in their native tongue. The warriors continued to surround them, but the attack stopped as quickly as it had began, with just the two mighty machines facing off against each other. Khan groaned and rolled over from where he'd crashed into the wall.

"Spartan, we've got a problem here. A big problem!"

CHAPTER TEN

The Jötnar of Prometheus and Hyperion performed the role of heavy infantry in the Biomech War. They had operated in groups before, but their deployment to Spascia, Helios Prime, Prometheus, and Mars proved once and for all that it was they, more than any other, that could provide the perfect warriors for the Alliance. Unlike the heavily trained and conditioned marines of the Alliance Marine Corps, the Jötnar were born warriors, with a toughness, speed, and strength matched only by the Vanguard Marines. Some speculated that this trend might see a new class emerge, one of a warrior elite that could provide an entire stock of warriors for the future. Some saw this as the ideal, but most dreaded the day that might come, one where only the strong would be given a voice in the Alliance.

The 1st Jötnar Battalion

A group of four Helion soldiers inched their way past the hundreds of dead Thegns and shattered machines. One of then stopped and vomited before being helped by the other three toward the Jötnar. Behind them moved a pair of Animosh warriors, but both groups kept a wary eye on each other as they moved toward Gun. It was the Animosh leader that spoke first. Like the overwhelming majority of Helions, he had to speak via a translator.

"Colonel, our forces are taking heavy casualties. We cannot..."

Gun placed his armor-plated foot on the head of a fallen Thegn foot soldier. He was balanced precariously atop the shattered remains of a ruined Bioray lander. Dozens of dead Thegns lay around the exit points, the few still alive hastily finished off by his bodyguard. He looked at his prey and pushed down hard with his foot. There was a sickening crunch, and the head tore off and rolled to the ground. He bent down, picked up the head, and raised it to the sky. Explosions off in the distance lit the face of the thing with frequent flashes, and he roared. It was a bloodcurdling howl filled with excitement and bloodlust. The Jötnar around him lifted their arms and weapons and joined in, much to the confusion of the NHA soldiers moving to new positions. As they filed past, they watched the monstrous warriors waving their weapons and then kept on moving, each trying to avoid catching the gaze of the super-human fighters.

"Don't tell me you cannot. If you can breathe, well, then you can."

He pointed to the barricades being hastily improved.

"Get the Khreenk back here to assist. I understand they have equipment we can use. This world must stay under our control. Do you understand?"

The Helion looked to the others around him and then back to Gun.

"The Khreenk, they are…"

Gun reached out and grabbed the Animosh leader by the arm.

"They are helping us. Now, are you in charge of this district or not?"

The Animosh struggled, but there was little chance of escaping the grasp of somebody like Gun. Finally, he relented, physically exhausted from his short ordeal.

"Yes, Colonel. I am in charge of all NHA forces in this sector."

"Good. I am sending you Khreenk forces. Establish a defensive line one kilometer from the chasm in a semi-circle. I want everything our side reinforced and dug in."

"What about the other side of the line? There is much cover for the enemy to use, and they are sending in troops through the tunnel system."

Gun sighed.

"Everything that side is to be flattened. Use thermite charges and breacher units to collapse every tunnel. I want a wall of steel and stone."

The group of Helions looked horrified at this

suggestion.

"Destroyed, Colonel? That is most of the city."

Gun pointed out to the north, then the west, and finally to the south. There was smoke in every direction, and the sound of battle could be heard everywhere.

"This city is already destroyed. This battle will finish what you never did in the last war."

"Colonel!" called out one of his bodyguards.

Gun looked back to the raised visor of his comrade. Like the rest of his Jötnar bodyguard, he wore a matt black variant of the standard JAS armor. This more primitive armor was still Gun's favorite and offered very heavy protection, as well as plenty of points for ammunition and weapons. Even as this battle continued, he felt strong and secure in this equipment. Even better, he knew it had been fabricated on Prometheus by the Alliance under the watchful eye of his own kin. All his guards wore this, and even the Vanguards had styled their equipment on this unit.

"What is it?"

"Have you seen the reports from Helios Prime?"

Gun had been so busy with his own battle that he'd forgotten to check the general reports on the war effort.

"No, why?"

"The enemy is due to arrive any moment."

"I know that."

The Jötnar shook his head furiously.

"No, Sir, it is much worse than that."

Gun looked at the reports on his visor and spotted the last general broadcast from Commodore Hampel, the acting Admiral for the Spascia Fleet. It was short and confirmed he was conserving his forces to assist when and where he could. It was the last part of the message that worried him the most, though.

They are sending some of their warships to the Helios Rift. Why?

* * *

ANS Conqueror positioned herself at the head of the inter-species fleet of now more than two hundred ships. It was a polyglot collection of vessels, with the majority being of cruiser size. Admiral Lewis surveyed his forces from the tactical display in the CIC. Some might have thought they were impressive, perhaps the largest a human had ever commanded in battle, but not him.

"What about the reinforcements? The Helions do understand the gravity of this situation?"

Captain Marcus, his XO nodded in agreement.

"They do, Sir. At least that is what they are telling us."

He then pointed to a number of blue icons in a lower orbit around the planet.

"There are eleven Byotai merchant ships moving in around the defense stations. It would appear the Khreenk have done the same and are sending armed civilian ships to protect them."

Admiral Lewis raised his eyebrows, more in irritation than surprise.

"So, they send ships to say they are doing their part, but don't send me enough to fight this battle. You've seen the reports coming in from Spascia, and we are facing the full weight of this comet. Who knows what they have buried inside? I think we all know though, don't we?"

He placed his hands on the tactical display and then rubbed his tired eyes. The unit showed the disposition of his forces. The bulk of the fleet was based around the remnants of the Narau contingent, with the largest number coming from the Helions. Their advanced cruisers provided the first layer of defense for their world. Behind them were the squadrons of Byotai warships. These large, black vessels were as different to each other as they were to the ships of the other races. Designed to match the shapes of creatures from their world, they looked much like the ancient sea monsters of old Earth. The XO walked around the board and then stopped.

"Sir, the message from Commodore Hampel said that the enemy was sending at least nine Biomanta ships through to the Rift. Are you sure you do not..."

He shook his head.

"No, that is a distraction, nothing more. The Helions have an entire station positioned right alongside the Rift. If any make it past them, well, we have more than enough ships to deal with them."

The XO had moved away and was now looking at the imagery of their primary target.

"Uh, Sir. Have you seen this?"

Admiral Lewis looked at the imagery intently. It showed the comet, the one that had arrived in the system to cause much calamity. The object was the focus of all their attention. The fleet had been positioned so that they would move in alongside the object as it entered a high orbit around Helios Prime. From there, he expected the battle to be fought, in and round the dense debris field that would make the battle more akin to combat in an asteroid field.

"Are you sure about this?"

Captain Marcus nodded.

"Completely, Sir. The comet has made a final course alteration. I don't know how they were able to gather so much thrust. We could never have managed to do that, not even with half the fleet providing the energy. All of our calculations for the last three months have shown it heading for a high orbital path around Helios Prime."

"Yes, I know. The comet would move into a high orbit just like the Ark over Spascia. What are you telling me? Is it moving away?"

"Sir, a section approximately one quarter the size of the comet has detached and has shifted its course by more than ten degrees. We are detecting massive gas emissions between the two parts. The rest of the comet is continuing on our previously calculated route. It appears to match the course pattern used by the Ark around Spascia, though much, much larger."

He then pointed at the larger object on the screen.

"The smaller fragment, along with a substantial debris field has been ejected away from the primary mass and is no longer moving into the same path. There are also spurious indications that there might be ships within the field itself. According to my calculations, it will head right here."

A red line running through the comet shifted slowly until it was positioned directly into the path of the planet itself. Admiral Lewis almost choked at the imagery he was looking at.

"How much remains of the comet?"

"The original core was over eleven kilometers in diameter, but the outer sections expanded well beyond this. But after the sections broke away, we've found our projections were way off. The core estimate was correct, but the debris field surrounding it hid smaller sections, as well as some of these Arks and ships. There is just as much flotsam around the core as there is to the comet itself. This new target, designated C34-1 is being aimed as a weapon, right at Helios Prime.

"The object, Captain, just give me the numbers. Also, Object C34-1? Are you serious?"

"I think we need to speak with the science team on this one."

The Admiral placed his face in his hands and sighed.

"This cannot be true. It just can't. We've had months to get the fleet into position to intercept this comet and now, at the last hour, this happens?"

Captain Marcus didn't know how to be more reassuring, so he fell back on what he knew. Sticking to the facts.

"Admiral, Captain Perry has also confirmed the trajectory changes and is the same as ours, to within three meters. Comet C34 has changed, Sir. We now have two targets, Comet C34 and the new secondary object on a collision course with Helios Prime. I've designated it Object C34-1 'Thunar' in our database."

Thunar? Well, it's good to know the computer has a sense of sobriety.

Most probably wouldn't understand, but he knew full well it was a regional variation of the old god Thor, the hammer wielding warrior famed for lightning, earthquakes, and other destruction. The ship's science officer began to panic and moved his chair along a line of panels as he checked the information from their sensors. Eventually, he turned around to face his senior officer.

"Admiral, the computers are working hard, but the variables…well, they are much larger than expected. I think…"

Admiral Lewis raised his hand.

"I don't have time for this; just give me the short version."

The science officer wiped at his brow and then moved back to the screen showing the comet imagery. Even after looking at it so many times, he still found it as fascinating and terrifying the hundredth time. Admiral Lewis took in a long, slow breath.

"Well, Sir, Object Thunar contains a core of approximately three to four kilometers in diameter. If it strikes at its present course, it will cause massive casualties on the ground."

Admiral Lewis didn't seem impressed.

"I need numbers, how much power are we talking about?"

"Power, Sir? Well…"

The man scratched his head and tapped at the screen before bringing up a model of the planet.

"Helios Prime is heavily urbanized, and the approximate impact center is within this area of the capital. The conservative estimate is approximately a forty terratonnes of TNT. It is the next thing down from what used to be known back on Earth as a Planet Killer. Depending on the angle, we might just be talking about massed devastation, rather than the destruction of all life on Helios Prime."

He'd heard the term before, and it conjured up horrific images of death and planet-wide destruction.

"What can we do?"

The science officer gulped a little at this question. He opened his mouth three times, but nothing came out other that something closer to a mutter.

"Well?"

"Uh, that's not really the issue, Sir. At this distance, there is nothing we can do other than break it up into smaller objects. The trouble is, even if we can shatter the core, the total energy will not change by much. The damage caused to the atmosphere and ecology will be devastating either way. By braking up the core, we simply create smaller targets. Only by reducing them to much smaller chunks would we be able to rely on the atmosphere itself to destroy them."

The emergency alert sounded, and the lights instantly dimmed to red.

"Admiral, new contacts coming through the Spascia Rift."

He looked up to the mainscreen.

"What, is it Commodore Hampel?"

A black shape shimmered and then lurched out from the gaping tear in space. It was shaped almost like a large bat and was quickly followed by many more.

"Biomech warships, Sir. They are preparing their weapons."

"Battlestations!" called the XO.

The Admiral looked back at the tactical screen, and the shape of the comet moving ever closer to Helios Prime.

You cunning bastards! You present me with an impossible problem, and then hit me with a distraction.

"ANS Kopis can send in a squadron of fighters to assist. Do not alter the disposition of the fleet. We have to maintain our position to intercept this…thing. Leave the warships to the Helions for now."

He moved his attention back to the screen and noticed something odd. The computer system had also picked it up and was tagging shapes and patterns around the core itself.

We need a way to deflect or break this thing up.

"How small do we need to make this thing to protect Helios Prime?"

The science officer heard him talking and lifted his hand as though in a classroom.

"Sir, if anything approaching the size of the comet hits Helios Prime, then the casualties will be catastrophic. The comet is moving at a little over fifty kilometers a second. A direct impact will create something like…well, a sixty to seventy kilometer diameter impact crater, followed by earthquakes, shockwaves, and fires for thousands of kilometers."

Admiral Lewis opened his mouth, but the science officer was too caught up in the explanation.

"It isn't the impact that will cause the real damage though, it's the debris thrown into the atmosphere that will darken the skies. These are known in history as extinction events, and for good reason. Our science teams disagree on the long term complications of this impact."

"Okay, so we make it smaller. What damage are we talking about?"

The officer looked confused and looked up as he made a number of quick calculations in his head. The XO spotted him and stepped closer.

"Use the computers. That's what they are…"

The man shook his head and stepped away from the XO.

"No, this is quicker…just wait…"

Captain Marcus would have pushed him again, but the Admiral signaled for him to back off. After a few more seconds, the man lowered his chin and looked back at him.

"Sections of comet under a kilometer will cause substantial damage to urban areas. The impact craters would be enough to wipe out a city the size of New Carlos, or even the Helion city of Spascia. The subsequent fires and damage would be substantial, but survivable. Smaller sections would destroy city districts, no more, assuming they made it through the atmosphere. Most would explode earlier, sending shockwaves to the ground. Some of our scientists disagree on the multiple target solution though. They say it would be better to let the planet take the impact rather than the worldwide bombardment that could potentially kick up even more debris to the atmosphere and block out sunlight."

The images in his head were of burning cities, destroyed buildings, and millions of casualties. All of this now rested on his shoulders, and it almost made him feel weak at the knees. The lives of the crews aboard two hundred ships paled to insignificance, next to the near loss of the entire population of Helios Prime. He approached one of the panels and brought up the list of personnel on the ground. Most were military, but there were also a significant number of politicians and scientists down there. He spotted a name almost immediately.

Sanlav Erdeniz, he's the man that developed the short-range railgun ammunition back in the war, wasn't he? What's he doing on Helios Prime?

He brought up the name, but for some reason the system was unable to connect directly. He had no time to waste and so called out to his communications officer.

"Get me General Daniels, immediately!"

The officer was fast, and in less than fifteen seconds a video stream was live between the two men. Colonel Horst Brünner had taken the 4th Heavy Battalion with him to Libuscha, but it was General Daniels who commanded the ground forces on Helios Prime, and he was the man that would definitely be able to make things happen down there.

"Admiral, I've been receiving regular updates. What is the problem?"

"The comet, a section of it has split away and changed

its course. It's on a course putting it directly toward Helios Prime. Our numbers have been way off. It will make contact in less than fifteen hours."

There was something strange about the General, and it took him a moment to realize the man was wearing full tactical armor. He wore his standard Alpha armor rather than his dress uniform, a measure of the gravity of the situation on the planet. Around him were the vast government buildings, all multiple levels that reached up to the sky with their massive spires and platforms. Groups of NHA soldiers marched about in the background, and the odd vapor trail marked the passage of various ships and aircraft.

"What can you do?"

Admiral Lewis swallowed and then spoke as calmly as he could manage.

"Right now, not a lot. The change of heading and velocity has completely thrown off our planning. My forces have been positioned to match their orbit upon arrival. Staying closer to the planet will allow the orbital station to provide additional firepower and air cover."

Come on, you fool. You have just hours, there has to be a military or scientific option available to us.

"I see. So, we have fifteen hours, and then what?"

"Then anybody within the impact site or on the surface will die. The fireball will be substantial, but the follow-up shockwaves, fires, and earthquakes will be even worse."

He looked to the initial damage assessments being made by the ship's computers. The information was fragmentary so far, but what was especially clear was that the casualties would be horrific.

"General, we must start an urgent evacuation of the surface. The initial impact will be devastating. Worse than you can possibly imagine. There will be much worse to follow, but avoiding the impact, shockwave, and fires will be the first issue."

He looked down as though not sure whether to add something else.

"This isn't the news I was expecting, Admiral. Let me know if I can do anything to help."

He wiped his lip.

"We can't afford to lose Helios Prime, not to lumps of rock and ice. Find a way to stop it. If you can't, then at least reduce the threat. You must be able to do something."

General Daniels thanked him and left, keen to get to work doing whatever he could to save as many of his people as he could in the very small amount of time he'd just been allotted. Admiral Lewis moved his attention to his personal screen and accessed his log of messages. There were the usual reports from Naval officers plus a small number of more personal items. It was the one forwarded from Admiral Anderson that he was looking for. The material seemed far from being practical, but it could be just what he needed. It took almost a minute to find the correct file from the Naval Research facility. With a quick tap, the image of Lieutenant Commander Sanlav Erdeniz appeared. He was one of the senior officers in Naval Research, part of the Alliance Navy.

That's him. What was it he said he was working on?

The dossier for the man was one of the most varied he'd seen. It wasn't just naval experience. The man was a certified expert in siege weaponry, defensive technologies, and had even participated in the early experiments with T'Kari technology to produce the artificial gravity units now used on the largest warships. He was so wrapped up in his read; he barely noticed the voice of the communications officer.

"Admiral, I have Lieutenant Commander Sanlav Erdeniz, from the Naval Research facility on Terra Nova. His ship is on course to enter the T'Karan Rift."

"What ship?"

"He's aboard ANS Endurance, I think. Yes, the Endeavour class engineering vessel. They are there to work on a classified project."

"Good work, put him on my screen."

The image of the Lieutenant Commander Erdeniz appeared in front of him. The man didn't look particularly familiar, but there was keenness, almost something frantic about his eyes.

"Admiral Lewis. We're about to leave the system, along with all other non-combat ships. Is there something I can help you with?"

Admiral Lewis almost choked as he tried to answer.

"That remains to be seen. You are part of the alternative project team, seconded to Endurance, are you not?"

"Yes, Sir."

"I take it you've seen the reports on C34?"

"No, Sir. We're running a closed loop here, no contact in or out unless authorized by High Command. We've been pretty busy for the last few weeks preparing for these tests."

Admiral Lewis checked a page of data relating to the project. Only parts of it were accessible to those outside of direct involvement. What he could see was that the ship had initially been stationed in T'Karan, where it had been siphoning energy from ANS Beagle for its projects. There was nothing about why it had been stationed inside Helion space, and he wondered if the subtle messages from Anderson had been intended to draw his attention to the mysterious ship.

"I see. Well, a section from C34 has broken away onto a modified course, and it will impact Helios Prime in less than fifteen hours. We have already checked its angle of attack, which is almost exactly at what would appear to be a ninety degree angle."

Commander Erdeniz shook his head in disagreement.

"That can't be right, Admiral. The energy required to change the course of a sizeable chunk of comet is, well, at that range it would be incredible. With what we know, it just isn't possible."

He lifted his hands and sighed.

"Son, I'm not interested in the science, right now. That thing has already ejected a number of Arks that are moving into position around four planets in this system. The first is responsible for a full-scale invasion of Spascia, and more will follow shortly. This enemy has a technological capacity far in excess of our own."

Erdeniz didn't seem particularly surprised.

"I understand, Admiral. My work here has been to assess the potential work of this project to be used in alternative ways. The information obtained from Hyperion confirms the enemy is vastly more advanced than we are. Their understanding of fusion technology and direct energy weapons and applications is incredible. This is why I was brought here on the orders of General Rivers himself, after the first trials of this system were reported."

That confirmed just one thing to Admiral Lewis, that this man and the ship might officially have been designated a science research vessel, but it had also been positioned there for something else, something that only an open-minded weapon designer might come up with.

"Commander, I'm more concerned with the remains of this comet. In fifteen hours it will hit, and based on its size, it will almost certainly be a…"

"Planet Killer, Sir."

"Not quite, but close enough. It will certainly cripple our ability to conduct an aggressive campaign against the Biomechs, let alone cause terrible casualties on Helios Prime. What I need to know is about this research of yours. How far along is it, and can you put it into the field?"

There was a moment's pause while Commander Erdeniz checked the Admiral's clearance for the project. It seemed excessive, but it only took a few seconds to confirm he was on the list.

"Well, Admiral, my research aboard ANS Endurance has just been a side project from the main research here. The team has been working on a miniaturized Rift generator system that incorporates elements of the technology taken from Hyperion."

"And?" Admiral Lewis asked.

"So far the system isn't working quite as predicted. We can produce Rifts that last a fraction of a second, but they are unstable and will not focus correctly at anything but short range. Worse though, the energy requirements are substantial. After three or four attempts, we have to reset the entire generator assembly. The cooling is an even bigger issue. If we don't…"

"Commander, what exactly are you trying to say?"

Lieutenant Commander Erdeniz looked intently at the camera.

"ANS Endurance has the ability to produce a tear in space, but only for a brief moment of time. So far, we've managed to send two drones through. All other tests have left them disintegrated when the Rift collapses. Every time the system is used there is a chance of major damage to the ship."

"That's it?"

"Yes, Admiral. Quite what were you hoping for?"

"Something I could use to deflect this comet with before it kills everything on Helios Prime."

"No, Sir, the system wasn't design to do that. Right now, we can only produce an entry and exit point up to a kilometer apart, and in a direct line from the emitters. Against the comet, we would have little effect in the time we can keep it open. We thought of using it in that way months ago, perhaps as a way of changing the course of the comet. The comet is more than just ice and rock though, isn't it? We know they have a means to control it, rendering our project useless."

Admiral Lewis looked almost crestfallen at this news.

"This is potentially the most powerful weapon in our arsenal, and your ship is near the T'Karan Rift entrance. There has to be a way."

"Uh, there is one other possibility, Sir. It is dangerous, but my research suggests it is certainly possible."

"Go on."

"If we create a Rift entry point inside the comet, and an exit point nearby, we can effectively move a section of the comet."

"And?"

"When the Spacebridge collapses, it will tear the section inside apart. My data suggests we would create a bubble of a size proportional to the energy expanded prior to the collapse."

Captain Marcus heard the last part and watched as the Commander showed them a short video demonstration. It was relatively simple, but showed an entry and exit point within two hundred meters of each other. A small ship moved halfway through and then the Rift collapsed. The middle section of the ship ripped apart as though a blade had cut right through it. Explosions struck both sides as the derelict vessel tore apart.

"You seriously think your research could be used like that from your science vessel?" Captain Marcus asked.

Commander Erdeniz inhaled slowly.

"If my research is correct, then there is an eighty-two percent chance it would work on the first cycle. Each additional use would suffer diminishing returns, and also increase the chance of major failure."

Admiral Lewis looked to his XO.

"Well, what do you think?"

Captain Marcus wasn't convinced, but that didn't give him even a moment's doubt as to what they needed to do.

"We need everything we have for this one. I say get them in position and fast, before it's too late. We can work out the details later on."

Admiral Lewis considered it, but not for long.

"Commander, get your research ready. I need to speak with your project leader and your Captain. I need you and your ship to join our fleet as far away from Helios Prime as we can manage. Every hour is critical, Gentlemen. This fragment is less than three million kilometers away from Helios Prime. Get to work!"

Commander Erdeniz vanished, and Admiral Lewis turned back to Captain Marcus.

"I want the fleet away from the planet and as close to Object Thunar as we can in the time we have."

The XO nodded and moved away. Admiral Lewis then turned his attention to his communications and science officers who waited patiently for their own orders.

"In the meantime, get me in touch with every science team we have within thirty minutes. I want you to coordinate everything coming in. We don't have time for passing information up for debate. Get me options and numbers, fast!"

Finally, he looked to the communications officer.

"I need to speak with Admiral Anderson in T'Karan and High Command on Terra Nova. This needs to be an urgent flash message through the Rift network. If we can't think of something, they'd better had."

"Yes, Sir."

The CIC had already been busy, but now they moved with a purpose unlike any so far. They were not getting ready for a space battle or a planetary assault. They were gearing up for a showdown with a massive comet and no workable strategy. The comet was a threat like no other, but that did little to interfere with their routine. He looked at them as they moved to their computer systems. They were fast and efficient, but he knew that didn't guarantee a workable solution.

We need a detailed plan, and within the hour.

He then moved his attention back to the image of Object Thunar and shook his head. He imagined the carnage caused by the massive object, and for a brief moment managed to forget about the fleets of ships and legions of enemy warriors that would also be arriving not long afterwards.

One way or another, we're bringing that thing down, even if I have to lose the entire fleet to do it!

* * *

Wictred and Vadi moved along the rubble that provided the last barrier to the open ground around the town. He'd patrolled this stretch four times now and was beginning to find the entire process a little boring.

"When will they come?" Vadi asked.

Wictred paused for a moment and looked out to the horizon.

"The Biomechs? Who knows? They will keep fighting

until more help arrives."

His intercom crackled. It was Captain Carter.

"Corporal, we've just heard from Helion Command. They are sending armored units to all outlaying regions. We've been designated two NHA units, and they'll be arriving by surface transport within the hour."

Wictred pointed off into the distance. Vadi watched and then nodded when he spotted the shape. It was the vessel from before, yet as it came down, it landed harder than expected, as though it was in some kind of distress.

"Biomechs?" he asked.

Wictred nodded and then activated his throat mic inside his helmet.

"Captain Carter, the Hunter-Killer is back. It looks likes it's landing two kilometers to the east, behind the dunes. They must be preparing for an attack on this location.

"Good work, get back here. We'll be ready for them."

Wictred considered his response, but something grated, something he couldn't quite put his finger on. The Bioray was a big craft, yet it hadn't been trailing smoke, and there were no fighters near it. There was no reason for it to have come down so fast and so heavily.

Fuel, they must have run out and landed outside of this area. That, or their crew is weaker than expected.

"Captain, what do you think about attacking the thing before they can organize themselves?"

There was a moment's pause as the Captain considered

his words.

"You want to move in on a grounded Biomanta?"

"Well, Sir, it's intact, and I suspect it's weakened since it first arrived."

"Good point, Corporal. The NHA are en route, so we could of course just sit it out until they arrive?"

"What if they were forced to land? They might simply go to ground and blow the ship. If we're fast, we could be there in thirty minutes. How useful would an intact Bioray be to Military Intelligence?"

"Son, you had me with your idea at the start. Meet me at the gatehouse. We move out in three minutes."

CHAPTER ELEVEN

The events of the Eos withdrawal had a profound effect upon the citizens of the growing Centauri Alliance. The casualties brought home the price of the battle but also reminded so many of the deprivations suffered in the Great Uprising. Support for anti-Alliance movements dropped substantially, and for the first time the Alliance was effectively united in its aim of unification and peace. All it would take would be final victory around Helios Prime and the total defeat of the Biomechs. For the first time in humanity's history, the only way forward would be in uniting with alien races, all for the greater good of mankind.

Rise and Fall of Interstellar Empires

Captain Perry had never expected the defense of Helios Prime would fall to him. With the disintegration of Object Thunar, only a quarter of the fleet had been left behind with him to defend the world. Any ships lacking the speed or endurance for the high-speed dash to Object Thunar had stayed back. Half of the ships were Alliance, and the rest were mainly the advanced Helion missile cruisers. His own ship, ANS Royal Oak, was now the flagship of the last line of defense for the planet. As well as the ships, he had the Helion orbital defense stations, a ring of heavily armed platforms positioned around the entire perimeter of the world.

"I'm waiting," he said impatiently.

Captain Harper moved as quickly as he could, stopped and saluted.

"The fighter wings have been briefed, Sir. They are ready to go."

"Finally."

He pointed to the mainscreen that showed the remainder of the comet. Unlike Object Thunar, this was the original comet and it was truly gigantic. He'd already sent a dozen probes as close as possible, but every single one had been destroyed.

"As expected, the course is going to place it in high orbit, perfect to manage a full-scale invasion."

He then altered the angle to show the Rift to Spascia.

"So far eleven ships have come through, and they are pinning down a disproportionate number of vessels. Three are fighting at our entry point as we speak."

He felt tense, and the complexity of the battle for

Helios Prime wasn't lost on him. There was the comet and its cargo of Biomechs just hours away, as well as a massive cloud of debris from the smashed Object Thunar fragment. On top of this, there were also the secondary attacks from Spascia.

"All of this is a distraction. They want us weak for the main event."

He was saying it aloud more for his benefit than for the CAG.

"That's why we're going to attack C34 right now. I want every single gun that we have firing. You've given the squadrons their orders. This is a full-scale preemptive assault. Fifty ships plus every fighter and station we can muster."

"But, Sir, the Rift to Spascia?"

"Oh, yes."

He moved the display to show the short battle that was taking place at the Rift. An equal number of ships from both sides fought a small skirmish. The control base to the one side added its own modest arsenal to the fight.

"I suggest that..."

The control station flashed blue as one of the Biomantas rammed the station at full speed. The Rift flickered, pulsed, and then collapsed even as another Biomanta moved through it. As the collapse completed, the remaining half of the ship spun out from the tear in space and collided with a Helion cruiser.

"Animals. Well, it looks like we're on our own now, doesn't it?"

"So is Spascia, Sir."

"Indeed. Check the squadrons one last time, Captain. In twelve minutes we will start the attack."

* * *

It had taken almost a full hour for the Helion Fleet to change course to a direct interception and meet with additional ships from the Rift. For the last four hours, they had been accelerating on emergency power, a level that pushed the ships and the crews to the limit. This powerful force included just under a hundred and fifty of the primary warships. Finally, they were closer to Object Thunar than they were to Helios Prime. They were in position though, and ready to begin what had been named Operation Lightning. It was more a joking name by one of the escort captains, but it was apt due to the time it had taken to put it into action. The original plan to intercept in orbit had been scuppered, and the initial strike by the Alliance drone force had failed completely in its attempt to destroy the target. Now they were escorting an unfamiliar ship into battle, with little idea as to what it would do.

As before, the Alliance warships took the lead, with the brand new Liberty Destroyers taking up the vanguard. Out on the right of the formation, and inside a cordon of Crusader class warships, moved the newly arrived Endeavour class science ship, ANS Endurance. The vessel was easily twice the size of the largest ship in the fleet, yet apart from her experimental Rift generators, she was completely unarmed. The small number of surviving drones from the failed Operation Needle circled the ship as a final buffer against a potential attack.

"It's true, then? We've lost contact with Spascia?" Admiral Lewis said.

His bitterness was easy to ascertain, as was his anger.

"Those Helions are a bunch of amateurs. They let the Biomechs get close enough to hit the station. That was their most vulnerable point."

He was angry, but more at himself for stationing Captain Perry and the others too far from the Rift to adequately protect it. He'd been thinking only of what was coming through, that small trickle of enemy ships. Instead, he should have considered what he would lose if it were to be lost.

No point wasting time on a lost cause. Perry will have to deal with C34 for now. Right now, I have this bastard to finish off, or all of this will be irrelevant.

He looked back at the information on the screen and tried to shake the images of the shattered Rift station from his mind.

"These numbers are not what I was expecting," he said.

The secondary display showed the projected damage

to the comet, based upon the information provided by Commander Erdeniz. According to the simulation, the Rift bubble would be open a short distance from the ship. He'd been hoping the entry would be wider than the projected five hundred meter diameter, though.

"I know, Sir," replied Captain Marcus, "Even if that ship can continue using its primary emitters, it will take many more of these Rift openings to cause enough damage. Erdeniz's calculations were much too optimistic."

"True. But you saw the damage assessments. A comet of that size will cripple much of Helios Prime. At least this will remove a large part of the threat for us. In lieu of a plan that will destroy it, this is the next best thing."

Captain Marcus rubbed his forehead, but he could think of nothing that would be better, not in the timeframe remaining to them."

Idiot! Admiral Lewis thought.

He looked back at Captain Marcus and nodded with a look of self-satisfaction on his face. It was a simple idea, but the more he considered it, the better it appeared.

"Why didn't I think of this earlier?"

He pointed at the display, specifically at the comet. He then rotated the three-dimensional model and stopped to point at its center.

"The report from Terra Nova said the comet's core could be split apart, didn't they?"

Captain Marcus nodded slowly.

"Yes, but this would only be possible by inserting enough atomic weapons inside the core itself. There is no way to get them inside, not to get close enough to burn, blast, and mine the thing. We don't have time for that. Don't forget the thing is heavily guarded as well."

Admiral Lewis grinned.

"We use the ship to create a temporary Rift inside the comet. It will need to be done twice. The first will create a hole, the second we'll use to send over every nuke we can spare."

The ship's science officer had been quiet for now. Instead of speaking, he'd been pacing, scratching his head, and doing a million other things as he calculated the data in his head. He stopped and noticed the two officers watching him.

"We don't have long to do this. If it's done right, it has a chance. The core is the real problem. If we can split it apart correctly, we can force the major elements apart. You do understand that at this distance there is no way to stop them hitting Helios Prime, though? Even if we break this comet into a hundred chunks, it will still devastate the planet."

Admiral Lewis shook his head bitterly. He'd forgotten the umpteen reports he'd already worked through extolling the virtues of deflection over destruction. He considered it more a short while, and then brought up several files to show the comet and its surrounding chunks of debris.

"In that case, we will fall back on the solution suggested by Anderson's team on the Admiral Jarvis Naval Station. We have neither the time nor the ability to do anything else."

The model enlarged to show just the comet. Even though it was substantially smaller than the original comet, it was still massive. Several chunks broke off, and were then shattered into fragments no larger than a human. It was an idealized model, and even Admiral Lewis found it hard to believe it would work quite as described.

"We will use all of the assets at our disposal. ANS Endurance will cut chunks of the comet way, much like a scalpel. These sections will still be large, but small enough so that the fleet can deal with them. Using a mixture of particle beams and atomics, we should be able to reduce the mass heading for Helios Prime by..."

He looked about for the figure.

"Forty-two percent, Admiral," said the soft voice of Commander Erdeniz.

He walked out of the shadows of the doorway and closer to Admiral Lewis. He stopped and saluted.

"Sir, it is good to meet you at last."

They shook hands, and the Commander moved to his flank to point at the model.

"My team is assisting the science crew on ANS Endurance for this operation. With a few tweaks, I can guarantee you at least four discharges before the coolant becomes an issue. That is more than enough to reduce the mass of this object. I've also managed to modify the expansion algorithm to increase the total surface area for the Rift. It reduces the time window, but it will allow us to eliminate up to thirty percent more per use."

He looked at the model and moved a number of sliders. The remaining comet reduced in size by a small amount. It wasn't much, but Admiral Lewis knew only too well how much even a few percent would make to those on the ground.

"With this revised data, the comet should break down to approximately forty-two percent of its original size. That is assuming we can focus the fleet on the target for long enough."

"Forty-two percent, are you sure?"

Commander Erdeniz almost looked offended at the question.

"Sir. The only unknown to me right now is how much firepower you will be able to maintain. Once they launch warships, you will have to make a choice. Will you continue breaking down the comet, or will you be forced to shoot the ships? Thereby reducing the available committed energy to its destruction."

Admiral Lewis was well aware of this. Even as he'd been looking at the numbers, it had been quite clear to him the scientists had made one mistake, a mistake that reminded him of the age old joke he'd heard back in the academy about spherical chickens. He almost laughed, but the gravity of the situation negated any possibility of that happening.

"Admiral, if we start the attack in the next fifteen minutes, then yes, we can do this. Any longer though and..."

"Uh...what's that?" said one of the officers toward the rear of the CIC.

Admiral Lewis looked back and watched the outer shape of the comet appearing to be vibrating in the middle of the tactical display, or at the very least emitting something. The shape vanished from the display and was replaced by nothing but noise.

"What the hell is going on?"

Admiral Lewis stepped back and turned his attention to the mainscreen. For some reason, the primary cameras were all pointing to the Spascia Rift. The heavily armed station was blasting away as the squadron of Biomech cruisers tried to force their way through. It was important, but nothing compared to the threat of the comet.

"Show me Object Thunar, right now!"

Lieutenant Vitelli, the tactical officer made two motions with his hands and turned the focus of the primary screen to that of the comet. The sensors were having trouble isolating the changes, but it was clear something was happening. Commander Erdeniz watched closely, his eyes widening with fascination.

"This is...incredible."

Admiral Lewis looked at him, having no idea as to what he was talking about.

"Uh, Admiral. Warn the fleet something is about to happen. Something very bad."

Captain Marcus looked at the two, nodded, and then proceeded to issue orders throughout the ship. Admiral Lewis pointed to his tactical display and connected to all the squadron commanders.

"This is the Admiral. Something is happening inside the comet. Prepare your weapons and launch fighters. I repeat, launch all fighters."

"Admiral, an urgent alert from Captain Perry at Helios Prime. He says the remaining Biomechs have been destroyed. His scouts have checked the area, and there is no chance of reactivating the Rift anytime soon. The station is completely destroyed. Spascia is alone. We can no longer reach them, Sir."

That was the news he'd been dreading. With the Rift out of action, it would be impossible to move ships between worlds, but even worse, it would take hours to contact Commodore Hampel.

"Understood. As you were."

He then looked to Commander Erdeniz.

"What's happening then? What is this thing up to?"

The man tilted his head a little as he considered his words.

"Those readings are colossal. I'd suggest either it is..."

The screen showing the view of the comet flash white and they stuck on the single color. All eyes shifted to the schematic produced by the ship's computer that showed the comet. Instead of the orb and its long tail, they now faced a massive cloud of rock, metal, and ice blasting toward them at an even greater velocity than before. Even Captain Marcus appeared stunned at the sight. Lieutenant Vitelli, however, remained completely calm and ran a quick assessment of the situation.

"Admiral, the Object Thunar has simply disintegrated. Something powerful built up in the rear of its structure and it shattered. The bulk of the energy has split the object into multiple targets, as well as massive levels of debris. All of this is traveling on the same course, but it is now moving slightly faster. The computer is counting over five thousand fragments plus six, no seven sections over a kilometer in diameter."

He looked back at the Admiral and shook his head.

"There's nothing we can do against that. Not in the time we have."

All of them watched the vast target as it moved at speed toward its meeting with Helios Prime.

"How long do we have?"

Lieutenant Vitelli was already busy checking the paths and velocity of the key fragments. The computer system concentrated on the largest parts and then expanded out, but the entire process took time.

"Three hours until they hit. Then it's all over. The smaller sections will be bad enough, but the larger ones will devastate massive areas of the surface."

Admiral Lewis ran his hand over his chin and then looked back to the small image of Commander Erdeniz.

"I think it might be an idea to find a way of bringing a few of those down to size, don't you think?"

"It won't stop the coming bombardment, Sir, but you're correct. It could mean the survival of the planet. I suggest you follow the backup strategy and work on the smaller sections. I will arrange to bring the Rift generators online shortly and see what we can do to the larger sections."

More alarms called out their song, but at this stage they were barely noticeable.

"Contact, multiple targets. The rear of the object has been protecting a large number of ships. They've just activated and are launching, Admiral!" said the XO.

All eyes turned to the tactical display, as one ship after another appeared. The XO wiped his brow as he added up the number of vessels. He began to shake his head.

"I...I don't understand. Somehow they have hidden this number of ships inside its core."

Admiral Lewis closed his eyes for a second. He had a strong fleet, but victory against the ships was no longer his primary goal. A few days earlier he might have relished the chance to take on the enemy in a fair fight, but not today.

"Get us back. I want the fleet moving away from that thing, now!"

He then looked to the tactical officer.

"Give me the numbers."

Lieutenant Vitelli was already ahead of them both.

"When Object Thunar shattered, it moved away from the rear of the debris. This large force of ships has been interconnected for some time, presumably part of the core, and also hidden inside this part of the tail. They continue to split apart, but already we have more than fifty capital ships, with perhaps as many still hidden inside the rest of the debris trail. My sensors can't get much of a picture inside there."

He stopped and then glanced at the nearest screen.

"Wait, we've got bigger problems. The fleet will take the full brunt of the debris field in seventy seconds. We're too close to avoid it. We have time to pursue but not to evade."

Admiral Lewis swallowed quickly. He'd completely forgotten that one simple fact. His orders were already being carried out, yet the shattered remnants of the comet would hit them while they were trying to maneuver. He moved to face Captain Marcus, but the XO was already there.

"Ready the ship, Sir?"

He nodded in agreement and then tapped the tactical display. It immediately connected him through to all the squadron commanders.

"This is Admiral Anderson. Coordinate with my tactical team here for a zoned box defense. The debris field is moving in close. Get your guns online and preserve your ships. Match your speed and heading with the debris."

He looked to Lieutenant Vitelli.

"If we travel with the field to Helios Prime, we can maximize our time inflicting damage."

"Yes, Sir. But what about their ships?"

Admiral Lewis looked at the growing number of ships moving through the rear of the comet's debris field and toward them.

"We'll make this as hard as we can for them, Lieutenant. The future of Helios will be decided inside this cluster of broken rock, ice, and metal. Our fleet will stay here until our work is done. Captain Perry will deal with whatever comes from the rest."

"Here is comes, Sir."

The passing of the layer of shattered comet was perhaps the greatest anti-climax in Admiral Lewis' career. Chunks of rock and ice rushed past at great distances from his ship. Even the smaller chunks managed to avoid contact so that apart from the sensors, there was no discernible feeling that they'd just traveled through something dangerous. All of them watched, many holding their breath as the wave of material passed by the ship. Incredibly, only a single Helion cruiser was struck. The guns from a dozen nearby ships helped cut down the offending chunk of rock so that the final impact was made by sections no larger than a meter across. Finally, the front cloud had passed, and the fleet found itself inside the heart of the massive field of debris.

"Admiral, we have finally matched speed. We're effectively in the middle of the remains of the comet fragment with a diameter of more than a hundred kilometers."

"And the rest of the fleet?"

Both of them looked to the tactical display. The XO spoke first.

"They all made it, Sir. Looks like a few took a few scrapes before they could match the speed."

" I see."

He knew what had to be done, but giving this order would guarantee deaths. It didn't dissuade him, but it did make him think one last time before he made contact via the ship's communications array. At least they had a few minutes before the Biomech ships could get close enough to engage them.

Yes, this field will make the job more difficult for them. Let's do what we can before they arrive. It is time.

"All ships initiate the closed-box protocol. Let's break this field down to size. All squadrons are free to engage."

The battle for Object Thunar was unlike anything seen before in the history of the Alliance. Over two hundred ships from the greatest civilizations yet encountered maneuvered inside a massive cloud of dust, rocket, and fragments larger than starships. Alliance Battlecruisers exploded chunks of ice with particle beams, while the Liberty Destroyers pulverized smaller chunks with their arrays of defensive flak guns. In just over two minutes, the entire area was filled with streaks of gunfire and missiles arcing back and forth. The cloud of debris was massive, and compared to the chunks of the ruined comet, the ships paled to insignificance. Still the one-side fight raged and minute-by-minute they moved closer to Helios Prime.

It was into this terrifying maelstrom that the opening wave of Biomech ships emerged to face the Alliance ships. First came five Biomantas vessels that must have already been ready for battle. Even as they moved past chunks of rock, they were pummeled by the heavy gunfire of scores of preprogrammed Avengers. The robotic fighters showed no concern for their safety, and three smashed against ice as they moved in and out of the newly arrived Biomechs. The badly mauled ships then came into the range of the capital ships that were already busy. Admiral Lewis watched all of this unfold from the comparative safety of ANS Conqueror. He looked at the mainscreen and the swirling dustbowl. It made the battle look more like a fight in a storm than in space. With his right hand, he pointed at the shapes of the Biomantas.

"Here they come. Get me Captain Garcia. It's time to

send in the next wave."

It was a risky strategy. There were few that would disagree. The capital ships continued their bombardment and left the fight with the Biomech warships to those ships unable to add much to the thinning of the comet. In reality, this meant the ships from the alien contingents would now be expected to pull their weight. Only the Klithi warships actually proved more than useful by using their powerful mines. Their defensive technologies were perfect for obliterating many of the smaller pieces of the comet. Even the Helion warships were mainly equipped with advanced missiles and modest particle beam weapons. They would best serve by attacking the cloud of debris.

"Admiral, I have Captain Garcia on the line. He reports his force is ready."

Admiral Lewis brought up the disposition screen. He could already see that most of his own ships were well engaged against Object Thunar. A quick glance showed the much smaller line of ships that had remained closer to the planet. He did notice six more Alliance destroyers had just arrived to bolster the line, as well as hundreds of fighters from all sides. They were supposed to be waiting, but instead, he saw more than half now in combat with Biomech ships coming through the Spascia Rift.

How many more damned ships do they have?

"Comms, send an urgent flashcom to Commodore Hampel in Spascia. I need to know what the hell is going on out there."

"Aye, Sir."

He might be busy managing the fine details of the unusual space battle, but that didn't remove his responsibility in keeping an eye on what else was happening in the system. As well as the trickle of ships from Spascia, there was still the main C34 comet that would reach its optimal position around the planet in just half a day. He knew that no matter what happened to his fleet, the remnants would have to move back and help tackle C34. It was a long, complex task, and one that so far had given him little thanks.

"Sir, I'm getting emergency traffic from the Spascia Rift. It's a message from the Admiral Jarvis Naval Station. It's Admiral Anderson."

"Put him on the mainscreen, now."

He glanced over to Captain Marcus to join him. Even as the man approached, he called out to the helmsman.

"Move us away from the fight. I need a clear signal for this."

The ship didn't need to leave the scene of the battle completely, but it did relocate more than thirty kilometers to the side of the debris field. Three Liberty destroyers moved with them for air cover. Even as they moved, the ships continued to add their fire to the battle. After nearly a full minute, an image of the Admiral appeared. He looked even more haggard than he might have expected. It was the group of alien representatives that really caught his attention though. He recognized Naglou, the newly elected leader of the Helion Executive, but not the Byotai figure alongside him.

"Admiral Anderson, good to hear from you. We're making slow progress, but the Biomechs have begun moving their ships into position to counterattack."

A low rattle ran down one side of the ship. It was an unusual sound, but everybody inside knew exactly what it was, small-caliber gunfire from one of the Biomech fighters. Although unable to penetrate the thick armor, it was more likely to be indiscriminate fire from a nearby dogfight.

"I know you're somewhat preoccupied, so I will be brief."

There was nearly ten seconds of lag, much less than normal due to the distances being shortened through repeaters placed at the Rifts. In that short time, a single Biomanta made it to within two kilometers of the Alliance starship before the Liberty class destroyers tore it apart with massed gunfire.

"General Rivers has put together a contingency plan for this campaign. We have ships and troops assembling, but everything that's ready is already being thrown into the line. I'm assembling a reserve in T'Karan space. This is a buffer in case of the worst. This is at the request of High Command."

Admiral Lewis raised his hand and turned to the

tactical display. He could see the ever-changing battlefield and quickly moved his hands to select different groups of ships to change their priorities.

"Admiral, the comet is taking longer to break up than expected."

He looked to his XO and then spoke quietly.

"Get Commander Erdeniz back here."

The Captain marched away to find the illusive officer who was lurking further back in the CIC. No sooner had he looked back to the screen than the Admiral was talking again.

"General Rivers is conducting a full review of security for our own colonies, in case the enemy manages to find a way back into our territory. "

He nodded in the direction of the aliens to his side.

"I have no doubt this campaign will be a long and difficult one. Our diplomats have been pushing hard, and they've at last come up with something. The politicians finally did something right. General Kolak from the Byotai has negotiated an agreement between us, Helios, the Klithi, and his people."

He looked at the camera.

"This agreement comes with a guarantee of nearly three hundred ships, the first wave of which will be at the Helios-Byotai Rift shortly. The rest are going to Micaya to open up a second front, if and when it would be prudent. The forces at Micaya will be under the command of

General Kolak, and he will report directly to you.

Admiral Lewis nodded slowly.

"What price have we or the Helions paid for this kind of gesture, Sir?"

Admiral Anderson looked pained to explain this in front of the others. He could see the commotion aboard ANS Conqueror and decided against dragging it out any longer than was necessary.

"Both the Byotai and the Klithi have long term grievances they want settled. They also want the Narau reinstated, but with new powers. It's going to be complicated. All we need to know is that when, and if this is all over, every race is going to want to relook at this entire arrangement, with fair involvement for them all."

Admiral Lewis listened and wondered quite how any of them could even be thinking of politics and details. Helios Prime was on the brink, and if the Biomechs were able to take control of the system, they would control the Nexus, the heart of the Rift connections between all the races in this part of the Orion Nebula. He shook his head and almost said what he was thinking.

"I've been monitoring your operation. Our figures show you've managed an almost seven percent reduction in the total mass approaching Helios Prime so far. That's good. I suspect you do not have much time left though before the main part of C34 is close enough to begin planetary assault."

"Yes, Admiral. I should get back to this."

He knew that wouldn't be it, but deep down he hoped he could leave this discussion and get back to what was important, the battle for Helios Prime.

"Admiral Lewis. There's another reason why the Byotai have offered to assist us in such numbers."

Here it comes, what's happened?

"The Anicinàbe have problems, big problems. One of their larger factions has crossed the Byotai border and raided two worlds. The news won't have hit you yet, but this clan known as the Red Scars have also attacked Anicinàbe ships from other clans."

He closed his eyes and slowed his breathing, doing his utmost to calm his frustration.

"The Byotai hit them hard, and it's looking fragile out there. But they suspect this Scars group poses a threat that could tip all of the Anicinàbe into a civil war. You must remember, they have no central control and are always fighting each other. They have asked for Narau assistance in keeping the Anicinàbe situation under control and away from their borders. That's the price, and in exchange they are sending us warships."

"I see. When will they arrive?"

"Admiral," said Lieutenant Vitelli, "A single Byotai ship has just arrived from the Helios-Byotai Rift. It's big, Sir, very big."

"Put it on my screen."

The image of a single ship was impressive, much like the dragonfly vessel they had already seen in the current order of battle.

"That's General Makos. He is bringing a dozen ships, all of them with combat experience. Make good use of them. I will be in touch."

He moved to leave and then looked back with a wry smile.

"I'll mobilize everything we have in the meantime, just don't let Helios Prime fall."

With that feed gone, he watched the arrival of the first ship that was soon joined by the rest of the black, insect shaped vessels. The rest were no larger than an Alliance cruiser, but the flagship was truly massive, perhaps fifty percent larger than even ANS Dreadnought.

"Get me their commander."

The communications officer looked back, surprise on his face.

"Admiral, they are already waiting to speak with you."

With just a nod of the head, the video feed was transferred to his own screen.

"Admiral Lewis. I am General Makos. My ships are at your disposal."

The figure had much in common with the Jötnar, just shorter and reptilian in look. This one wore thick plating on key parts of its body and a dull helm that covered its forehead and ran down to its neck.

"Good. You are closer to C34 than I am. One moment."

He sent a short request to communications, and in less than five seconds, a poor quality feed reached Captain Perry.

"Admiral, we've detected these new ships. What can you tell me about them?"

The man sounded nervous, not that Admiral Lewis could blame him.

"This is General Makos. I want him to assist your forces with C34."

The translator on the Byotai was unable to pass on the confusion, but his expression worked just as well.

"Attack, with just my twelve ships on the forces around this world? We don't have the firepower."

"No."

Admiral Lewis concentrated on Captain Perry.

"There's a reason I left all of the troop transports with you, Captain. I want a coordinated assault put into action within the hour. Hit them hard and get marines inside that thing. Both Captain Perry and General Makos looked stunned.

Yes, that is exactly why you're going to do this, he thought, *because that's just how the Biomechs will see this plan.*

* * *

The fighting around Object Thunar had reached a critical

stage. Every second a chunk of the massive object was torn apart, yet the Biomech warship now moved in to stop whatever chance the defenders might have. The task of dealing with the debris field was one that left few ships able to deal with them. While the cruisers and Battlecruisers continued their one-sided battle, the task of the ship-to-ship battle fell on the Lightnings, Hammerheads, and Maulers of the Alliance. The only capital ships to assist then were the black Byotai warships, each of which was modeled on a flying creature from their own worlds. At the center of this group moved three large dragonfly shaped Byotai heavy merchant ships. All of them had been modified to carry significant numbers of large caliber railguns; every one helpfully donated by the Alliance from old war stocks.

The lead position was taken by an entire wing of Maulers, each of them being shadowed by two or more fighters. They were in among the first wave of Biomantas just as they smashed into the debris cloud.

"Do it, now!" Captain Garcia ordered.

He shook his head in amazement as the first two nuclear warheads impacted on the nearest Biomanta. The first missile failed to detonate, but the second erupted just after it punched through the outer armor of the ship. The subsequent explosion tore the vessel in half, much to the cheering approval of his modest crew.

"Great work."

The craft spun about on its axis and accelerated to the side, just as an unguided rocket surged past and struck a chunk of hardened ice. The Mauler leveled off and moved back to its original trajectory. Captain Garcia sighed and looked to his co-pilot who smiled sheepishly. Lieutenant Takeda might be the youngest Mauler pilot in the fleet, and perhaps the shortest, yet her skill was without question the best.

"Damned good, Takeda, that's what I'm talking about!"

More than thirty fighters of mixed types moved in around the group of Maulers. Behind them followed the Byotai Dragonflies, as they were being nicknamed by the crew. They were dark and almost beautiful to look at. The massed gun batteries built into their hulls dispelled any myths at their lack of effectiveness. More than a dozen of the sleek Helion fighters moved on the one flank, and four Khreenk Corsairs moved with them. Two Helion cruisers protected the rear of the force and unleashed a barrage of missiles and then pushed on.

"Ready for the Cephalon?"

Takeda nodded firmly. Captain Garcia tapped the intercom button on his console. He'd been granted full tactical control of this part of the battle, and he could feel the stress already building. The shape of the huge Cephalon command ship filled their view from the cockpit, and at this range it looked like a Kraken moving from the ocean to devour them. There was little else to see from their current position.

"All attack wings move on the targets. Break and attack!"

The Maulers were large craft, much bigger than any Alliance fighter, and originally designed for use in landing operations to put marines into battle. Their powerful engines, thick armor, and multiple gun turrets had proven useful as support gunships in ways never envisaged. Even better, the Maulers all contained a large cargo area that could carry a multitude of mission modules, such as drone control, missiles systems, and even enough space to carry a single Avenger drone.

"Captain, I've got fighters coming this way," said Takeda.

Captain Garcia wasn't surprised. The Cephalon class ships were something new, but already the basic schematics and capabilities had been spread through the Alliance computer databases. These ships functioned as heavy battleships and command vessels. Many suspected they were the fortified homes for the Biomech Steersmen, the leadership caste of the enemy.

"Clear a path for the Byotai!"

The Maulers split up to run down the flanks of the massive ship and raked it from all angles with continuous gunfire. Biomech fighters tried to intercept them, but the flanking Alliance fighters easily beat them back. With most of the gunfire concentrating on the fast moving small craft, the Byotai warships were clear to launch their own attacks. One by one, they launched a barrage of unguided torpedoes. Each projectile was the size of a fighter and blasted away at hypersonic speeds. Half were cut down by defensive fire, but enough struck the bow of the Cephalon to start a series of explosions that ran a quarter the way down its hull.

The Byotai Dragonflies followed the Maulers to the rear of the Cephalon and then broke out to face the rest of the Biomantas. Captain Garcia was the first to spot the second Cephalon leading a huge column of ships. A bright white light forced the cockpit glass to darken for a moment then a dozen streaks tore past them to cut away a Dragonfly's wings. Another burst hit the Helion cruiser.

"Bring us in closer; we need to thin the herd!"

CHAPTER TWELVE

Who was Spartan before the Uprising? The only public records of the man show that he'd been one of many involved in the underground gladiatorial combat circuit. A veteran of multiple bouts, it wasn't until his killing of a public servant that brought him to public attention. Who were his family, and where did he come from? There were rumors of an accident involving his family, and many more described a variety of misadventures while in care. Few of these could be corroborated, however. These were questions that would never be satisfactorily answered until the events of the great contest with the Biomechs in the Orion Nebula. The greatest mystery to many remained the origins of his name. Who was Spartan, and where did he come from?

The Rise of Spartan

The bright flash of the Helion cruiser's engines detonating announced the arrival of the rest of the Biomech vanguard. More than ninety warships streamed past the wreckage with their guns blazing. A single Cephalon command ship proved so massive that it merely crashed directly into the flank of the crippled ship and tore it apart like tissue paper. This wave of ships was not there for the invasion of Helios Prime. Their task was a simple one, the complete destruction of the ships defending Helios Prime so that the next wave could make it unscathed.

"I want four destroyers providing overwatch for ANS Endurance now!"

Admiral Lewis almost stumbled as a double volley from a passing Biomanta tore a chunk six meters long from the flank of the ship. An emergency alert sounded and was quickly drowned out by the shouting of the officers in the CIC. He looked at them as they conducted their work. Every single one concentrated on their tasks with all their attention on the battle. He turned back to face Sanlav.

"Tell me this is working? Our ships are taking a pounding here, and there is not one chance in hell we can do this on our own," he snapped.

"I put us right here, based on the figures you gave us. You're sure the tech on your ship can do this?"

Instead of answering, it was his XO that spoke.

"Six fragments destroyed. The largest is too big for us to damage. ANS Endurance is maneuvering alongside us to take the first shot. She's taking fire from their fighters."

The mainscreen showed the massive space battle, and

now both sides were fully engaged. Biomantas fought Crusader warships and exchanged volleys while fighters dashed in and out. Maulers moved in small groups, but Biomech fighters harried their every move. Even the alien ships had done their part and fired on Biomechs and chunks of Object Thunar with equal gusto.

Commander Erdeniz moved his hands with surprising speed and dexterity, as he coordinated his controls with the new readings coming back from the engineering vessel.

"Tell me you can do this?"

Sanlav looked to the Admiral and gave an odd, almost sinister smile. It wasn't what he'd expected, and he found it a little unnerving. He'd heard things about this man before, about his unusual past that mixed combat, research, and more than a few scandals. Even so, his reputation for improvisation was something of a legend in the Alliance.

"If it doesn't, the feedback loop will destroy the ship and anything within a kilometer."

"Admiral, we've got a clear shot through the field," said Lieutenant Vitelli.

The imagery on the mainscreen showed a large, oval shape covered in spikes and odd fissures. The computers were already running detailed scans, but it was Commander Erdeniz that recognized it instantly for what it was. He spun about and made a number of changes to the settings for the engineering ship.

"That is more than the largest section, Admiral."

He turned back and pointed at the screen.

"That is another Ark, just like the one carved out of rock and ice that hit Spascia. It's an Ark constructed for one reason only. It's what is going to control the invasion of Helios."

Admiral Lewis nodded in agreement.

"I think you're right. Is Endurance online and ready?"

Sanlav made a few more configuration changes before finally looking back. He seemed confident, but there was something else, perhaps the faintest hint of doubt.

"Yes, Admiral, she's online, and her capacitors are already fully charged."

"Good."

He turned about and moved to his horizontal tactical display. Captain Marcus was alongside him, waiting patiently for the order. Admiral Lewis tapped the icons for any ships in the flagged area and gave them their new orders. Their captains had been waiting for the signal, and as one, they split apart to create an open corridor to the target.

"Now!"

* * *

The Mauler shuddered as the guns from the passing Biomanta raked its hull. They twisted about to avoid the fire, but a following Helion fighter was cut clean in half.

More rounds tore the rear left engine from its mount and sent the internal alarms into overdrive. The two Maulers on each side also took a pounding, but although damaged all three came through in relatively one piece. Captain Garcia and Lieutenant Takeda maneuvered the craft through a bewildering series of movements as they avoided yet more fire, and then they were out of danger, for now. Captain Garcia looked to his co-pilot and shook his head in amazement.

"That was close, too close."

She nodded in agreement.

"Not over yet, Sir."

He looked back and spotted the pair of Biomech fighters. They were being pursued by the sleek Helion fighters and coming right at them. There was no need for any orders to the gunners, and before the fighters could get too close, they were targeted by three of the turret mounts. Round after round smashed around them and managed to catch the first. The second veered away and vanished into another massed dogfight on their flank.

"Sir, urgent flashcom from Admiral Lewis."

Captain Garcia looked at the short text message that showed on the overlay of the front screen. The text was relatively large and contained only the most pertinent information. Either way, it sent a cold chill through his body.

"About time. Get us back to ANS Conqueror. We need

to rejoin the picket, and fast!"

Dozens of ships and fighters moved about and split off from the battle with the Biomech ships. Most made it, but a small number were too badly damaged to cut off as the Allies gave ground. Even as the first made it back, a Biomech Ravager rammed a stray Crusader class ship. Both vessels ripped apart, their wreckage sparking and flashing with secondary explosions. Small shapes burst from the hull of the Alliance ship, marking the escape of its surviving crew.

"Captain!" cried Takeda, as she pointed to the bow of ANS Endurance.

Both looked as an odd energy pulse built up around its bow. Blue flashes that had more in common with lightning arcs than weapons licked about the cold empty space near the ship. Both of them knew the ship was there for a reason, but neither had much faith that it would do anything substantial.

"I don't like the look of this!"

The energy surge continued to build.

"Put us between the capital ships and that thing, fast."

"Aye, Sir."

* * *

Admiral Lewis held his breath as the bright light appeared in the distance, and only a short distance from the Alliance engineering vessel. Both of them watched as the light pulsed and then vanished in a flash of white. At the same time, a Rift entrance opened up directly in the path of the Ark, but then vanished as quickly as the computer system detected it.

"What the hell is happening?" he demanded.

Sanlav looked to him and shuddered, but said nothing. He looked back at his screen and began muttering. His face looked paler than normal, and a bead of sweat dropped down from his temple.

"Commander, tell me dammit!"

"The…the emitters…overloaded, and the entrance shifted focus. Give me a moment…"

He moved a number of wheels and sliders on the screen and sent the data directly to the ship. There was a short delay between him sending the information and the engineers aboard the ship putting them through the system. Three seconds later a green icon flashed and then appeared directly in the middle of the model of the station. It expanded quickly and soon engulfed nearly a third of the station.

"There!" he announced triumphantly.

"Why is it expanding?" asked the science officer nervously.

The screen's overlay added a dotted line from the Alliance ship and directly to the Ark. It was wider than expected, and with each passing moment the corridor expanded.

"Any moment now."

Even as he said the last word, another icon appeared, but this one was directly over the stern of ANS Endurance. The green icon pulsed and shifted about, but only a few meters in any one direction. Admiral Lewis didn't wait for confirmation and instead hit the emergency alert button on his console.

"All ships, get away from Endurance, now!"

It was too late though. Even as those nearest activated their maneuvering thrusters, the dotted line flashed and quickly expanded as the Rift in space-time was created between the two points. The Rift looked almost perfect, but only for the blink of an eye before the entire Rift structure collapsed in on itself. The ship vanished, to be replaced by a massive explosion then engulfed both points of the tunnel. The intense heat that flashed outwards with the energy of a hundred tactical nuclear weapons instantly vaporized three Alliance cruisers. Dozens of fighters from both sides also vanished.

"Brace for..." were the last words from the XO when the debris and heat slammed into the flank of the warship. Only the powerful radiation shielding prevented the entire crew from being instantly killed. Admiral Lewis was thrown to the wall, and the Battlecruiser was left powerless in space as it spun out of control away from where ANS Endurance had once been. In its place sat the shattered remnants of sections of the comet, Biomech ships, and a few select pieces of the Alliance vessel. In a single blow, the heart of the Biomech force, including the Thunar fragments and the Ark, was shattered. The Allies suffered almost as badly, as an equal level of damage was inflicted against any craft unfortunate enough to be caught in the massive blast.

* * *

The Mauler spun between two Byotai Dragonflies when the blast struck. The vast heat bloom rushed past and dissipated in seconds, but not before cooking the nearest Byotai ship from one side. Hundreds of small explosions ripped through its hull, as it lay lifeless. The Mauler shuddered and then leveled off.

"What the hell was that?" Captain Garcia asked.

Lieutenant Takeda pulled the craft around and kept it positioned firmly between the two vessels. They had a perfect few of the battlefield, and to their shock they found nothing intact within the blast zone that marked the last location of ANS Endurance.

"Sir, look."

They both looked out through the cockpit toward the Biomech fleet. The massive Ark had been replaced by hundreds of smaller chunks that now drifted amongst the battered Biomech ships. Dozens were burning, and even more had been smashed by the close proximity collapse of the entire station.

"Is it gone?"

He looked back at his small command team inside the Mauler. The tactical officer was already running the numbers as he called out.

"No, Sir. The Ark has sustained massive damage with ruptures on all sides. The remaining Biomechs are falling back to defend it."

"And ANS Endurance?"

The man looked up and shook his head.

"The feedback loop destroyed them both. Looks like we lost a few ships as well."

He could already see that on his own overlay. Unlike the Biomechs, most of their ships had been spaced out in the debris field and sustained minimal losses.

"Who's in charge? Can you reach Admiral Lewis?"

The small team on board did their utmost to reach as many of the remaining ships. Many replied, but none of the heavy Alliance ships responded. As each acknowledgement came in, it became clear to Captain Garcia that both sides had suffered losses, and there were many ships out of action, or partially disabled.

"No command ships in action, Sir. ANS Conqueror has fluctuating power levels, and the same goes for most of the ships near the blast radius."

He reached for the intercom and opened up a general

channel to the fleet.

"This is Captain Garcia of the Alliance Mauler ANS Tempest. I am assuming command. All available ships and fighters follow me. We need to end this, now."

He looked to Lieutenant Takeda and realized he hadn't even spotted the blood dripping from a small cut to her forehead.

"You ready for this?"

She did her best to smile.

"Good. Set a course for the Ark."

The craft shuddered as the three remaining engines pushed the craft away from the wrecked Byotai vessel. Once they moved into the open, they were greeted by the shocking view of scores of their own ships and all moving slowly toward the Ark. Even as they flew past the lifeless shapes of cruisers, they began to reactivate. They made it halfway to the target when a transmission came through.

"This is Admiral Lewis. We're back in commission. All ships take Tempest's lead. We're running these bastards down!"

The large group of ships moved faster and faster toward the shattered Ark and its reduced force of ships. More tried to untangle themselves from the stricken Ark, but the Rift collapse had done its job well. In eleven minutes most of the remaining fleet limped toward the shattered remains of the Biomech Ark. Missiles and torpedoes began the assault and were quickly followed by every weapon system still functional in the fleet. The final phase of the battle for Object Thunar was not a fight; it was a complete rout. One by one the Biomech ships tried to hold them back, and one by one they were smashed by the combined firepower of over a hundred of the remaining ships. Less than twenty minutes later, the remnants of the Biomech force was in tatters, leaving just two Cephalon command ships and a dozen other ships to escape on a direct course toward Helios Prime.

Instead of pursuing them, the fleet remained to break down the last fragments of Object Thunar. Even though fully engaged, the Crusader class ships still maintained pressure on the Biomechs trying to flee. The direct energy weapons of the later tranche of ships were easily able to travel vast distances and still cause damaged. It wasn't enough to decide the battle, but it was enough to give a parting shot to the hated enemy. As the ships set to work on the broken pieces of the comet, Admiral Lewis relaxed, even if just a little.

So, we stopped the apocalypse. What comes next?

"Admiral, an urgent message from Captain Perry. He says there's something happening to C34. He's on an attack vector."

The Admiral wiped his brow and then nodded.

"Put him on my screen."

I guess this is my answer.

* * *

Captain Carter moved ahead of the small group and made his way around the side of the dune. He'd told them all to specifically avoid climbing the peaks and presenting targets backlit by the bright skyline. It was the kind of material they'd all learnt by rote in basic training, but as always, it was easy to forget in actual combat. He stopped and noticed an incoming flashcom from the temporary facility currently being organized nearly a hundred kilometers away. It was short and sweet, nothing more than the last Biomanta vessels were making a break for the surface.

Good, he thought. *That means they know they're beaten.*

He lowered himself carefully and looked down at the incredible sight before him. There were pieces of broken metal all around the crash site, but there were also many bodies from a short and violent battle. Some were Thegns, but most were Helions. He could only think they must have been transporting prisoners.

Maybe they tried to escape, or just crashed the thing.

He watched and could feel nothing but bitterness toward the machines. They'd taken civilians and forced them into an impossible situation. It made what needed to be done next much easier.

"Well?" Wictred asked.

Both he and Vadi waited further back at the base of

the sand dune. Their bulk made them far less suited for the task of discreet reconnaissance. Instead, they brought up the heavy weapons and waited for the word. Two more marines were waiting with them while Lance Corporal James joined the Captain along the edge of the dune with an L48 resting on a bipod. Captain Carter said nothing, but gave a simple set of hand gestures. Wictred nodded at the last one.

"He wants us to go in. Follow me!"

Wictred didn't even check to see if his comrades were with him. He knew them well enough that they would be ready. He moved out from cover and around the side of the dune. There was a subtle dip, and the different gravity and change in height almost made him lose his balance. He managed to regain his footing and lurched ahead into plain view of the crashed vessel. It was in a much worse state than he'd expected, with hundreds of bullet holes and dents running along the nose section. Two massive doors lay wide open, and a handful of Thegns were trying to drag something from out of the inside. A single eight-legged war machine spotted him and raised a firearm.

"Yes!" Wictred howled.

With his bloodlust up, he increased speed toward them. Two short cracks from the dune announced the precision marksmanship of Captain Carter. The first blast struck the machine right in the center of its torso. It dropped to the ground belching a cloud of heated vapor. Another double shot blasted out, and two Thegns fell to the ground. The surviving three dropped what they were doing and moved to stop Wictred. None carried firearms, but they all swung their retractable blades at him, each trying desperately to keep away the monstrous warrior. The first forced Wictred to jump to the side, but Vadi ploughed on and threw himself at the nearest. Both hit the ground in a tumble of bodies, leaving the remaining two to Wictred. He took their blades on his armor and then yanked the first Thegn to his chest. More gunshots rang out, as the rest of the marines surged toward the Bioray and cut down the remaining Thegn.

"Clear!" shouted one of them.

"Clear," repeated Captain Carter as he watched from the dune.

The other marines fanned out and moved closer to the crashed craft. Vadi and Private O'Hara climbed inside. The marine quickly turned back, opened up her visor, and vomited onto the ground. She choked and coughed for a moment before settling down.

"What is it?" shouted down the Captain.

Wictred cast the remaining Thegn over to the two nearest marines and then climbed inside the wreckage. He glanced about for a moment and then stepped back to look to the officer.

"Bodies, lots of them. Mainly Helions. Looks like they were taking prisoners somewhere."

Captain Carter stood up straight and lowered his carbine. He began walking toward the craft while continually looking for signs of danger. Something black moved overhead, followed shortly by a sonic boom. The speed was so great that it kicked up dust as it moved overhead. He looked up and examined the craft as it moved off into the distance.

"Alliance Hammerhead. Looks like we're back in control again."

Wictred moved back inside the craft and made his way past the dozens of mutilated bodies. Most had clearly been killed by external gunfire, but a good number must have died in the rough landing. He kept on moving and then reached the broken armor of a Biomech. It was the size of Wictred, but the armor had been recently torn open, and blood and fluid ran freely from inside.

"Nasty," said the Captain, moving alongside Wictred.

"Yes. What do you think did this?"

The Alliance officer pointed lower, where a line of eight finger-sized holes had been punched through the plating.

"Looks like medium caliber cannon rounds. I'd say a Hammerhead strafed them on the way down."

He straightened his back as though stretching and then nodded to himself.

"Either way, his fight is over. We've got ourselves a piece of Biomech tech, so we'd better get in touch with Command about this. Who knows what use it might be?"

Wictred nodded in agreement.

"Yeah, this is going to be a long war. Anything we can strip from their tech might be of use."

Captain Carter grinned.

"Corporal, you might be right on that one. Hyperion brought us the Rift technology, and the war exposed us to direct energy weapons."

He looked back at the massive craft and wondered what secrets the craft might hold. Vadi, the Helion synthetic emerged from one of the hatches and held up one of the turret guns in the air above him and roared.

"Well, if nothing else, you've found some new guns."

CHAPTER THIRTEEN

What will be the weapon of the future for the Alliance? The Wars of the Confederacy were decided with railguns, and those before that with kinetic auto cannons, missiles, and atomic weapons. New developments in the 4thcentury of the New Colonies brought in the use of particle beams and mass drivers. These were hardly new technologies, but their use in battle would be tested in the great struggles with the Biomechs and their insidious forces.

Naval Cadet's Handbook

The formation of ships moved at high speed through the cool stillness of space. Around them moved smaller capital ships and more than two-dozen armed civilian clippers, all desperate to do their part to defend Helios Prime from the coming assault.

"Captain, I'm picking up a radiation bloom," said

Lieutenant MacTyler, ANS Royal Oak's tactical officer.

"What? Show me!" Captain Perry snapped.

The computers had already flagged the energy signature and immediately cross-referenced it with similar events over Eos, and more recently at Spascia. As expected, the information closely matched the more recent attack. Captain Perry's face changed from confusion to outright panic.

"They're not preparing to fire on us. Look at the position of their primary weapon emitters and gun ports. Over eighty percent of their entire arsenal is pointing ahead."

The tactical officer nodded in agreement with his assessment.

"They are about to launch an attack on Helios Prime."

Captain Perry scratched at his cheek, a nervous affliction he'd picked up over the years, and a mark of clear frustration. He was too far away, and his angle of attack was wrong to be able to cause damage to that part of the comet. His orders had been to pin down the enemy and ensure they were unable to launch ships unmolested. That was why he'd elected to intercept the target from the rear. There was no reason to see the forward guns as a threat to the planet, safe behind its thick atmosphere.

"I don't understand. The bloom effect and the atmosphere will render the direct energy weapons of this...thing, well, redundant."

He twisted about to face his XO and the tactical officer.

"Uh...well, that's assuming they are using a particle beam type weapon."

"That's true," added Commander James Durham.

The man had only recently transferred from the Admiral Jarvis Naval Station, amidst rumors of a near breakdown following the news of his brother's death. Although potentially a problem, his experience went back nearly a decade, and he'd seen action in more the a dozen minor engagements prior to Helios Prime.

"All the data we have suggests this kind of attack would be completely wasted."

The Captain considered what both of them had said. Commander Durham listened carefully before speaking.

"What about more conventional weapons? Atomics are a possibility."

Lieutenant MacTyler nodded in agreement.

"True, but don't forget the Helions have a sophisticated air-defense system across the entire surface of Helios Prime. Missiles, guns, and even satellite based laser weaponry can burn through and disable that kind of technology before it strikes. The Biomechs will already know this."

Even as they considered their next move, the entire fleet moved ever closer. Not a single fighter had been launched; each lay in wait inside the bowels of the larger warships. Pilots sat in their seats, strapped in, and waiting for the word. Even the heavy Maulers waited in multiple hangars with massive mag-clamps holding them in place.

"We're missing something. We must be."

Captain Perry looked at the imagery of C34 for what must have been the twentieth time. With Object Thunar destroyed, the immediate risk of a devastating bombardment had been averted; that was clear. The rest of Admiral Lewis' forces were moving back to the planet as fast as their engines would take them, even at the expense of sustaining long-term damage during the high-speed redeployment.

He'd already seen the reports from two ships forced to stay back as the strain on their engines had been too much. There was a temptation for him to order a halt to his own forces, but the Admiral's orders were clear. He just wanted to know what the enemy's plan was, and more than anything else, why had they not launched their ships?

"Sir, those energy blooms have stabilized but still no sign of attack."

Commander Durham pointed at the current position of the comet, as it reached the end of its long journey to Helios Prime and began its first high orbit around the planet.

"Based upon what had happened at Spascia, we can assume this larger Ark will hold an invasion force of substantial size. We're talking hundreds of thousands of warriors, perhaps even millions. What if they are just getting their weapons ready in case we move to interfere with their operation?"

It was a simple assessment, and Captain Perry could hardly deny his thoughts matched the facts.

"You think they consider us to be so insignificant a threat that they won't even bother trying to keep us away?"

The look on his officer's face answered his question clearly enough.

What if they're not afraid of us for a reason?

It was his job to stop the attack long enough for the rest of the fleet to arrive. Only with all of their ships combined, could they hope to actually bring some kind of conclusion to the inevitable battle for the control of Helios Prime and the area of space around it. Even so, in the last hour, his motley collection of fifty ships, plus the reinforcements from General Makos, had moved ever closer to the target. The cloud of ice and rock made it hard to move near enough to obtain a detailed scan, but his ships were well prepared and had taken on as much information as possible from the fight with Thunar.

How long can we survive against that thing?

The comet looked barely any smaller than the first images he'd seen when it had been detected. The object was already being drawn in by the strong pull of Helios Prime and moving into an orbit of just over twenty thousand kilometers. It wasn't the size that really made him nervous, though of course that was of concern to him. Unlike the objects at Spascia, or even Thunar, this one seemed different. It was the largest, and as far as his scanner could tell, the most developed.

"Sir, their gun ports are still active. We've detected over three hundred along the dorsal section and multiple emitters and turret systems deploying. They're readying for combat."

"What about the landing bays, though? Are they close to launching ships or fighters yet?"

His tactical officer looked back over his shoulder.

"No, Sir, just their weapon system. So far there are no target locks on our ships. We've only had a cursory look from them so far. It's almost as if they don't see us as a threat."

So why are they opening their gun ports? What exactly are they aiming at?

His thoughts were interrupted.

"Captain Perry, this is Admiral Lewis. Do what you can. Helios Prime must survive. The Biomechs are moving into position around every inhabited world in this system. We have to make sure they can never obtain a foothold here. I will be there soon. Good luck."

With that he was gone, and the Captain found himself alone in a CIC filled with officers. All of them had a task to do, but all he could do was give the command to send them into battle. He reached for the intercom, and the mood shifted ever so subtly around him.

"This is Captain Perry. Comet C34 is deploying weapons

to strike the surface. All ships execute Attack Plan Alpha. Keep their guns busy and get boots on the ground."

There was no need to issue anything more specific; the entire opening phase to the battle had already been planned in excruciating detail. Now that the comet was in line of sight, the particle emitters fitted to the larger ships rereleased their powerful particle beams. A hundred explosions ripped through the rear of the massive object but did little to reduce its effectiveness. Even the massed projectile bombardment from the railguns did little more than rip chunks of rock, ice, and metal.

"They are launching, Sir."

The great hangar doors opened in two-dozen places at once. Each was large enough to release an entire warship. Unlike before, the massive object released fighters. This was not a trickle of craft but hundreds upon hundreds of them. As soon as they were free of the debris field, they accelerated toward the approaching Alliance Fleet. Captain Perry watched with growing unease as his ships were forced to divert some of their fire toward the hundreds of rapidly approaching fighters. He contacted Captain Harper and his image opened up on the nearest screen.

"I want our fighters to move in on the lower structure of the comet. It's up to them to stop the bombardment. Go in low and hit their missiles with turret fire, understood?"

"Yes, Captain, they're already on the way."

The CAG waited no time in sending out the revised

orders to the accelerating fighter wings. In just two minutes, the two sides met in what may have been the largest fighter action in Alliance history. Every model of fighter in service was involved, and the casualties proved equally horrific. Forty-six fighters were lost in the first minute as the no-man's-land between C34 and the fleet filled with the ruins of fighters. Behind them moved the Liberty destroyers, who saturated the Biomechs with a continuous cloud of deadly shrapnel.

Just look at them, Captain Perry thought.

The space battle was confused, but it was General Makos and his own wing of black monstrous vessels that caught his eye. Every time they fired, the ships released a relatively low velocity mass of energy that rushed out and vaporized whatever it hit. Each of the alien ships unleashed a massive bombardment of pulsed energy, and for a moment at least, Captain Perry though they might have a chance. Then the larger hangars opened up, revealing a monstrous dry dock filled with scores of defensive turrets.

"Captain, scanners are picking up Biomech capital ships beginning to deploy."

The tactical officer looked over his left shoulder, his brow tight and nervous.

"It's beginning, Sir. Scanners detect a Cephalon deploying and powering up weapons."

Yes, and the rest will surely follow.

The man's face tightened as he watched new data coming in.

"Oh, no, I was wrong. It's not missiles."

Both of them looked at the screen giving a massive overview of the fast comet based Ark. It looked like some hellish black monstrosity, surrounded by razor sharp chunks of debris as big as a space station. Fighters swarmed about it like fleas while it opened up scores of channels that ran deep inside the surface.

"What are those things?"

The tactical officer wiped his brow and shook his head just as the first volley began. From where they watched, it was like an Earth ship from the ancient past firing a broadside of cannons. From each of the deep shafts rushed out a solid lump of material harvested from the heart of the comet. They slammed downwards into the atmosphere with a powerful crash. Long streaks of gunfire from the circling fighters did their best to intercept them, but the massive objects easily shrugged off the fire as they dropped down.

"Sir, those are chunks of the core, each one between fifty and a hundred meters. They must be using mass drivers."

One after one they crashed into the upper atmosphere, with many breaking apart while the fragments fell down leaving great trails behind them.

"Sir, if any of those fragments make it through, they

will be able to destroy a small city."

Captain Perry was already in direct contact with both Admiral Lewis and General Daniels. They all watched as over a hundred objects were thrown down into the atmosphere with tremendous force.

"Captain, do what you can against that Ark. I'm coming as fast as I can."

The video footage of General Daniels was completely different, however. At first the imagery was clear, but then the interference and distortion began to make it almost unwatchable.

"Sir, I'm reading massive impacts in the one-hundred megatons yield. It's playing merry hell with our comms."

"Captain, I'll be there within the hour. Can you stop this bombardment?"

He looked to imagery coming from the CIC of ANS Conqueror. It was from inside the CIC of the flagship, and it was clear they had been in a tough battle. Half of the lights were out of action, and multiple computer systems were offline.

"I have fighters and escorts moving below the Ark. My boarding parties will arrive in…seven minutes."

"Good, good."

Captain Perry checked the status of his advancing squadrons before moving the tactical display to show the position previously occupied by Thunar.

"Is it true, ANS Endurance is gone?"

Admiral Lewis nodded glumly.

"Yes, but their system took a large part of the target with them. Their failure is our benefit; the remaining segments of Thunar being dealt with by the ships unable to keep up. That means another of these mobile Arks is offline and unable to perform a massed bombardment of Helios Prime."

"So Helios Prime is safe from Thunar?"

"Safe enough. My science team tells me that nothing should hit Helios Prime that is larger than an Alliance landing craft. Any that make it through should break up once they hit the atmosphere. The Helion defense systems can deal with the rest. It's nothing compared to the close range bombardment from C34."

"My boys are on it. At least you've eliminated the terminal threat."

"Yes, but at a heavy cost. My fleet has been mauled, and we still have the primary threat to deal with. Your ships are almost in range. It is imperative that you stop the enemy from deploying their ground forces. You don't need to beat them, Captain, just pin them down until I can arrive. Exchange ships for time until I can reach you."

"Understood, Sir."

"Good, as soon as they emerge from behind Helios Prime, I will be able to provide you with a particle beam corridor. Make sure you keep everything out from the attack vector we'll be using."

"Yes, Admiral."

The image flickered and then vanished. Captain Perry looked to Captain Harper, the ship's CAG who had brought up two displays showing the precise deployment of the fighter wings on the mainscreen. The craft were well out in front of the fleet, and as with Thunar, they were mainly formed up around the heavy Maulers. The capital ships followed their pre-selected paths to engage the comet while keeping clear corridors for boarding parties to land.

"All wings report as ready, Sir."

"Good."

Both of them noticed something changing in the middle of the screen. At first nobody seemed sure what it was until the computer identified several moving parts of the target structure.

"It's opening up, Sir. We have clear access into the superstructure. They are releasing Ravager and Biomanta assault vessels. I think this is the beginning of their assault."

Captain Perry needed no further encouragement. He tapped the general transmission button to all vessels under his temporary command.

"All vessels, engage the enemy!"

He then indicated to his XO.

"I need to see what's going on at the surface."

There was something about the man's face that stopped him in his tracks. He looked back to the mainscreen and the continually changing shape of the vast comet. In the last minute, a number of large petal type shapes had extended outwards, and the structure seemed even larger than before. With each passing moment, another gantry, tower, or wing deployed to change its shape into something more resembling a super-sized starship. It was unlike anything either of them had seen before.

"Incoming fire!" shouted the tactical officer.

At first there was nothing to see, but the mainscreen attached the direct energy overlay to show the path of the beam. As with the weapon system on the station at Spascia, this one linked its fire together to unleash a single stream that struck the nearest Crusader class ship. It cut the ship in half and then moved directly to the next vessel.

"Evasive action!" roared the XO.

The mighty battle Conqueror class Battlecruiser groaned as it twisted about on its axis. More fire hit the layered armor, but as the ship moved, it pulled the damaged section out of the way and put in the untouched underside of the ship in the way. Two Biomanta ships moved past the stern and raked the Alliance ship with cannon fire. At the same time, ANS Royal Oak hit back with her stern chasers, an ancient concept, but one that meant four heavy railgun batteries had been retained for such occasions.

"More targets, they are deploying en masse, Sir."

Additional objects appeared on the tactical display. Each one was flagged with a red diamond as soon as the computer system identified the model of vessel. Dozens and dozens of cruiser class ships appeared, but as before, it was the hundreds of fighters that the computer system found almost impossible to monitor.

"Sir, we're now counting three hundred plus fighters, and more are launching. Our fighter cover is on its limits. We need to move the capital ships closer to support them."

"Or fall back," he said quietly.

We need marines on that station and fast.

"How long till the Maulers get there?"

"Not long," replied Commander Durham.

"Get us closer. We need that station occupied to give our people time."

"Sir, we're losing ships every minute. The firepower from their Ark is too much. By my calculations, we'll lose the fleet in less than an hour."

As if to emphasis the tactical officer's comments, the ship sustained a dozen heavy impacts from the aft gun mounts on the station. A final impact struck much harder and ripped through multiple decks. Red indicators marked a number of key systems that were now offline from the damage.

"What the hell was that?" Captain Perry demanded.

"Their capital ships. They have more warships moving out. It looks like we're a threat after all. It's worse than that though, Sir. Look!"

The tactical officer altered the view to the tail fragments

moving near the comet. From a distance, it looked like nothing more than debris, but on closer examination there were multiple ships attached to the rock itself.

"I'm detecting at least six cruiser class vessels on that segment alone."

"How many more are there?"

"That's the problem, Sir. There are over six hundred fragments, all of them held into place around the station, and many of them are sheltering ships."

Six hundred? This is impossible!

"Very well. Keep the guns firing; we'll buy Admiral Lewis the time he needs."

Another volley slammed into his ship, and the damage alerts showed that three decks had been penetrated. Captain Perry knew he could put up a good fight, but the numbers in front of him had just confirmed a simple truth.

I don't have enough ships to protect Helios Prime.

Even that wasn't the revelation that hurt the most. It was that the battered ships of Admiral Lewis would make little more than a dent when they arrived. He looked at the monstrous Ark warship in front on them. It was like looking at some ever-changing monster, one he seriously doubted they could affect.

It's all in the hands of our marines now. God help them.

* * *

Sergeant Ashley Payne looked back to his platoon and checked they were ready for the hundredth time. He wore a black beard across his chin, and a thick scar ran down his cheek to his neck. He was a veteran of the insurgency on Carthago and showed little patience for tardiness of slackness.

"All right, marines, we land in thirty seconds. Remember, this is a zero-g assault. We go in fast and we go in hard. This is a Biomech Ark, so the rules of engagement are simple."

He smiled, a short, cruel look that inspired nothing less than fear in the entire unit.

"You will shoot anything you find. I want a body count that the General can only dream of."

The Mauler shuddered as it altered course just a fraction. All external video feeds had been deactivated so the marines could only see exactly what their officers had presented them. More light gunfire hit the frontal armor, but the Mauler was tough. Unlike the fighters used by the Navy, this vessel could take heavy punishment and still keep going. There was a reason they were technically classified as ships, even if they were not much larger than the much older models of landing craft.

"Ten seconds!"

The Mauler seemed to go motionless and then struck something with force. The craft shook violently, and then everything returned to calm as before. The side hatches opened up, and every marine inside made for the exits. Sergeant Payne was first out, using the grab rails to pull himself out and then using the thrusters on his suit to move though the massive landing area. A thin layer of dust from their arrival, mixed with dust and dirt from hundreds, perhaps thousands of years obscured his vision. He looked back and concentrated on his unit.

"Marines, fan out and put them down!"

More marines surged out of the craft and spread out to his flanks. Half a dozen moved up to the ceiling and a single SAAR robot drifted out before clamping itself firmly to the ground. Guns flashed, but there was neither sound, nor useable gravity. Sergeant Payne concentrated on the dispersal, noting with confidence that in less than forty seconds, the craft was empty and his entire platoon had deployed. Further to the right another two Maulers had landed and done exactly the same.

That's a company of marines on the ground. Now we'll do some damage!

He looked back at the target, the vast interior hangar. The dust was already beginning to move, and in its place were a dozen Biomechs. Each stood upright, a vast machine covered in thickly layered armor. Around them moved scores of the eight-legged Decurion war machines. Unlike the marines, they were easily able to move throughout the hangar, but they didn't attack. Instead, the Biomechs masters lifted their arms and opened fire. The first pulse of energy vaporized five marines and left nothing but charred armor and pieces of melted flesh. More shots slammed into the three platoons as they scattered in panic.

"Stand your ground, and put these things down for good!" he shouted.

While the marines scattered, the battle-hardened marine lifted his carbine and took aim. He even managed to loose off a short burst before a pulse of energy struck the ground in front of him, sending his shattered body backwards and against the Mauler in a spray of broken bones and organs.

"Fall back!" screamed a corporal.

Through the intercom system his voice was as loud as any of the others. Some retreated while others did their best to find cover in the vast open space. Any useful cover was held by the machines, though; and unlike their usual practice, they stood their ground and continued to fire on the outnumbered and outgunned marines. By the time the first wave of Thegns emerged from their hiding places and swarmed over the hangar, there were less than twenty marines left alive.

A young female private with two holes in her left arm, managed to reach the Mauler. Hands pulled her inside just as a massed volley of gunfire cut apart the last survivors trying to join her. The door clunked shut, and an officer grabbed her and activated the clamps. Even as he did so, the Mauler pulled away. They sustained multiple impacts, but incredibly managed to get away from the bloodbath.

"How many did we lose?" she asked with a cough.

"Too many. The fleet's been given the withdrawal order. The Biomechs control Helion space now. We're joining Admiral Lewis at the secondary assembly point."

They sat in silence as the Mauler joined the tiny number of surviving craft back to the capital ships. Even as they moved through space, the volleys of gunfire from both sides left ruined ships and bodies in all directions. The battle of C34 was over, and the Alliance had little to show for it other than a shattered fleet, broken morale, and a planet now suffering the throes of a devastating bombardment from space. The marine opened her visor and wiped her brow.

"I thought we would have won this fight. Helios Prime will fall, and we'll be next."

The Lieutenant shook his head.

"No chance, Private. We'll do what we always do. We'll regroup, and we'll come back and hit them twice as hard."

"And what about Helios Prime?"

They both watched the screen on the front wall that showed the hundreds of meteors streaming down to the planet below. Some were small chunks, but others were big enough to destroy large swathes of the city. The sky showed up red, and black smoke rose from a thousand fires burning away.

"They will suffer. Be under no illusions though, we will

return."

The mixture of Alliance and alien vessels moved out of orbit and accelerated away from the planet and toward their rendezvous with the remnants of Admiral Lewis' fleet. Fighters from both sides continued to battle, and the planetary defense platforms took severe punishment from the hundreds of Biomech warships now in orbit over Helios Prime. Like Spascia before it, the world of Helios Prime was now under the Biomech blockade.

* * *

Spartan had led three assaults on the Biomech defenses, and still they'd been unable to break through. Each time the marines had reached the sets of barricades, the defenders had triggered a series of charges that had left more than a dozen marines wounded. He moved back and knelt down alongside Teresa and Captain Rivers.

"They are entrenched back there. We will not get inside."

The young Captain looked confused.

"I don't understand. This is just a diversion."

Spartan leaned around the pillar and took aim at the distant doorway and sprayed it will coil rounds.

"You can't hit them like that," the Captain sighed.

Teresa struck him on the head.

"You've fought them before, and you know how they

work. If they believe this is a feint, then they will redeploy, and the others will suffer badly. We need to drawn in everything they have and now."

Spartan looked back and grinned at his wife.

"You should listen to her. Teresa knows what she's talking about."

Another of the Decurion machines pushed out a prisoner, this time a man in his thirties. It lifted the barely moving man into plain sight and moved its pincers around the man's throat. The gunfire stopped as though a switch had been flicked.

"Animals," hissed Spartan.

He moved out into the open and lifted his carbine in a single fluid motion. There was no hesitation or mercy. The muzzles flashed, and a hole appeared in the man's arm. The machine dropped the wounded man as the pincer arm was ripped from its joint.

"Marines, forward!"

Spartan and Teresa were on their feet first and rushed toward the flailing machine. More marines moved from their hiding places and charged the numerous barricades held by the machines. Three were knocked down, and then they were over the rubble and vanished into the darkness. Captain Rivers watched them go and shook his head. He'd never seen Spartan in action, and his nerve and willingness to sacrifice others so quickly was not what he'd expected. Even more surprising was the Colonel. Since he'd arrived,

Colonel Morato had transformed from the cool, calm commander to a violent officer, one that seemed to exude an aggressive attitude he was just not used to.

Spartan landed on the other side of the barricades and found three Thegns waiting with their firearms pointing right at him. The first fired and penetrated his thigh armor. He stumbled and then put a triple blast into the next warrior's chest. Teresa landed alongside him and held down her trigger. The long burst cut into all three. More marines fanned out around them, firing at any sign of the enemy. That was when they came across the first of the prisoners. Spartan groaned and looked down to check if he was bleeding. There was definitely a hole. He could only assume the projectile had either passed and missed his limb, or more likely, it had embedded itself in the PDS Alpha armor.

"A young lieutenant stopped by the two of them, looked to Spartan, and then to Teresa.

"Colonel, the machines are falling back to the base of a secondary shaft. Large numbers of their Decurion machines control the two floors above this level."

Spartan smiled, but it was a bittersweet look. He pointed off into the distance.

"They're establishing a kill-zone. The Core will be right behind them."

Teresa was already speaking with Khan via the digital communications network. It took only a few seconds before she was done. She looked back to Spartan.

"They agree. The machines are falling back to contain us. They have a clear run to the crash site identified by Z'Kanthu."

Teresa reached out and grabbed Spartan's shoulder.

"Are you sure we can trust it…him?"

Spartan looked back at her and shrugged.

"We'll find out soon enough. It's time to let them think they've pushed us back. We'll have to make it look good. This is now the diversion."

Even Teresa looked confused at this part.

"I…uh, I thought this…"

Spartan placed his hand on her shoulder.

"They can hear us," was all he said.

* * *

Z'Kanthu pushed ahead like a metal god, his large size and powerful limbs making him all but impervious to melee attacks from the machines. A long distance behind him waited the bloodied figures of Khan, Tajt, Olik, and Knaprig. They had made use of the wrecked equipment and storage units to find as much useful cover as they could. Around them moved dozens of marines moving into the darkness offered by the low lighting. There was no real need for the Jötnar to participate in this part of the fight, but even after Olik's bloody wound, and Knaprig's severed arm, they refused to give up. The Alliance forces had moved up to the first of the many bodies and dug in throughout the mall inspired structure. The ceiling had partially collapsed, and a thin layer of dust along the ground seemed to drift up around their feet. Z'Kanthu stopped and looked back at the four wounded Jötnar off into the distance.

"They are ahead, are you ready?"

Khan signaled with his right arm. Z'Kanthu lifted his arms and roared in a high-pitched mechanical scream. He then hunkered down on his haunches and took aim with his weapons. Ahead of him, just where they suspected lay the immobile Core, came the flicker of light. It started as a dull orange that quickly became yellow. Hard, black shadows cast on the ground and then they came. Decurions poured forth from the darkness and directly at the Biomech warlord. He opened fire, but the machines came on thick and fast.

"Fall back!" Khan shouted.

From his position much further back, he could see the machines were swarming out like bugs. If he weren't quick, he would be completely overrun. Z'Kanthu fired a final volley and then turned and ran as fast as he could. His great size meant he crashed through barriers, display stands, and parts of staircases as he moved. Two Decurions managed to leap onto his body, and he was forced to crash into the nearby wall to force them off. More came closer still before the gunfire from the four Jötnar picked off the nearest. Still he ran, finally stopping just a few meters from his new friends.

"The machines, they are here," he said without a hint of emotion.

As the hidden marines lay in wait, the four Jötnar and Z'Kanthu opened fire. The sheer weight of numbers was substantial, as machines and Thegns surrounded them on three sides. Only with their backs to the wall stopped them from reaching them on all four sides. Khan looked quickly to his comrades and then to the machine they had only so recently befriended.

"Well, you said they would want you. Now Spartan can secure the Core."

The marines opened fire from dozens of hidden positions. A mixture of coilguns and L48 rifles tore holes in the Biomech horde, but only a few could return fire. Instead of shooting at Z'Kanthu, they hurled themselves at him, desperate to disable rather than kill him. Three Thegns and a Decurion knocked Khan to the ground, and he roared with laughter, smashing his fist through one of their backs as he lay there.

"Spartan, take the Core!" he shouted over his open channel.

CHAPTER FOURTEEN

The Empires of Ancient Earth included some that lasted for hundreds or even thousands of years. It was those that could survive in the face of new and powerful threats that could truly be considered great. The Samurai of Japan suffered at the hands of the more tactically aware Mongols, and the Celts of Europe were ultimately crushed by the mechanical efficiency of the Romans. Technology wasn't the only requirement for victory, however. In the twentieth century, the dogged resistance and industry of its enemies defeated the advanced armies of Nazi Germany, just as much as its own leadership destroyed it from within. The Alliance was something new, yet its foundations were the Confederacy and the early pioneers that had set out from Earth so many centuries before.

Brief History of the Alliance

Jack's hands were shaking as he tried to drink from the warm flask. The marines had now held the trench works around Gun's command post against three determined assaults. The outer regions of the old city were well and truly lost, but no matter how many warriors they threw at them, they seemed unable to break the last few strongpoints this side of the chasm.

"Son, I need you on the line."

He looked up and saw the hard lines running along Sergeant Stone's face. The man was tough, one of the toughest he'd met. Yet even now he was sure the man had some sympathy, or perhaps concern for his marines. He reached out and helped Jack to his feet. Lieutenant Elvidge was next to him and a single fireteam of battered looking marines. The fighting had been so confused that Jack realized he had no idea where he actually was. Trenches ran in all directions, and most of the buildings were nothing but rubble.

"Son, it's time," said the Sergeant.

The man turned and spoke to Lieutenant Elvidge, leaving Jack stunned. Private Jenkell grabbed him, pulling him down a mound and to the right where another group of marines were dragging a machine gun into position. Behind them came the booming sound of Helion artillery. They were close, and the gray and black streaks from their missiles and rockets arced overhead to drop down into the enemy controlled parts of the city.

Jack slid down into the nearest breastwork and went immediately to his carbine. His mind felt completely shattered at this point, so rather than think, he forced himself into routine. He checked the mechanism, ammunition feed, and power pack. All the while Jenkell watched him work. She was clearly worried, but he noticed nothing outside of the work he was already doing. He slowly looked up and saw her watching him.

"Jack, I know what…"

"Marines!" roared a familiar voice.

Both of them twisted about and looked up at the armored form of Gun. Two black armored guards flanked him, all bearing the symbol of Hyperion proudly on their chests. A squad of Khreenk fighters ran past them and moved into a forward trench. An odd four-legged machine, like a small version of a Biomech Decurion followed them and disappeared behind a wall.

"The Biomechs have pushed everything they have within six blocks of our lines. We are all that stands between them and the chasm."

He pointed at the dark mountain that ran up from the city.

"If they make it past us, they will be inside the mountain in less than three hours. We will stop them cold."

More rockets rushed overhead like a violent salute to their synthetic leader. The low rumble in the distance marked out the initial impacts of the ordnance amongst the enemy's positions.

"Our aircraft are hitting their landing zones hard. We

will break them on our armor."

Some of the marines shouted, but most stayed quiet. The time for triumphalism was long past; now it was simply butchering work. The Khreenk worked methodically on their equipment, and the marines dragged whatever heavy weapons remained to the frontline. Gun and his party moved from the high ground and toward one of the many shattered buildings. They were more shells than buildings anymore, and the irregular shapes proved more than useful for the larger size of the Jötnar. Jack watched as his old friend moved to his new position and then, just as before, he felt the coldness and the nerves return.

"Targets, two hundred meters and closing!" said one of the sharpshooters waiting in a raised position on one of the remaining third floors.

The final assault on Spascia City began not with gunfire, or even a bombardment. It began with something even Gun hadn't anticipated. Even though the underground tunnels had been filled, there were still two shafts accessible to the enemy, and one ran directly beneath Gun's command post. The opening attack began with a massive blast that tore a hole fifty meters wide in the middle of their defenses. Any man or woman within the blast radius was killed immediately. Less than thirty seconds after the blast came the gunfire, and then the Thegns came at the defenders in waves. Most hit from the surface, but a large number also emerged from the pit in the center of the defenses to strike into the heart of the Alliance position.

"Fire!" Sergeant Stone ordered.

Jack and his nearest comrades had no time to worry about the pit behind them. Hundreds of new targets appeared as the Thegns moved from cover to cover. This was no simple wave attack. It was a carefully timed assault, using every inch of available cover. Jack aimed at the first target, fired, and then moved to the next. Even as he tracked to his right, he noticed the first Thegn he'd shot was still alive and took aim back at him. Something tugged. He found himself on his back, and Gun looking down at him.

"Watch your head, Jack."

The mighty warrior turned and ran back toward the pit, his guards following right behind. Some of the Khreenk join in, and a vicious hand-to-hand brawl broke out as the first Thegns reached the surface. Jenkell helped Jack to his feet as he watched in awe at the figure of Gun. He didn't just kill or incapacitate nearly a dozen of the enemy, but he then leapt down into the pit and vanished.

"He's insane," said Private Jenkell.

Jack shook his head.

"No, he's a Jötnar. That's what they do."

Feeling calmer and more levelheaded, he moved back to the line and took aim. This time he made sure he put one of the enemy down before moving to the next target. Decurion war machines crept about, all of them staying low and scuttling about like spiders before leaping out and overrunning the outer defenses. Two of them reached Jack's position and jumped over their shattered wall. The first landed right behind him and stabbed at his back. A pair of Khreenk warriors blasted it apart with large, short-barreled cannon that they carried low about their hips on gyro-stabilized mounts.

"Thanks," was the best he could manage.

The second machine landed further back and unfortunately for it, directly in the path of a single Jötnar warrior. With a yell and a roar, he grabbed one of its arms and then blazed away with his multi-barreled cannon at the machine. In seconds, the thing was a smashed ruin. More Thegns now reached the line, but the marines return fire was so great, not a single one was able to climb over.

"Keep up your fire!" Lieutenant Elvidge cried out.

Jack looked to his right and spotted the officer, with Sergeant Stone nearby. Both were directing the marines who lay crouched along the wall like some ancient Earth battle. It was all close range, and both sides were taking casualties from the stray rounds. Movement caught Jack's eye, and he glanced left, but it was more marines running ahead to join the rest on the line. Two dropped down along side him and lifted their guns to fire. The first took a blast to the face and snapped backwards, the impact killing him instantly.

"Shoot, damn you!" Sergeant Stone shouted, for what

must have been the hundredth time.

More Thegns moved nearer and nearer until they were just a block away and exchanging continuous gunfire. Even as they fought back, it was clear the marines' numbers and ammunition must have been suffering. The center of the line was already firing at a reduced rate when mortars knocked out its two remaining machine guns. Two Thegns climbed over the tripods, and Jack raked them from the side with his carbine. Both fell, and he reached down for his next clip, to find them all gone. Sergeant Stone spotted his firing and nodded in acknowledgement.

"Good shooting, Son, keep at it."

Jenkell passed over another clip and pushed it into his left hand.

"Make it count."

A salvo of mortar bombs crashed into the defenses, and one of the SAAR robots exploded in a bright flash. Two nearby Rams also exploded, and their cargo of ammunition caught fire and blasted apart in all directions. Then came a sound none of them had ever heard, a kind of warbling, high-pitched screeching that would have caused any of them not wearing helmets to crawl about on the ground. Jack pulled back the loading level on his L52 and took aim. The sight of the last wave of enemy warriors stunned him. Hundreds of Thegns lifted up from their cover and rushed in a final great surge for the marines' defenses.

You can do this, aim low and squeeze.

Jack fired and the emergency alert activated in his visor. For a moment he was dumbfounded, and then he realized it was an overheating transformer in the coilgun. Just as he'd been trained to, he pulled out the bayonet from his sheath and slid it onto the notch, as the wave of Thegns crashed into the wall. Heavy gunfire from behind them scattered the Thegns, but more came on. One threw himself at Jack, but in a single stabbing action he stepped back and thrust into the thing's throat. It gurgled incoherently before being pulled off and shot by Jenkell.

A moving shadow covered Jack as he looked for another target. He looked over his shoulder and watched the bulk of Gun and his guards emerge from the pit. They were all covered in blood and gore. With one arm extended, he pointed to the outer barricades being held by the marines.

"Run them all down!"

With that simple order, he set off along the ground and jumped over the defenses, right into the mass of Thegns. His guards did the same, each hacking and shooting simultaneously.

"Marines, advance!" Lieutenant Elvidge added.

Jack didn't even realize what he was doing as he rose to his feet and climbed out of cover to join the crazed Jötnar. More marines did the same, and then they were rushing across open ground and through the scattered line of Thegns. Jack moved one foot in front of the other, his carbine out in front, and his eyes focused on keeping moving. He legs felt like jelly and his heart pounded, but every step took him away from the firefight and closer to his comrades who were running about wildly.

A single one of the Eques walkers stood its ground and blocked off the debris-strewn street. Two marines vanished in a blast of gunfire, but the Khreenk flanked the thing and put down such a weight of fire that its badly damaged body was forced to face them. At that moment, Gun and the rest charged at it with guns blazing.

"With me," said Sergeant Stone.

Jack had lost sight of the marine for the first part of the counterattack, but now a full platoon of marines was advancing down the side street and picking off any stray Thegns they could find. Occasionally, one would rush them, and a mixture of bayonets and gunfire soon finished them off. Meter by meter the marines pushed on until the defenses were clear, and the Thegns were broken and falling back into the city outskirts, their attack smashed and their forces fleeing for fear of total annihilation.

As Gun tore the electronics from the very heart of the fallen Eques, the enemy's forces withdrew as fast as they could move. He watched with a mixture of pride and pleasure as his exhausted warriors chased them to the very edge of the city and out into the open. Only then did he give the order for the remaining fighters and drones to hit them.

They'll be back, and this time they won't be stupid enough to try a direct assault.

He looked up to the sky.

How many more soldiers do they have up inside that Ark?

A dozen Alliance fighters screamed overhead and then split into three groups. All moved down low and fired long bursts of fire at the ground. Some anti-aircraft fire came back, and at least a missile battery that must have been ten or more kilometers from the city struck one. It served as an important reminder that the battle was far from won. He looked out at the ruins of the city, the place where the Helions, Khreenk, and humans of the Alliance had made their stand, and held. He dreaded to think what the casualties had been.

Gun looked back at the mountain and smiled as scores of automated guns continued to blast away at the small number of remaining enemy aircraft. Most of the higher peak was covered in the black smoke trails of the Helion rocket batteries that continued to bombard the retreating Biomechs. The figures of several officers approached, the nearest one being Lieutenant Elvidge.

"Colonel, I think we've done it."

Gun smiled.

"Your marines fought well, Lieutenant. Pass on my praise."

He raised his eyes and spotted the distant shape of the enemy's forward base, their orbital Arks from where the battle for Spascia was being fought.

Yes, we saved the city. Now the battle for this world will truly begin.

* * *

Spartan didn't waste time, and as soon as he spotted the vast numbers of warriors stream away, he moved ahead. A handful of Thegns defended the open ground, but he also knew about those much higher. He ran ahead and slid to the right behind a fallen Decurion. Teresa was alongside him and lifted herself up from the metal to look at the gently moving shapes.

"What now?"

"We give them something to shoot at."

He turned around and waved to those moving into position behind them. Four bright yellow lamps announced the arrival of a pair of SAAR robots. They trundled forward and out in front where the marines were waiting. As soon as they were in the open, a great volley of gunfire tore down at them. The first was knocked out instantly, but the second was able to rotate its tracker and perform a full radar and acoustic assessment of the area. Spartan watched with a wry smile as the data circulated through the visor overlays of every man and woman present. He looked to Teresa who waited ever so patiently.

"See, I said the tech would work."

Few probably realized at that very moment that the networking technology was based on a system developed in their old private security company. Like all other assets owned by the Corporation, they had been taken on by the state. Spartan had caught most of the details during his trip from Earth to Mars, and it had angered him greatly. He hadn't spoken about what had happened yet to Teresa, not even about her new position in the Marine Corps. She looked at him and knew exactly what he was thinking about.

"The tech is good. That was never the problem."

She looked back to the heavy response coming back from the enemy. It was deadly, but nothing as strong as when they'd first arrived. Spartan waited just a little longer to give time for the remaining SAAR robot to finish its sweep. The machine even managed to unleash three bursts up high into the shadows before it was knocked out.

"Now! Put them down."

Marines surged from their hiding places and lifted their weapons high. The enemy was almost all tagged and instead of aiming at the targets, they simply fired at the pre-stored locations on their visors. Over half the Thegns were killed or wounded, and the rest immediately pinned down by the accurate suppressing fire.

"Follow me," said Spartan.

He and Teresa inched past the fallen enemy and around the side of the over shaft. Even as they moved, they could make out the broken metal girders ahead where something heavy had fallen through. They reached the double metal doors that were barely attached to the frame and hanging to the sides. Inside was filled with a thin mist that all but obscured their vision. Spartan looked to Teresa and spotted Captain Rivers and five more marines who had joined them. Projectiles clattered about them, but once past the main opening they were relatively safe.

"So, is it in there?" asked the Captain.

Spartan checked the details the Biomech had given him. It wasn't much, but the energy configuration inside the mist matched what he had been given exactly. For the briefest of moments, he wondered if this might be one of the easiest ways he'd come across for him to be captured, but then completely discounted it.

"Yeah, it's here. Your guys, are they ready?"

"Guys?" complained the nearest.

The visor on her helmet flipped up to reveal a pale white face and piercing white eyes.

"We're not guys, Spartan. Not all of us. The name's Corporal Tindall."

Spartan grinned with just the right side of his mouth.

"Of course not. You're ready though, aren't you, Corporal Tindall?"

In answer to his question, the marines pulled out their standard issue tactical bayonets and slid them onto the lugs of their carbines. The blades were razor sharp and serrated along the cutting edge. The mere sight of the sharpened metal sent a shudder through Spartan's body. There was something cruel, almost primeval about such simplistic weaponry.

"Always," answered the Corporal.

"Let's do this."

Spartan moved into the mist first, ignoring the gun battle still raging behind them. The mixed overlay of his visor integrated thermal imaging and infrared, producing a sophisticated combination that allowed him to see nearly ten meters ahead. A warm, partially glowing object was obvious nearly fifteen meters away and partly buried under cool metal objects. He looked up and tracked the damage leading into one of the shafts that went right up to the surface. The area around them looked like a large loading and storage area, quite possibly designed for the retail premises located around them.

"Spartan, look," said Captain Rivers.

The man had moved off to the right of the open space and past one of the many thick columns supporting the low ceiling. Metal storage bins were stacked throughout, and some had been tipped over or ransacked. Then Spartan noticed the odd shape in the direction of the Captain's hand.

"What is it?"

Teresa moved past him and stopped, dropping to her knees.

"I've seen one before. It's part of a Biomanta. The vessel must have crashed on the next level up."

She pointed to the shattered ceiling above the broken parts of the spacecraft. The shape was impossible for Spartan to make out, but Teresa appeared certain of what she'd found. Chunks of the vessel looked as though they'd been ripped out, and multiple Decurion war machines moved all over it, continually checking for signs of danger.

"Get down!" Corporal Tindall called out.

A great flash of white light moved along the far side of the storage hall and struck around the marines. At the same time, a large number of Thegns emerged from the wreckage and fanned out in a mirror of the marines' own position.

"This isn't working!" Captain Rivers complained.

Spartan took aim, put a burst into a Thegn, and then ducked down as three rounds narrowly missed his armored head. Teresa spotted the puff of dust near him and struck him hard in the chest with her fist.

"Don't do anything stupid. I've only just got you back."

Spartan winked at her and then glanced down to his thigh, checking the electronic component given to him by Z'Kanthu was still intact. He had no idea exactly what it was, but from what he could see the metal housing was scratched but undamaged.

* * *

Z'Kanthu was surrounded, and this time he had no idea
how, or even if he could survive the fight. At first, the
Thegns and Decurions had tried to force him to yield,
but after killing his fourteenth Thegn something had
changed. One of the Decurions had damaged his left leg,
and another managed to tear a section of his gun system
apart, instantly rendering his targeting system inoperative.

Khan left his wounded comrades to the protection of
the marines and raced out from cover to help the battered
machine. By the time he reached him, Z'Kanthu was on his
knee. Two Decurions stabbed at his torso while a dozen
more Thegns blasted at close range, each shot ripping off
chunks of metal.

"I thought you said..." started Khan.

He grabbed one of the Thegns and spun it about.
The half creature, half warrior looked at him with an
expressionless stance, which Khan found even more
repellent than normal. All it took was a quick snap, and its
neck was cracked with sickening efficiency.

"...these Biomechs wanted nothing more than to take
you alive?"

He moved on to the nearest Decurion that continued
to attack the Biomech, even as Khan grabbed a leg. The
machine snapped at him and stabbed with a single leg.
Khan kicked it and then threw himself on the machine.
The two tumbled down to the ground where they stabbed
and struck each other like a pair of industrial pile drivers.

"Khan!" Knaprig yelled.

Tajt and the wounded Jötnar staggered away from the continuing gun battle and extended the combat blades from their armor. The short, slashing weapons pushed out like little scimitars from mounts along the back of the wrists. Tajt dove headlong into the fight and embedded both his fists into the first Thegn he found. Knaprig, on the other hand, was reduced to fighting with a single arm. It seemed to increase his rage even more as he ran amok, stabbing and kicking at those attacking the fallen Biomech.

"Stay down!" Olik called from further back.

The injured warrior was suffering with his chest wound and leaned against a pillar, picking off any Thegn that moved into his sights. Occasionally one moved in on him, but the concealed marine marksmen quickly finished them off. Just after he fired, he heard a scream and looked up and behind. A Decurion had made it to the next level and had butchered two marines where they stood. A third was trying to wrestle it, but he had no chance against the machine's power. Olik made to move, but three Thegns reached him due to his distraction, and he was forced to fight with his own blades. Even as he fought, he managed to connect on the secure channel with Teresa.

"Colonel, we're running out of time here."

* * *

Spartan took aim once more, but a fusillade of gunfire crashed around them. He ducked back, and sparks and flashes jumped about the hidden marines. He looked to Teresa and then the marines. It was some time since he'd seen such large numbers of them, yet even though their armor was new and improved, they were essentially the same as when he'd left the Corps. Even the L52 carbines hadn't changed, not that it bothered him. They were amongst one of his favorite weapons.

"We need to use some good old fashioned shock and awe," he said quietly.

Teresa felt her heart almost stutter at this. She knew him well enough to know that meant something wild and dangerous.

"How many grenades do you all have?"

Four of them plus Teresa pulled out a small cylindrical proximity grenade. The device was standard issue, and most of the marines had already expended them.

"Okay. I give the signal, and you all scatter them out at the line of Thegns. On my mark, we move out after them."

He looked at the grenades for a moment.

"Oh, set them to timed mode. Proximity is not gonna help us today."

All it took was a short twist to change the setting.

"Activate your helmet blast shield and run them down. This is gonna be close up and personal."

The five, including Teresa checked the small devices and activated them ready. Spartan nodded to the one remaining marine that hadn't fitted her bayonet.

"Put some steel on that thing. You'll need it, I promise."

A burst of fire clattered against the pillar, reminding them quite how precarious their situation was. Spartan seemed unaffected by any of it. He gave the nod and each of them pulled their arms back.

"Covering fire!" Spartan said.

He and another marine leaned out and fired long, continuous bursts with their carbines.

"Now!"

Teresa threw her grenade first, quickly followed by the other three. The fourth almost left the Private's hands when he took three rounds directly to the face. Killed instantly, the man dropped to the ground in plain few. Two more rounds struck his lifeless body, and the grenade rolled off to the side. Spartan was already counting down in his head, and without consideration for his body, hurled himself into the open and onto his stomach next to the grenade.

Five, four...

He grabbed the object and hurled it barely in time. It made it halfway and then bounced on the ground before stopping just in front of the Thegns.

"Go!"

The marines leapt from their hiding places and activated

their blast shields. An additional micro-fine plate dropped down in front of their visors that completely blocked out their view. Now they were totally dependent upon the data coming in from their sensors. All of them made it two or three meters before the grenades went off. The timing was near perfect, and all five exploded within half a second of each other. The precision weapons were powerful and sent a blast of heat, followed up with a small burst of electromagnetic energy and burning hot fragments of shattered metal.

Here we go, Teresa thought.

She deactivated the blast shield and found herself in front of a wounded Thegn. Without hesitation, she stabbed it in the chest and then yanked back the carbine and moved to the next. Spartan didn't even bother using his bayonet and swung his carbine like a club. The others spread out before being engulfed in the mass melee where they were still outnumbered. Two of the marines were cut down by short-ranged fire, but they'd done their job. Spartan was inside the wrecked craft.

Almost there, he thought hopefully.

Being inside something like this reminded him of the great battle on Terra Nova. That sent a shudder down his spine. The final fight of the bloody civil war was hardly an occasion he wanted to be reminded of. He looked about the smashed metal and felt a pang of doubt. There was broken metal and bulkheads warped beyond recognition.

Then he spotted it, a metal sarcophagus protected by a hex of metal bars. They were undamaged and glistened like newly polished steel. Dozens of tubes ran from the sacred object, each filled with an odd, semi-translucent fluid.

"So, this is another of their Cores. Why can't they just have a man controlling this stuff?"

He knew full well why not, of course. These AI Cores were pieces of technology unique to the Biomechs. They used them instead of crews to command captured ships, and in this case as the backup way to control the bandon of troops fighting outside. Spartan moved closer to the thing even as the battle continued to rage outside. He pulled out the device given to him by Z'Kanthu and looked up at the Core.

"You!" hissed a metallic voice.

In front of him was a single Thegn, but this one was larger, much closer to Khan in shape and size. Like all the other Thegns, its skin was fused metal to give it a permanent suit of armor. It carried a maul shaped device in both hands and stepped in front of the Core to protect it. It looked at the object in Spartan's hand.

"If you destroy the Core, you will lose this world. Without its leadership, my warriors will fight until every last one of them is dead."

Spartan looked at its face and laughed loudly. The creature rocked slightly on its feet, waiting for the inevitable clash of weapons and flesh.

"Bullshit!"

The creature paused, perhaps confused for a brief moment. That was the moment Spartan charged forward. The Thegn warrior swung at him, but Spartan dove to the right and brought his carbine down on its shoulder. With a crack, the weapon's stock snapped in two, leaving him holding just the muzzle and forward grip.

"We know your past, Spartan. Even if you live, you will still serve us. Remember your parents…"

The Thegn swung again, and this time the mace struck Spartan's shoulder. It should have simply bounced off, but the object burned through the plating as though it was a plasma cutter. Sparks burst from it as the thing push its weapon further still.

"Hey!" came a familiar voice.

Spartan tilted his helmet slightly and spotted Teresa entering the wreckage. She held her carbine close to her hip and fired a single blast that struck the Thegn in the chest. The round easily punched through the armor, yet the warrior barely moved.

"You will both die," it said angrily.

Teresa seemed more surprised it was speaking, than the fact the magnetic rounds had simply passed though the warrior unnoticed. This was the first time she'd ever heard a sound from a Thegn, not that this thing looked that much like them. Its coloring and armor was unique. It moved to face her, and Spartan lurched away at the Core. Teresa saw him go and ran forward at the Thegn commander. She made contact with her bayonet on its shoulder. With a cackle, it brought its left arm down and slammed the other mace into her helmet. The massive impact sent her to the floor, unconscious. It turned about and looked at Spartan who was busily fumbling with the panel to the right of the Core.

"You have no chance, Spartan. Destroying the Core will not save you."

It lifted both of its arms high, preparing to dash Spartan's helm with the powerful weapons. Spartan ignored him and pushed the unit into the panel, precisely as described by Z'Kanthu. He spun about as the maces came down for his face. It took every ounce of energy and skill for him to twist away from the attack. Even so, both maces scraped across his chest and crashed into his shoulder. The impact was heavy, and Spartan staggered to his side before collapsing to the ground. The Thegn looked at the Core and then turned to face Spartan, his back to the thing he had been protecting.

"The Core gives us orders, but any commander can override them. You must know this."

Teresa rolled to her side and tried to stand, but she was still stunned and her body failed her. It was more like working under heavy sedation. She reached down for her pistol, and her hand dropped down loosely to her side.

"Spartan," she said weakly.

* * *

Khan couldn't move, yet still he laughed. One after another, the Thegns pushed him down with sheer weight of numbers. Blades and fists smashed him over and over, and still he refused to die. He lay there on his back and grabbed the nearest Thegn with both hands. Two more pulled on his arms, pulling back his left. With all his remaining effort, he smashed his right fist into the nearest. A great puff of metal fragments and flesh signaled the creature's demise, but another two threw themselves into the gap.

"This is exactly how I wanted…"

The Thegns slowed their attack and then the closest loosened its grip. Khan found his leg was free, and with an almighty effort, he raised himself to a knee and grabbed the Thegn still attached to his left arm. With a quick motion, he brought it down on his bent knee and snapped its back.

"Khan, look," said Olik from the other side of the battlefield.

At first Khan felt his heart drop. There were scores of Thegns between them, and even more around the fallen Z'Kanthu, yet each had slowed their movement and stood about watching them. If he could have found a single word to describe them, it would have been sullen. Only one, a badly damaged Thegn with half an arm staggered toward Khan. It made an odd noise, and Khan felt almost sorry for the thing. His gun was still non-functioning, and the blade on his left arm was gone, presumably embedded in one of the many bodies around him. He looked right and smiled at the happy sight of a single reaming blade.

"Good."

Khan walked at the thing and then built up speed. The Thegn did the same, but its severe damage made it shuffle more like a zombie than a warrior. In its remaining hand was a curved piece of sharp metal that it lifted high. Khan reached it and took the Thegn's blow with a twisted hanging parry from his right arm. At the same time, he stepped out to the left and brought his blade back down in an arcing cut that hit the Thegn in the back of the neck. With perfect technique, the weapon sliced through metal and tissue, instantly decapitating the final threat. The Thegn dropped to its knees and then toppled over to land on its chest. Olik laughed.

"The thing was broken down, was that really necessary?"

Khan looked like a demonic war machine, his body and armor bent, scratched, and damaged on almost every surface. His helmet was dripping with blood, yet when he opened his visor, he could do nothing but howl with delight. Finally, he stopped and looked to his comrade.

"My friend, it is always necessary."

A dull crunching sound made both of them turn their attention to where a mound of bodies marked the fall of Z'Kanthu. First a single chunk of metal lifted up, and then he pushed up onto his feet. Dust fell from his shoulders as he staggered and then placed a damaged arm on a pillar.

"It is done. I now control the bandon. Only one remains, the Thegn officer. I can sense it, but I cannot control it."

Khan smiled.

"Good, now let's find Spartan before he gets himself killed."

Z'Kanthu tried to move, but his legs were too badly damaged to do more than hobble.

"I suggest you hurry. The Thegn commander will not let him escape."

Khan was already on the way, but he had time for one last quip as he left the scene of battle.

"Spartan has no intention of escaping."

* * *

Spartan lifted himself up from the ground and shook his head. With a click he deactivated the helmet visor, and it hissed open to reveal his scarred face. He wore a thin black beard that covered his chin and ran up his cheeks. His unkempt hair pushed down over his forehead, yet his eyes oozed an emotion, one the Thegn could never have understood. Anybody else might have thought it was rage or anger, but Teresa could see from where she lay that it was something very different. He stretched his back ready for the fight and then spotted her watching him. It wasn't anger, fear, or bitterness. It was elation.

"It's time..." he said.

Spartan burst from where he'd been on the ground and directly at the Thegn. As he moved, he darted fractionally from one side to the other, throwing off his position to the enemy. Closer they came, and the Thegn began a complex series of rotating actions with both arms to present a continuous threat with the super-heated mauls. Finally, he made it to within two meters of its front and lurched to the left. The Thegn spotted the movement and altered its direction just as Spartan shifted his footing and passed right by to the right. He was now alongside the thing and twisted about to grab at its arm. At the same time, he stamped into the gap behind its knee. The Thegn's left leg buckled and it lost balance. Spartan grabbed the finger and thumb of its hand and wrenched them apart, instantly snapping bone and muscle.

"...time for you to die."

He yanked the maul from the smashed hand and brought down its full weight into its head. It screeched in a mixture of what must have been terror and anger, but Spartan ignored the sound. He rained down one hit after another until nothing remained above the neck. He finally let the limp body drop to the ground and turned back to

Teresa. She'd managed to drag herself up into a partial sitting position. He bent down and tapped the visor access button. It flipped up to reveal her face.

"Feeling better," she coughed.

Spartan almost laughed.

"Much."

More noise announced the arrival of numerous Thegns that pushed through the breached vessel and fanned out. They were all armed, but so far not one had fired.

"Looks like your Biomech friend screwed us over," said Teresa.

As more moved inside, she reached out for a weapon.

"What did it mean, about your parents? I thought they died in a crash when you were a child."

Spartan thought back and then shrugged. He had far more important things to contend with right now.

"Who knows? Last thing I remember was waking up in a hospital bed with no memory."

It was the first time Spartan had ever mentioned anything to do with his childhood. Teresa had always avoided the subject, yet for some inexplicable reason he threw that bombshell at her.

"You remember nothing as a boy?"

Spartan shook his head while checking for a weapon.

"Nope. Just the hospital and then they moved me from place to place."

"So how do they know you?"

Spartan found that odd, and on any other occasion, he might have wanted to examine it further. Their predicament right now took precedence, however. He looked at the Thegns and tried to decide which one he would kill first. More steps, these were louder and came from outside. He moved in front of Teresa and lifted his hands as though readying himself for a boxing match. The light from the entrance dimmed and then in came a great shape, a blood covered metal monster.

"Khan?"

"Of course."

His friend continued forward and embraced Spartan like brothers. Finally, he broke free and beckoned to the many Thegns waiting and watching.

"What do you think of our new friends?"

Spartan looked to Teresa who smiled reassuringly.

"I say it's time we found them something useful to do."

He felt relaxed, but there was something she'd said about his past, and it unnerved him. Not because of what he had no memory of, but because every time he tried to think back to before the hospital, he could see nothing but blackness and a pain in his body.

What the hell is that?

* * *

General Rivers paced back and forth as the video stream

footage played out once more. He'd only just arrived on board ANS Warlord, the newest warship from the Alliance shipyards. In theory, she was based heavily on ANS Dreadnought, but there was a single major difference. The hull comprised of two assembles, both fused together during initial construction to create a vessel with double the mass and capabilities. She was an Alliance Super-Battleship and the only production version of the experimental Warlord class. More were planned for the future, but with war already underway, production had shifted to the more easily produced models like the third tranche Crusaders and the Liberty class destroyers. Many more cruisers waited in orbit, as well as scores of different Liberty destroyers. It was an impressive number, made more so by their commander, Admiral Churchill. For all their numbers, it was the footage that stayed with him. He'd been watching it for almost twenty minutes now and still could not find the words to describe his outrage.

"Where the hell are they? We have a war to fight."

It had been twenty minutes of watching and waiting until finally the virtual presence projector activated. Around him appeared the forms of Admiral Anderson, Admiral Churchill from T'Karan, and the newly elected President Harrison there on Terra Nova. A tall, commanding figure that had made it through on a platform of victory and expansion. He looked to his right where the three Chiefs of Staff sat patiently, their presence only betrayed by a slight glimmer.

"General. Thank you for convening this meeting. Please continue," said the President.

The General nodded and then pointed into the middle of the room where a holographic model of the systems and planets of the Orion Nebula were shown. Blue shapes marked out planets, while flashing red colors indicated ongoing operations.

"Our forces have secured Alliance space. Mars and Prometheus, as you know, are back under our control. Patrols are back to normal, and the Rift Network is fully operational, but only in our territory."

"And Orion?"

General Rivers licked his lip and considered his words.

"The Helios system is under a systematic assault by the Biomechs. The planet of Spascia is cut off and under full military blockade. They have Arks heading for Libuscha that will arrive in just over eight weeks, and another making for Micaya."

He pointed at the center of the display where a single planet flashed continually.

"We've not heard from any of our people on Helios Prime for six hours now. Our fleet has withdrawn, and their Ark is conducting a continuous mass-driver bombardment of the surface. Nothing is getting on or off that planet."

There was a long pause, mainly due to the time delay involved between all parties, but also due to the terrifying scenario they were in.

"There is always the issue of the Black Rift. It's twenty-seven astronomical units from the Helion homeworld, just over two weeks for our conventional vessels on full burn. In the last few hours, the Helion and T'Kari task force at the Rift has detected the approach of a substantial force."

The President shook his head in irritation.

"Where the hell did they come from?"

General Rivers looked to Admiral Anderson.

"Some are the survivors of the fighting on Spascia. We knew some had broken away. The rest must have been dormant in the asteroid belt. All we know is that a flotilla will arrive within three days. If they succeed in disabling the defenses, then the only way to collapse the Rift will be from the Helion planetary Doomsday systems."

Again there was a long pause. The situation was worse than the President had been expecting, that much was clear to the military commanders.

"And this situation with the Byotai and the Anicinàbe. Is that under control?"

General Rivers nodded.

"For now. There is no immediate danger in the Byotai systems, but it does mean that most of their forces are being held back to defend their fifty plus worlds."

"Can we win?" asked the President.

General Rivers didn't even need to think about it.

"No, Sir. We cannot. The Arks are all but impregnable

to our weapons, and each one carries sufficient vessels to hold back our combined military forces. We can hold them, for weeks, perhaps months. But if we want to come out of this alive, we will need to put something else into action. Helios needs help, and soon."

"Operation Citadel?" Admiral Churchill asked.

"That is one option, replied General Rivers, "There is also the possibility of making use of the information obtained by Spartan and Colonel Morato on Mars. They have access to…"

"No," President Harrison said in a firm tone, "I've spoken with my own advisors on this one. We cannot condone involvement of Biomech forces in our long-term strategic goals. Bring them to Terra Nova as planned. They will be properly debriefed."

General Rivers looked taken aback, but it was Admiral Anderson who spoke exactly what he was thinking.

"Mr. President. I concur with General Rivers' assessment of the information coming from Mars. We would be foolish if we chose to ignore the…"

The man lifted his hands in annoyance.

"That is enough, Gentlemen. I have seen the reports concerning this man, a man that has been missing and in Biomech custody for months. No, when he gets here, he will be kept somewhere safe and secure until such time as this crisis is over."

"And the Biomech?" Admiral Anderson asked.

The President considered that for a moment.

"You lost one of theirs during the operation at Prometheus, did you not? It might be wise to keep this one for a rainy day. You never know when a bargaining chip might prove useful."

He made to continue, but something caught his attention, and he looked away. It was only for a moment, but long enough for General Rivers and Admiral Anderson to share a look. Neither said a word, but both knew immediately what the other was thinking. The President finished talking to the unseen person and turned his attention back to those present.

"Right, where were we?"

Admiral Anderson spoke first.

"We were discussing how we are going to win this war."

The President nodded.

"Ah, yes. So Helios and its planets are under siege, and the Black Rift will come under attack at any moment. A few more men or ships will make little difference. There will be no reinforcements traveling through the T'Karan-Helios Rift, not until we have sufficient numbers to tip the scales."

The President scratched at his temple, an odd affectation, and one that hadn't gone unmissed to the others present when he had something to say that seemed at odds with his body language. General Hammerstein rose to his feet, but the President waved him down.

"We cannot sit back and wait for the next engagement. We must be decisive, Gentlemen. The public is behind us for now, but we must act, and when we start, we must be successful. One major defeat in the field, and I will be forced to withdraw all that we have left to our own borders. Operation Citadel is, in my opinion, the way forward. That means a massive build-up on the border, and the creation of the greatest military expedition ever mounted by mankind. It is my opinion that..."

He continued speaking while Admiral Anderson gave the General a quick glance. General Rivers nodded ever so slightly at the look. Not even the other Joint Chiefs could make out the subtle movement of his head. Unlike them though, the two old senior officers had spent considerable time in the last war. There was a degree of respect and acknowledgement amongst them and people like Admiral Churchill that the others could never understand.

Yes, I know. If we want to win this war, we'll need this Biomech, and there's only one man that can make that happen. Spartan.

www.ingramcontent.com/pod-product-compliance
Lightning Source LLC
Chambersburg PA
CBHW051318250626
47155CB00007B/2369